You're a New Yorker if you fold your slice of pizza before eating it; if you don't mind paying more for the "Sunday Times" than a ham sandwich; if you never owned a car and (gulp) don't know how to drive.

I'm a hopeless city rat. I know New Yorkers, and Ron Ross is a true New Yorker; read one page of his prose and there's no hiding the fact.

Who better, then, to pen a collection of short stories, "Tales From The Sidewalks Of New Yo          \on?

Good stuff. Fun stuff. Anc          uff from a guy who's been on those same sidewalks.

**Steve Farhood**
Showtime boxing analyst

\*\*\*\*\*\*\*\*\*\*\*\*\*\*\*\*\*\*\*\*\*\*:          \*\*\*\*\*\*\*\*\*\*\*\*\*\*\*\*\*\*\*

Open the pages of "Tales from the Sidewalks of New York" and you will smell the goods of the pushcart peddlers, hear the elevated trains rumble by and understand what it was like to grow up in a special place during a special time. The neighborhood was tough, the people tough and beautiful. Ron Ross takes you to places in New York that no longer exist. It's an incredible, 217-page journey. And the poems? The poems are a knockout. –

**Bobby Cassidy Jr.,** Newsday

\*\*\*\*\*\*\*\*\*\*\*\*\*\*\*\*\*\*\*\*\*\*\*\*\*\*\*\*\*\*\*\*\*\*\*\*\*\*\*\*\*\*\*\*\*

Having read Ron Ross' "Bummy Davis Vs. Murder, Inc." no less than six times, I believe it's the best book written about Brooklyn, boxing and the Jewish Mafia. Therefore, I couldn't imagine any encore to match "Bummy's" level of read-ability. Now, along comes Ross with ten "Tales From The Sidewalks of New York" – plus three bonus poems. Not only has Ron done it again – brilliantly – only this time with short stories that capture the Big Apple's flavor as well as any native of Brooklyn or elsewhere in Gotham. It proves that the genius of "Bummy" was no accident!

**Stan Fischler**, author, "The Subway And The City", sports announcer, journalist

\*\*\*\*\*\*\*\*\*\*\*\*\*\*\*\*\*\*\*\*\*\*\*\*\*\*\*\*\*\*\*\*\*\*\*\*\*\*\*\*\*\*\*\*\*\*\*\*\*\*\*\*\*\*\*

Ron Ross grew up on the sidewalks of New York, specifically the sidewalks of Brownsville, Brooklyn, in the 1930s and 1940s. Fortunately for the reader he is also a born story teller who knows how to weave a delightful tale that is at turns poignant, hilarious, and hopeful. In his latest book, Tales From the Sidewalks of New York, Ross has written an engrossing and highly entertaining collection of 13 short stories that make you feel as if you have entered a time machine into a New York City that is no more. Several stories revolve around a boxing theme, a subject the author knows very well, having been a boxer, manager and promoter. Ross not only captures the gritty feel of the streets but also the romantic yearnings, fears and dreams of his colorful cast of characters. He creates powerful images with his prose, especially when he delves into the minds and hearts of his characters, be they male or female, Child or adult, hero or bum. As in his previous work, Bummy Davis vs. Murder Inc.—The Rise and Fall of the Jewish Mafia and an Ill fated Prizefighter, Ross's word pictures give you the feeling that you are watching a film noir classic.

Reviewed by **Mike Silver**, Author of The Arc of Boxing: The Rise and Decline of the Sweet Science

*Kirkus Review of Tales From the Sidewalks of New York*

In 13 short stories based on real life, Ross (*Nine...Ten...and Out! The Two Worlds of Emile Griffith*, 2008, etc.) mines the memories of his life to create memorable characters struggling to survive against unfavorable odds.

To Ross, the boxing ring and its "gallant performers" have always seemed "to be a microcosm of life." In "The Journeyman," Ross' opening story, the author portrays the weary existence of a seasoned prizefighter named Billy Dumas, aka "The King of Plain." A "Model-T in a world of Corvettes and Porsches," Billy's been beaten so badly he develops what appears to be dementia—and a tragic belief in his own ability. The succeeding trio of tales revolves around the street-wise, Brooklyn adolescence of future Jewish prizefighter Al "Boomy" Davidoff and a gang of miscreants, such as Brownsville bully Billy Belch and "soda bottle-cap legend" Bitsy Beckerman, who act as if they're on "the farm team of Murder, Inc." "The Cashayfelope Man," about the mystery surrounding a foreign-born ragpicker, takes place around the desperate time of what 6-year-old protagonist Dovie Mendelson calls "the Limberg baby." Brownsville, the Brooklyn neighborhood of pushcarts and punch-ball games, reappears along with another set of pugilists and promoters in two of the book's stronger pieces, "An Entrepreneurial Act" and "The Glory Days." The former is a touching eulogy for Monk, "who throws as many punches with his face as he does with his fists"; the latter is a love letter, alternately heartbreaking and inspiring, to the camaraderie of boxers and trainers. The final three tales are told in rhyming verse, which detracts slightly from the power of the author's wise-guy vernacular and polished prose. For the most part, Ross writes like a Steinbeck trained as a boxing columnist in the Lower East Side. Humorous turns of phrase keep sad inevitabilities at bay: "[T]his whole world ain't made up of ditch-diggers and pugs," says Monk—a thought that runs contrary to the world Ross handily creates.

A lithe, lyrical collection that packs more than a few punches.

# TALES
## FROM THE
# SIDEWALKS
## OF
# NEW YORK

Ron Ross

Published by: Bedell Books

ISBN: 1470002191
ISBN: 13:9781470002190

Library of Congress Control Number: 2012902104
North Charleston, SC

*This book is dedicated to my adored and adoring wife Susan*
*For understanding and sharing in those solitary hours of confinement*
*That is part of the creative process of an author's life.*

# ACKNOWLEDGMENTS

*With special thanks to:*

*My very talented and courageous daughter Lisa Ross whose derring-do and accomplishments as a globe-trotting photographer are a source of everlasting pride as well as a bit of paternal apprehension.*

*My daughter Wendy Ross Woods and son-in-law Richard Woods. first, for creating our three wonderful granddaughters and also for being the talented and devoted educators that have established you both as pillars of the community.*

*My three beautiful and exceptional granddaughters, Jaime, Justine and Julia for bringing such joy and love into our lives. I want to tell you to reach for the stars, that there is nothing unattainable – but it seems you already know that.*

*My late but never to be forgotten dear friend Budd Schulberg, who served not just as an inspiration, but also as a role model.*

*My good friend Stan Fischler, known to the sports world as "The Hockey Maven" but known to me as an all-around great guy. The three stories of a kid called Boomy are dedicated to you!*

*And last, but very, very far from least – Hank Kaplan – the dean, mentor and guiding light to all boxing writers, historians, archivists and all who knew him. Hank's presence is sorely missed but his memory and friendship live on in my heart.*

# CONTENTS

# PROLOGUE

Things do not just happen; they happen *because*. "Because" takes in a lot of territory and in this case it began with a number of readers of BUMMY DAVIS VS MURDER, INC. asking if I had any more stories, anecdotes or information of growing up in Brownsville back in Al "Bummy" Davis' time.

About four feet from my desk is a closet that I use for storing everything from old manuscripts, current projects, ideas for future projects, promotional material and every kind of paperwork relating in any way to my work. I call it my main file storage. My wife calls it a major disaster zone. It's all in the eyes of the beholder.

After receiving a call from an especially excitable former Brownsville resident and neighbor of Bummy Davis' family I went to the "Bummy Davis" file pile in the closet and pulled out original notes, interviews and the first draft of the book that was 635 pages, eventually edited down to 418, retaining only the material that met the qualifications of a non-fiction work – factual information based on interviews and articles. From the remainder, the edited-out portion, I gleaned three short stories about this kid Boomy's growing up years. I took incidents that were related to me but not described in detail and from that I created the fiction-based-on fact stories.

So there I was, sitting at my desk with three short stories that I was going to do what with? There was no hesitation. It was not an unfamiliar situation. Often, in the past, the germ of an idea would burrow into my consciousness firing me with a fervor that took precedence over all else. The cure was simple but effective. I would tend to and nurture the idea until it was molded into a full-blown story. Sometimes the "cure" took a couple days, usually quite a bit longer. When I was finished I always followed the same routine – read the story, smile with satisfaction or re-write until I was satisfied – then take it from my desk and place it on a shelf in the file closet, and back to work.

Call it an accident or an intervention of fate or maybe just a klutz in action. Bottom line, the pattern was broken and the cupboard became a bit less cluttered. As I went to place the three short stories about a kid named Boomy on the closet shelf my elbow brushed against a pile of papers on the same shelf, sending them spiraling to the floor. I could have just picked them up and placed them back on the shelf. Instead I brought them to my desk to see what was there and make sure that all the papers – whatever they might be – were in proper order. I skipped lunch, begged off dinner, finally permitting myself to be force-fed a bowl of soup and a half of something that may have been a tuna fish sandwich – or possibly roast beef, as I read stories – all tales that sprouted from the sidewalks of New York - that I had written over the years for an audience of One – me!

I knew then that the shelf would remain clear and what was on that shelf now has a new home between the covers of this book,

*TALES FROM THE SIDEWALKS OF NEW YORK*

# THE JOURNEYMAN

*by Ron Ross*

When Billy Dumas came into town there were no brass bands to greet him. In fact, he drew about as much attention as a piece of scrap paper blowing in a wind gust. That's the way it is with an old punched out and banged up heavy who rides the rails east to west and north to south but whose ride to the top never was and never will be. Even on his good days ... actually, with Billy there were warm days, cold days, rainy days, sunny days – but good days? Only, if you call it a good day when no growling mutt was looking to take a bite out of his ass and there was a stool or bench somewhere for him to flop out. Otherwise, good days? Not for Billy Dumas.

He wasn't the kind of guy people didn't like. Actually, he was a likeable guy by default, mainly because there was no reason not to like him. The King of Plain, that's what he was. Oatmeal or a doughnut and coffee for breakfast, whatever the daily special was at Woolworth's for lunch and beef stew or meat loaf for dinner – if there was change in his pocket. And depending on that same pocket, a double feature every

Saturday. That's all it took to make Billy happy. Well, maybe a cold schooner of beer didn't bring a frown to him on a hot summer day and neither did a steaming cup of Java when snot icicles were hanging from his nose. Let's just say that Billy Dumas was okay with the simple pleasures of life. And let us also say that life could probably have treated him a little better, but it didn't.

Billy was a prizefighter. A no frills that's-what-you-see-that's-what-you-get prizefighter. A lot of guys who grow up in neighborhoods like Billy's become prizefighters but it's like an evolution; they fight for a few months or a few years, then, win or lose, they move on. It's like a stepping-stone to the real world where people are mechanics, truck drivers, stevedores and get a paycheck every week without spilling blood and running every morning before the sun gets up. But not Billy. He was a prizefighter.

Billy would go eight to ten rounds with anyone, anywhere, always giving the best that was in him. He had sturdy legs - like tree trunks, punched like a mule, knew all the moves and never ran out of gas. The major problem was that Billy was like a Model-T in a world of Corvettes and Porsches, a big old sedan that kept chugging along but had only one gear. He'd keep on going, looking okay, holding his own, but once the pace picked up Billy couldn't accelerate. Sometimes it seemed like he was stuck in the mud with his wheels spinning – Billy Dumas was going nowhere.

But even nowhere is somewhere and for Billy somewhere was anywhere a railroad track passed through. Which is how he winds up in Evanston, from where he'll move on to Sioux City, then Omaha. A journeyman fighter whose home base was any whistle stop with a fight club. You could say he was a storybook fighter with the story usually following the same plot. He comes in as the spoiler against a local favorite. Sometimes he gets cheered as the loser. Other times he gets booed as the winner. In the overall scheme of things, whatever the result, it was not earth shattering. However, life in general was not going too well for him lately. He wanted to dig in and turn things around and the only way he could think of doing it was by fighting. It was the one thing he knew and did ... and depended upon. So, now, in his mind, whatever fight would be coming up was not going to be just another fight.

Billy Dumas may never have been a top ten and maybe he never could shine the shoes of a Louis or Sharkey but whenever he climbed between those ropes into a ring he knew he was being paid to fight and that's what he did. There was a time Billy didn't have to travel – at least not more than a subway ride away. 'When there were so many fight clubs in New York that you had a card every night of the week except Sunday, a local guy with the heart and punch of a Billy Dumas was bread and butter for every promoter, and for the fans he was usually the icing on the cake ... at least for a while, anyhow.

The first time Billy hit Evanston was ten, maybe twelve years ago. His hazel eyes still had a sparkle that shone from the hollow of his high, angular cheekbones joining brow ridges that were criss-crossed with jagged pink lines of scar tissue. His nose, with a little knob at the bridge, bent slightly to the left. He would have been an easy guess on "what's My Line?"

Billy was the kind of opponent who, when going against a local favorite, the fans were willing to plunk their money down to watch. His record was pretty good back then mainly because he was quite a kindergarten standout. Against four and six round apprentices his punch and condition kept him close to the top of the class. It was graduate school where his A's and B's were replaced by C's and C minuses. He still shuffled forward in that classic, upright stance, working off the left jab, an occasional left hook searching for a soft spot in the belly and always looking for an opening for the right hand. But in the eights and tens the targets that he was shooting at were a bit more elusive, the punches came back in greater numbers with a lot more sting and Billy learned that oak trees don't fall like saplings.

And the fans learned something, too. They learned that Billy Dumas was one tough son-of-a-bitch who could make anyone sweat and huff and puff but he couldn't pull in that brass ring. He was on the merry-go-round just for the ride. Pretty soon one Billy Dumas fight was just like every Billy Dumas fight. The bell rang, Billy came forward, always moving in. He'd land some punches, miss a lot more, bodies would collide and there'd be some snorting and grunting. It was never an easy night for Billy or the other guy. But the real lesson was that down the stretch there was nothing for Billy to turn on. All his cylinders were already opened up so when his opponent reached down for his bootstraps, called on those extra ounces, Billy was there to watch the show. After a while, not too many others were interested in watching Billy's show. They knew the ending. He became a piss-time attraction. When Billy Dumas was in the ring it became a good time to take a break, answer Nature's Call and get ready for the next fight on the card. That's when Billy began taking his show on the road.

So, Billy arrived on his maiden voyage to Evanston with a letter of introduction. He would rather have arrived with his manager, but Hammy Sorenson was a guy with a very fragile constitution who very easily got carsick, airsick, trainsick and seasick – unless accompanied by a contender or at least a reasonable facsimile. It did not take Jake Flood, Evanston's one-and-only fight promoter, very long to read Hammy's two-liner about "a good, tough earnest heavyweight who always gives the fans _and the promoter_ their money's worth" but it did inspire him to look up at Billy and go into his "dime a dozen fighters" and "if you're willing to work cheap" spiels.

"I don't know ... . I wanna do Hammy a favor but I got kids crawling outta the woodwork. Good tough kids, crowd pleasers who are willing to work with me, you know what I mean."

"I know the score, Mr. Flood. I'm no pig. I know you'll be fair with me, and I promise, you won't be sorry. Here, just listen to this." With which Billy pulled a billfold out of the back pocket of his pants from which he very carefully removed a neatly folded newspaper clipping and, after displaying it to Jake, read to him,

> **"Billy Dumas showed me something last night as he starched up-and-coming Doug Rafferty in 2 minutes and 8 seconds of the 5<sup>th</sup> round at the Broadway Arena in Brooklyn. What he showed me was that he could stop a freight train with his right hand."**

That's all that Billy read. There was more to the article but it didn't register with him so he simply wiped it from his mind. So what if the guy that wrote it thought that

> *"...problem is that everyone in the arena knows when that right hand is coming, including his opponent. He's a hard-nosed warrior whose best will probably always be a little short of the mark ... "* Billy felt that he made his point. "That's from the New York Journal-American. You won't be disappointed with me, Mr. Flood."

Actually, what disappointed Jake Flood more than anything else was paying the price. The cheaper the cost, the happier he was. Seeing a bargain basement special, Jake gave out with this great big "Okay-I-Give-In-Out-Of-The-Goodness-

Of-My-Heart" sigh and inked Billy in for the semi-final eight on that Friday's card.

As it turned out, Billy and Jake were very compatible. When it came to paying out, Jake squeezed quarters into nickels and Billy, on the other hand, was strictly a retail buyer. Whatever the price tag was, that was it. They got along just fine. Even when Billy, in his Evanston debut, belted out a young local favorite, Jake was not unhinged. Then again, he did not shed tears when, two weeks later. Billy went oh-for everything swinging at a slippery, side-stepping dude from the South Side of Chicago who played a medley of his favorite hits on Billy's face.

After mailing Hammy his one-third share (which his manager magnanimously cut from fifty per cent because, not being there, he had no overhead), paying his hotel bill and deducting his train fare, Billy cleared a little more than forty bucks in Evanston before deciding it was time to move on. Jake Flood shook his hand and wished him luck, thinking he would never see him again and not caring whether he did or not.

That's the way most people felt about Billy, but not Molly. She cared. Maybe if her old man hadn't boozed away the super's key money at McSorley's Ale House they would've gotten the apartment that was promised to them up in Washington Heights and growing up with and caring about Billy Dumas would not have been in the cards. But much of life is a crap shoot and whether winding up living one floor below the Dumas family on West 37th Street would be considered coming out with a seven or rolling snake-eyes is open to conjecture.

Even though their lips never touched until they were eighteen, thirteen years after becoming neighbors, theirs was a match made in Hell's Kitchen. At 8:30 each morning they'd walk to school together. No one ever teased or got fresh with Molly. Not with Billy Dumas at her side. After school Molly double-dutched and hop-scotched the hours away while Billy began learning his trade at the C.Y.O. gym on 14th Street.

The second looks that came Molly's way were mostly at how she was dwarfed by Billy even though she looked taller than her five-foot-four with her head always held high and shoulders squared away. She was pleasant enough to look at but a bit of an upturn to her nose and fuller lips would have helped to draw double-takes. Just by looking at them, it was easy to assume that this big sheepdog of a guy watched over and took care of her but everyone who knew them understood that it was Molly who took care of Billy. And taking care of Billy was no easy task. Molly outgrew the street games but Billy never moved on from the gym.

There never was a proposal of marriage. Billy had all kinds of courage but not that kind. It took his fourth professional fight, a sliced eyebrow and a busted nose to bring that about. Molly never asked Billy why he wanted to be a prizefighter. It was as common among the boys growing up in her neighborhood as chicken pox or whooping cough, but in Billy's case, not as curable. Billy was in third grade when Jack Dempsey climbed back through the ropes at the Polo Grounds to knock out Luis Angel Firpo and from that moment on he knew what he wanted to be. He didn't care if he was a Dempsey or a Firpo – he just wanted to be in that ring.

After watching her best friend win his first three fights, Molly sat far back at the Star Casino, but not far enough, as Billy got all busted up for twenty-five bucks. She went back to the dressing room and watched as they stitched up Billy's cut and put icepacks on his nose. The next day Molly led Billy to City Hall where they took out a marriage license. She knew that she had to take care of him.

☆ ☆ ☆

Before he left Evanston that first time, Billy found out that problems he never could have solved in school came to him pretty easily now. He didn't even need a pencil and paper to figure out that without Hammy's one-third cut and the cost of a train ticket he'd have cashed out with better than a hundred bucks in his pocket. Hammy? He was like death and taxes but when it came to railroads, there were options, especially when there were freight yards around. As a matter of fact, it was a lot more comfortable sprawling out on the floor of a freight car than sitting cramped up in a seat made for a ballerina and gagging on a blend of cigar smoke and cheap perfume. And the price was right.

So, he wrapped up two tens in a Moon Mullins comic strip, put it in an envelope and mailed it off to Molly, leaving him with $20.42 and a future that no self-respecting fortune teller would ever want to know about, let alone, dare to predict. It was a future that Billy chose and that Molly shared. She had a good job at Klein's and was able to open up better futures for Billy, but Billy explained that he was a fighter, not a truck driver or stock clerk. When he was at home he would wrap her in a gentle bear hug and explain it to her and tell how, as long as he had that right hand, his future was in front of him. When he was on the road he explained it with an occasional envelope of bills. At first, the tough part for Molly was when Billy was away for long stretches. Soon, that became the easy part. The tough part was when he returned home, each time with a face more unrecognizable, eyes that had become mere slits, shadowed by layers of scar tissue, lips and ears swollen and a slur to his speech that made him sound like a stranger.

✧ ✧ ✧

Billy looked at the woman behind the counter and hoped she wouldn't ask him anything until he was able to rest for a few minutes. If every muscle in his body didn't ache it was only because it was a muscle he couldn't feel anymore. The floor of the Union Pacific car that he rode in on was harder than a city street and he was bounced around like the train had square wheels. Usually, he folded up a topcoat under himself and used it as a mattress. but Billy didn't have a topcoat any more.

He felt that he couldn't walk another step when he turned onto Dempster Street and then he saw Moe's Diner; he blinked his eyes to make sure it wasn't a mirage. "Hi, Sweetie. You look like you can use some coffee."

He stared up at her and thought she looked a little bit like Molly. Lately, he thought that about a lot of women. "I was just thinkin', it's not far from dinnertime and I shouldn't ruin my appetite," he lied. With less than a dollar's change in his pocket it was a lie of expedience and they don't count.

"First time in Evanston?" It wasn't a bad guess considering the held-together-by-tape-and-string cardboard suitcase on the stool next to him.

"No, I've been here about four or five times over the last ten years." He put out his hand to stop her as she placed a cup of steaming coffee in front of him. "No, I told you. I don't wanna ruin ..."

"Do me a favor," she leaned over and whispered. "I put up a fresh pot. Not that this ain't, but the boss don't like to see two pots out there at the same time. Do me a favor. It's on me."

Billy looked at her. She was a better liar than he was. His hand shook as he raised the cup to his lips and felt new life surge through his body just like a transfusion of energy.

"You a wrestler?" she asked, trying not to stare too obviously at a face that resembled a map of the Rockie Mountains.

"Nah, I'm legit. What makes you think that?"

"Well, you sure do look like a big, strong guy. I wouldn't think you're a traveling salesman," she smiled.

"I'm a prizefighter," Billy smiled back.

"I'll bet you're really good. Are you'?"

Billy reached into his pocket, pulled the still-in-one-piece clipping from his wallet and read, " `... **he could stop a freight train with his right hand.**' I ain't bragging and that don't make me the best in the whole wide world. It just tells you something about me."

"It sure does, Sweetie. I am very impressed," she said, batting her eyelashes. "By the way, I am Sally. And you're ..."

"Billy Dumas."

"I think I heard of you."

"I don't think so. Not unless you read the Fight Results column in the sport pages every day or Ring Magazine. It's in real small print. I ain't that big a name."

Sally walked to the back and when she returned she was carrying a large slab of apple pie that she carried over to a table in the corner. "What happened to the guy who was sitting here?"

"What guy?" Billy was pretty sure that no one had been sitting in that part of the diner. In fact, the place was empty except for him, Sally and a mailman nursing a doughnut and coffee at the other end of the counter.

"What a creep! That's what it is in this business. Thank God he didn't order a steak dinner. Well, I can't put this back. Against the law." She walked back behind the counter and dropped the pie in front of Billy. "Knock this off for me, will ya, Champ?"

Billy didn't argue. His stomach didn't let him. Billy looked at the clock on the wall. He wanted to find Jake Flood before the day was over. As he got up, he reached into his pocket and pulled out a handful of change which he was about to deposit on the counter.

"Hey, Sweetie, put that back. You're embarrassing me. You help me out of a tight spot and you wanna tip me for it? I should be giving you the tip." She looked at his crumpled, dust-covered clothes and dug up the courage to ask, "Listen, I know you don't get paid until you fight. We can always use a guy to wash some dishes ..."

"I'm a fighter. I don't get paid for anything else. But what I can do is, you let me eat here and I'll do your dishes."

Sally and Billy shook hands. He was very careful not to squeeze too hard.

✱  ✱  ✱

Billy thought to himself, "Either I got bigger or this office shrunk."

Jake Flood thought to himself, "Why me?" but said, "Billy Dumas, a ghost from the past. What a pleasant surprise. You are looking so good." He was the third person to lie that afternoon.

"I need a couple of fights, Mr. Flood."

This time Jake said it out loud. "Why me'?"

Billy didn't understand the question. He wasn't supposed to. "What do you mean? You're the promoter."

Jake wanted to make it short and sweet, so he leaned back and thought for a minute. Actually, he had grown to like Billy Dumas. He had grown to like and appreciate a lot of the boys that climbed through the ropes in his arena. But Billy was like a contemporary. He came to Evanston the first time not long after Jake Flood turned his vaudeville palace into a sports arena and over the years, while other of Jake's early fighters became fathers and some, grandfathers, Billy Dumas remained a prizefighter, returning every couple of years, always giving it his best. Neither one ever made it big, but they both tried. Jake's downfall was that he began to appreciate the sport and the men in it too much for his own good. Sometimes it's difficult for a heart and a brain to get along in the same body. About three years back an old washed-up middleweight from Youngstown pleaded for Jake to put him on a card so he could make enough to keep his landlord from evicting him and his crippled mother. The crippled part must have been hereditary because the way this guy moved it looked like the biggest betting action was going to be on whether he could climb through the ropes. The only way he was going to pass the physical was if he wasn't there to take it. Which he wasn't. Jake got a stand-in to take the physical and arranged for a sweet-natured, compassionate oppo-nent, who, in exchange for the promise of a big main event almost got a hernia carrying this Youngstown relic around the ring for eight rounds while the crowd crooned "Let Me Call You Sweetheart". There was a very happy ending for almost everyone. The old fighter from Youngstown was happy because he walked out of the ring unmarked (with some assistance to be sure) and was able to save his home; his landlord was happy because he came into this money that he never expected to see; and the very compassion-ate opponent was happy because he added an easy win to his record and became a main-event fighter in the process; Jake was happy for doing a good deed, but only for a very short while.

Jake figured that the doctor, after examining some twenty fighters, would never realize if one fighter in the ring that night was not the fighter that stood before him that after-noon. However, as it develops, this doctor had seen many fighters who had to be helped down the steps from the ring but never before had he seen a fighter who had to be helped *up* the steps.

The six-member athletic commission had a hearing at which they said that Jake had done a very bad thing which made him a bad person. Jake said, on the contrary, he had done a very good thing and was therefore, a good person. It was decided by a six-to-one count that Jake Flood was a bad person and as the state of Illinois did not license bad people, Jake Flood was no longer a boxing promoter. Feeling he had been greatly wronged, Jake appealed to the powers-that-be or the powers-that-were and recognizing all the good intentions on Jake's part, the decision was reversed – to a degree. Jake Flood was eligible to apply for a license – just not as a box-ing promoter. So, Jake journeyed to the Division of Licenses, checked to see what career opportunities were out there for a guy with such unique qualifications as he possessed and became a notary public. At twenty-five cents a signature Jake realized he would never make the cover of Fortune Magazine but, on the other hand, much of the stress would he removed from his life.

"Billy," Jake hid behind a cover of blue cigar smoke so that the rancor and bitterness would be masked as he tried explain-ing his descent from grace, "I am no longer a promoter. I have branched out and am now a notary public." It is possible that Billy was impressed but it was a time when his thoughts revolved mainly around himself. "Jeez, I was really bankin' on a couple of good pay days. I really need it Mr. Flood."

Jake looked at Billy and what he saw no couple or any amount of pay days were going to make up for. There was no longer any definition to his once finely structured face which now more closely resembled a half-blown balloon and the wide hazel eyes had been hammered into two chinky slits. Suddenly, Jake felt guilty but all he could think of doing was tamp out his cigar and wave the bothersome smoke away from Billy's face. "Billy, if I could help you, I would, but it ain't my business anymore. I got no say in it." Then Jake made an offer that he did not make very often in his life. "How about a few bucks to tide you over?"

"I'm not asking for any handouts. I wanna earn what I get. If you're not the promoter anymore, maybe you can take me to the guy who is."

☆   ☆   ☆

The outside of the Crown Hotel needed a little more paint than it did two years ago and the smell of mildew in the lobby was slightly stronger but there weren't many places in town that Billy could afford even in the best of times. The five-bucks-for-a- single was about four and a half bucks more than he had in his pocket but Billy did have prospects. It was the two nights in advance that was the real problem so he found a bench at the Greyhound terminal which may not have been as comfortable, but it was affordable.

He had no problem getting up early in the morning because he wasn't able to fall asleep, so at 5 AM he left his cardboard suitcase with nothing worth swiping and went out for his run which was more like a drunken sailor staggering in a windstorm across a rolling, tossing deck. From the first day he started training as a boxer. Billy Dumas never missed a day of roadwork except for when he was on a moving train or on the day of a fight. It fell into the same category as breathing, eating and sleeping, all of which he did better and enjoyed more. It was his one activity, though, that gave him the opportunity and time to think and sometimes to even use his imagination. He did both as he plodded down Main

Street and circled Grey Park. First he thought of how things were going to start looking up when Mr. Flood brings him over to the new promoter later that morning. Then he had a little daydream about Molly and smiled as he pictured her behind her counter at Klein's Department Store. His vision blurred and biting down hard upon his lip, he tried convincing himself that the moistness in his eyes was because of a cinder and not the deep sadness that had been coming over him so often lately.

Billy Dumas took his beatings and came back for more. But the pain was not his alone. Molly shared in it. Some called Billy courageous, some called him a stoic, others called him stubborn and a guy who didn't know when it was time to hang them up. About a year ago he came back from Toledo with a busted ear drum and a lip so badly split that all he could eat was what he could suck in with a straw. Billy was able to handle it. Molly wasn't. The beatings had taken their toll. Billy's hurt was her grief. She told him again about a good, steady job at Klein's, how she wanted to spend her time with him instead of constantly worrying about him. Billy told her what he always told her, that he was a fighter and that was his job. He told her that he was good and he believed what he was saying. He believed it because he believed Hammy and it was after he lost his third fight in a row, a tough ten-rounder to Bulldog Curtis at Ridgewood Grove, and he was wondering about himself, that Hammy made him understand things.

"You know what a champ is, Billy? A champ is being the best at what he does. And you are the roadblock, the hurdle for every fighter lookin' for that crown. You are the big test,

Billy, and no one is better at that job than you. You are the champ at what you do." He walked to the promoter's office, picked up the two hundred buck purse, put a hundred in his pocket, gave Billy his half and a pat on the back. It was good to be the manager of "the champ".

Molly shook her head sadly. She said she couldn't take any more. It was as much a plea as an ultimatum. Billy looked at her and came back with a plea of his own. "It's what I do, Moll. It's all I know how to do.

And it was over. She ran her fingers gently across his broken face, gave him a hug, and kissed him goodbye. That was it.

✫   ✫   ✫

For Billy, life moved on because that was his style. Shake it off and keep coming forward. No matter how hard the punch, no matter how great the hurt, Billy Dumas knew only one way. But this was no ordinary blow. He couldn't quite grasp the reason why. It was like getting tagged with a punch you never saw – and never expected. Billy countered with hope. He was good at that. It was hope that kept him climbing through the ropes all those long years. It was also hope, though, that blinded him to what was real.

He moved his belongings into the Y and spent his nights staring at the ceiling, wondering why Molly didn't understand and believe in him. When he'd finally drift off to sleep he would dream dreams that weren't very grand. They were plain, simple dreams of the way things were before. Just dreams of him and Molly. Nothing special or exciting. They brought happiness to his sleep and sadness when he awoke.

If one-half of all the people living in Evanston came up to Jake Flood's office every single day to have their signatures notarized maybe then he would be able to pay the butcher, the baker and everyone else he owed money to. It was only a maybe. So it was very fortunate that Jake also had the rental income from the arena to supplement his cigar-box-half-filled-with-quarters operation. Actually, he did much better as a landlord than he ever did as a promoter. The change in occupations also gave him a totally different perception of prizefighters. It's funny how much easier it is to like a guy when that guy is not banging on your door for money.

Still, Jake thought what a nice day it would be if Billy just got lost and didn't bother him. That "what-did-I-do-to-deserve-this" feeling came very naturally to him. But, then, looking at this caricature of the prizefighter he once knew, he felt a twinge and wished he were made of tougher stuff. He didn't know who to feel more sorry for – Billy Dumas or himself

So, when Billy told Jake he needed a fight very badly, Jake, knowing that the veteran was on the down side of yesterday, tried to talk him out of it. Especially when he heard that Hammy Sorenson no longer took a cut from Billy's purse even though he was still his manager of record and it was no secret that Hammy had only two charities - his left pocket and his right pocket. The thought never entered Jake's mind that Hammy Sorenson, too, could have found a cricket sitting on his shoulder.

Jake was not Billy's Dutch uncle. He just acted that way. It was difficult for him, just as it was for Molly or almost anyone, to comprehend that for Billy Dumas, fighting was the affirmation of who he was. His stamp of identification. The mold of himself without which he was no one ... nothing ... dust to dust. For Billy Dumas, prizefighting was just as necessary as the blood coursing through his veins. But Jake tried. He gave

Billy some well-intended advice. He told him it was time to get out, to hang up his gloves before he got hurt. Then he thought back to how, after each of his fights in Evanston, Billy used to set aside half his purse and mail it to his wife ... Molly ... he even remembered her name. And he remembered how proud Billy was the couple of times he talked about her. So he told him to go home to his wife and Billy told him he didn't have a wife to go home to.

At first Jake didn't understand. For one brief second he felt that maybe the punches took their toll, then he saw the look in Billy's eyes and he knew that, yeah, the punches probably did take their toll but not the way he had thought. And he sensed that, once again, he was going to get involved in something that he knew was wrong but doing the right thing was even more wrong. He told Billy he'd see about getting him a fight and Billy thanked him. Jake did not say "You're welcome."

The next day, Billy put in a grueling workout at the gym. So did Jake. Billy searched out the toughest heavies to spar with, while Jake searched for someone who looked like a major patty-cake performer. They each worked up a good sweat and came out satisfied with their performances.

It's funny how two guys can look at the same menu and each salivate at the other guy's dish. But that's how it was with Jake Flood and Jim Garrity, the manager of Tony Saldino. As soon as Jake laid eyes on Saldino, a local product who would probably go off at even money if matched with the heavy bag, he knew he had the blue plate special. For Garrity, when he saw Billy's gray-streaked hair and flattened out face lined with enough furrows and old scars to make it look like a road map, he was thinking dessert with whipped cream but absolutely no cherry. He would be getting no cherry.

It turns out that Saldino was scheduled for the semi-final on next Friday's card against a man-mountain named

Malousek who was causing Saldino to have bad dreams at night but just a couple hours ago, Garrity learned from B.T. Huskins, the promoter, that Malousek's manager called to say his fighter was very unhappy with the purse and was pulling out of the fight.

Recognizing that timing was everything in life, Jake wasted none of it as he whisked Garrity's dessert to Huskins' office while the blue plate special looked on approvingly, happy that he would now be able to sleep better.

✵ ✵ ✵

When Jake and Billy got to B.T. Huskins' office it was an easy observation on Billy's part to see that these guys had no intention of kissing one another. It might have had something to do with the fact that Huskins, former deputy boxing commissioner, current promoter and also Jake Flood's tenant who leased the arena, was one of those instrumental in drumming Jake out of the promotional business, which he then took over, or it could just have been normal landlord-tenant relations. Whatever, they were more like oil and water than bread and butter, but it didn't matter because the bulldog-faced guy sitting behind the desk needed a fighter and Billy Dumas was a fighter.

✵ ✵ ✵

When Sally found out from one of the Greyhound bus drivers who was a regular at Moe's that her dishwasher slept in the bus terminal the night before, she had another favor to ask of Billy.

"Sweetie, I hate to impose, but our watchdog died last week ..."

"Gee, that's too bad. How'd it happen?"

"Uh, chicken bones. Poor thing choked on chicken bones. Anyhow, we don't feel safe leaving the place unguarded overnight. So, until we get another dog, would it be too much of a favor if you'd sleep here? It may not be as good as a hotel, but we got a nice cot in the back. We'd really appreciate it."

Nobody was more willing to be imposed upon than Billy Dumas was then. He told Sally about his fight at the Arena the next week and she asked if it would be okay if she came to watch him.

"It won't make you nervous, will it?"

He thought for a moment. To a guy who's climbed into that ring nearly two hundred times, another fight is something you take pretty much in stride. But, in his mind, Billy Dumas had built a stage, a set and a scenario. This was the fight that was going to set his life back on course. "Nervous? Nah, It'll be like a walk in the park."

So, Billy stepped up his normal routine and worked very hard getting ready for another fight that he convinced himself was not really just another fight. Each morning he'd bounce out of his cot before the roosters had a chance to crow, run two loops through the park, come back for a breakfast of oatmeal, rye toast and black coffee. Then he did his work in the back washing the dishes and Sally kept looking around for the tea kettle when she realized there was none. Instead of a tea kettle, she had a whistling dishwasher/prizefighter. She smiled but hoped he wouldn't break into song.

After a three hour break, there was a long, sweat-filled afternoon at the gym where eyebrows raised as they watched a worn out old veteran seemingly transformed into a twenty-one year old bundle of energy. A local heavyweight named Saldino was beginning to have misgivings.

At night, sleep would come quickly, filled with dreams of his hand being held high by the referee in fight after fight as the crowds cheered for him, and always, emerging from the crowd would be Molly, trying vainly to reach out and tell him how proud she was of him. In this dream his face was youthful and unmarked and his eyes were bright and clear. It was as good a dream as he could want to have.

☆　☆　☆

On Thursday, after three days of looking and feeling better than he had in ages, Billy tapered off with a light workout. On the way back to Moe's he stopped under the marquee of the local movie house. "City For Conquest" was playing. He had seen it so many times that he could shut his eyes and recite the follow-up to any line in the movie. He couldn't pass it up so he spent the evening watching another old fighter, played by Jimmy Cagney, show them all what he was made of. As he sat back comfortably in the dark, nearly empty theater, he slowly began to realize that there was something he never really noticed before. It was how much Ann Sheridan resembled Molly. He thought that was strange, because a couple of weeks ago he had the same feeling about Paulette Goddard.

He wanted to stay and watch the picture again but he knew he should get to bed early. It had been a really good week. It would take Friday to make it perfect. Friday got off to a good start. The sun rose exactly when it was supposed to. Billy didn't. Fight day brought one luxury with it. No road-work, so he stayed in the sack until seven. Even the clanging of dishes and the barking of breakfast orders up front didn't bother him. Everyone else was on schedule.

Sally got to the diner and opened up for the breakfast crowd at 6:30. She was surprised to see Billy still asleep, then figured out that on the day of a fight he rests. She called her cousin Claire to make sure that she was prepared to fill in for her that evening so that she could go to the arena. Everything was set.

Tony Saldino started the day off with a big win by slapping the hell out of his wife for letting the baby wake him up. He was feeling tough and ugly. Looking at himself in the bathroom mirror, he snorted and sneered, psyching himself up for that old tub of lard Dumas.

Doc Halvorsen packed his medical bag and was about to begin his two block walk to the arena at ten minutes to eleven when he turned back to his desk, hearing the phone ring. He knew it was B.T. Huskins calling with any last minute changes. Now he'd have to walk a little brisker than he liked but he would still be there at eleven on the dot, like always.

When Buck Stracey pulled his engine into the Chicago terminal right on time at 9:03 AM he got some good news. Instead of taking out the 12:10 he was switched to the 8:30 PM to Sacramento. That gave him a whole day in Chicago which meant at least a good show and a steak dinner. Nothing gave Buck more pleasure than being at the throttle in control of a powerful, surging, dynamic locomotive. But a blood-rare steak smothered in onions came a close second.

For Jake Flood, any time that he got in was on schedule. After a haircut and a shave followed by a philosophical discussion with the bootblack on the corner he found himself inking his notary pad and getting ready to settle in behind his desk a few minutes before noon when Jim Garrity came storming in.

✰　✰　✰

Billy Dumas knew that mistakes happen all the tune. Still, the stone settling in his stomach was getting heavier and heavier. When Doc Halvorsen called for "Saldino and Malousek, going eight rounds, step up to the scale", Billy called out, almost like a prayer, "Excuse me. It's supposed to be Saldino and Dumas". He kept telling himself it was a mistake, but he was having a problem believing himself

Tony Saldino also decided to do some praying after seeing the man-mountain, Malousek. "That's right. It's supposed to be Saldino and Dumas." He left out "Please, God."

Doc Halvorsen thought to himself, "Wow, these two really want at each other. Probably put on one hell of a show." But orders being orders and the good doctor, knowing where his paycheck came from, explained, "Got this list from B.T. Huskins less than two hours ago, fellas."

Billy started to say something, but, instead, removed the towel from around his waist, got dressed, turned and headed for the street. He walked slowly around the corner to Huskins' office. His legs were unsteady beneath him and he kept squeezing his eyelids tightly shut, hoping to snap himself awake from what he hoped was a terrible dream.

Billy Dumas had enough street smarts to know that more often than not, it was *who* you knew rather than *what* you knew that got you what you wanted. He didn't know there was a reverse gear in there somewhere. When Malousek's manager called the day before and told Huskins that his fighter reconsidered and would fight Saldino after all, ordinarily the promoter would tell him which body of water to jump into, but as one of his greatest joys was sticking it to Jake Flood, he chose happiness. Malousek was in and Dumas was out.

Huskins was sitting behind his desk and looked at Billy like he was a dirt smudge on his wall. Billy was not too good at making speeches but he spoke slowly and tried his best, without begging or pleading, to explain that this fight was very important to him and how he would make sure that the crowd got more than their money's worth. He tried to impress him with how hard he worked at his trade.

When he saw the jowl-faced promoter follow a yawn with a sigh he felt like it was the tenth round and he was way behind on points. Desperation time. Billy pulled out his yellowed Journal-American clipping and read about the night when he clocked Rafferty at the Broadway Arena — "... **he could stop a freight train with his right hand."** He turned his eyes from the paper – "That's me they're talkin' about." - and looked at Huskins who was so impressed that he yawned again, and informed Billy in very plain, but not so easy to understand english to forget it - he couldn't use him. Then he looked at the old warrior and told him it was time to hang them up. He could have told him to stop breathing or he could have grasped his heart and stopped it from pumping. Instead he told him to hang up his gloves. A good message from a bad messenger.

But, when you're a guy named Billy Dumas and all you know is to be a fighter and you can't even think of being anything else a message doesn't always hit home the way it's supposed to. One thing was for sure, though. For Billy Dumas Friday was not a good day. He wasn't sure of when or how he left Huskins'office. He took off on a trot, not knowing where or why he was going.

✫　✫　✫

When Jake Flood came huffing and puffing his way into Huskins' office it was not with the idea of changing his mind. He was too much the practical pig to entertain the notion of miracles. He was there to unburden what was on his chest,

e mugs coming out to root him on. As the cheers and noise
he crowd cascaded over him, Billy waved his right hand
cknowledge his following and all the trees along the path
ed and bent as the wind whistled through their branches.

✲ ✲ ✲

etimes your gut knows more than your brain. Jake felt
this was one of those times. It was like a baked beans and
bage syndrome, but the gnawing ache was not indigestion.
had no idea how he was going to ease the hurt that Billy
to be feeling but he knew he had to find him and try.
Actually, even though he wouldn't admit it to anyone, he
w that Huskins was right — Billy Dumas shouldn't be fight-
anymore. Huskins may have had the right answer, but he
it with the wrong formula. His bouncing Dumas from the
had nothing to do with the fighter's welfare or to protect
. Nothing noble or anything like that. B.T. Huskins' only rea-
for shelving Billy Dumas was to stick it to *him* — Jake Flood.
lizing that filled Jake with a strange kind of guilt and a strong
se that he was committed to help Billy. But first he had to find
. He was too fat and out of shape to run, but he ran anyhow.

✲ ✲ ✲

y was calm as he bounced on the balls of his feet, rotating
hips to keep his tone but his jaw was clamped in a tight set
determination. There was no quickening of his pulsebeat,
deep breaths. Just a narrowing of his eyes as he focused
full being on the task confronting him. It should be just
ther night's work, but it wasn't and he knew that. Why he

to let the contempt that was bottled up inside of him for so
long come spilling out. He was there to leave no doubt in the
mind of Jim Garrity that it was B.T. Huskins alone who sold
him out. And mostly, he was there because he felt so goddam
lousy for Billy Dumas.

Jake Flood's world suited him very well. It was simple
and uncluttered, made up only of knights and fire-breathing dragons. Being that it was his world, he was the one who
designated who were the knights and who were the dragons.
Not surprisingly, even though any suit of armor would have
made a tight fit, Jake was a knight and by a unanimous vote of
'One', B.T. Huskins was a very credible reptile.

B.T. Huskins also had his own world. It, too, was simple
and uncluttered. It consisted of a God (self-appointed, of
course) and one commandment – "Thou shalt do the right
thing." And the right thing to Huskins was that a rule was a
rule. There were no ifs, ands or buts. In fact, there were rules
that B.T. Huskins added to the book and these rules were
sacred and unchallengeable.

One rule was that anything Jake Flood endorsed was to be
unendorsed, not to be granted. Another was that the bottom
line governed everything. For Jake Flood, it was much more
important to do a good thing than to do the right thing. The
two were not always the same. To Jake, it was okay to break or,
at least, bend a rule if it made things come out good.

So, when he asked that Huskins have a little compassion ...
feeling for a guy who gave everything he had to this game,
a guy who fought from bell to bell, not a single tear trickled
down Huskins' cheek. He looked Jake squarely in the eye and
told him that Dumas was a washed-up has-been. It wasn't that
"compassion" was unknown to B.T. Huskins and it wasn't that
there was no compassion in his heart. It was simply that it was
reserved for himself. He crowed, "You never learn your lesson, do you?" and reminded Jake Flood how "compassion"

cost him his license. And Jake Flood corrected him as best he knew how. "Bullshit. You stole my license." The pointless meeting had come to an end.

Jake felt it was a good idea to find Billy.

So Sally went to the fights to see and cheer for Billy Dumas, but there was no Billy Dumas to cheer for. The mimeographed program only cost a dime but, still, Sally felt she was entitled to the correct information. There were eight bouts listed, none with the name Billy Dumas. Sometime during the second four-rounder she questioned an usher who pointed her to someone who he said was the matchmaker and would know. He *did* know. He knew what she already knew - that there was no Billy Dumas fighting on the card. Then he remembered that there had been a Billy Dumas scheduled but there was a last minute change. Sally decided she was not a fight fan and left.

It was almost nine o'clock when she got back to the diner. Her cousin Claire, somewhere between shaken up and confused, told her that Billy had stopped in early in the evening, picked up his suitcase, then hugged her and mumbled something like "Gotta go now, Moll. You'll see, it'll all be good" and left. Sally walked to the back. Billy's few belongings were gone. She was about to leave when she saw on top of the bed, neatly spread out, the old newspaper clipping that she was sure Billy Dumas never was without. Carefully, she tried picking it up but it was so dry and brittle with age it crumbled at her touch.

✧   ✧   ✧

Buck Stracey went over his check-list once more, then uncapped his thermos of hot, black coffee. His train began picking up speed and he smiled as he could never get over

the thrill of seeing the lights of Chicago f settled back and took a big swallow of the st It looked like another long, dull night bi made sure to stay alert on the job and caffei

✧   ✧   ✧

Billy Dumas got to Grey Park when he triec where he was going. It was always a journey tc another town, another fight. Suddenly, it al him and he put his suitcase down. This wasr fight. He had something to prove. Billy smil in a lungful of air. Suddenly, he was alive again. Everything was stored in a memory ba out effortlessly. There was nothing to think al routine took over. It was important to be w when he climbed into the ring. Fifteen minut left jabs, short hooks and an assortment of ri uppercuts had his perspiration running freely relaxed and calm with the juices starting to fl right mixture of excitement and anticipatio to his trainer, letting him know that he was re Park maintenance man turned away, uncomfo strange guy punching the air by the big oak tre him like he was a first cousin. He ignored him emptying the waste baskets along the lane.

Billy started the long dressing-room-to-ri he bounced towards the east gate of Grey Pa believe the turnout. There was Trini Alvarez, a El Paso; Dom DiGiacomo, that plug-ugly son broke his nose in Peoria. Joey "The Red" Baro hook! And even Doug Rafferty! Would you be

had to prove anything, he couldn't understand, but tonight he was going to show them what Billy Dumas was all about. He would show the crowds, he would show the Huskins and the Floods, and he would show Molly.

Even the sounds of the crowd couldn't drown out the snorting and the heavy, pounding approach of his adversary from the far side of the large arena. Something very much like a smile played its way across Billy's distended face but it wasn't a smile. It was a look of longing for ... what? It was an answer that Billy Dumas knew but didn't want to. He turned and lifted his face toward the intense, luminous stare of his opponent.

✫   ✫   ✫

When the clerk at the Crown Hotel checked the register and said he was certain that no Dumas was staying there, Jake was about to give up on finding him and, instead, head for the Arena to watch the show when he remembered Billy saying something about eating at Moe's Diner. So he took a cab to Moe's and found out that Billy Dumas had once again taken his show on the road. No forwarding address. Just a squeeze of the wrong lady and – Poof! Gone. As it turns out, Jake does not need a hunter's cap, a magnifying glass or a bloodhound.

It was the kind of beaten, battered suitcase that no eager but principled rag-picker would bother sifting through. Sitting there, at the entrance to Grey Park, it did everything but whistle and point the direction that Billy Dumas had taken. Jake had already checked the Greyhound Terminal and was heading for the commuter train station when he saw the very unforgettable suitcase that first caught his attention on Billy Dumas' first day in town. That's when Jake remembered that Billy Dumas chose not to travel first-class. He headed east, through Grey Park, towards the Union Pacific tracks. A sense of urgency caused him to increase his pace and his heart pounded in his chest.

✡ ✡ ✡

Billy squeezed his eyes shut. He had to close out faces of Huskins, Jake Flood, Molly, even Hammy Sorenson ... all telling him to hang up his gloves ... none of them understanding that this was his life ... that Billy Dumas was a prizefighter. Slowly, he opened his eyes and they were gone. They should have believed in him and respected him more. But that's why he was here now. Soon they would understand.

The crowd was roaring, awaiting the bell for the first round. The sounds engulfed Billy and bathed him in a comfort and glow that he had never felt before. They were there for him. They stamped their feet and roared for him until he felt the ground under him vibrate. He remained calm and determined as he turned to face his opponent.

✡ ✡ ✡

Jake Flood reached the top of the rise. He froze when he saw the sight confronting him. "Billy! Stop. Don't do it!" He was shouting as loud as he could but didn't think he could be heard.

✡ ✡ ✡

Billy Dumas squared away in his upright style, his left hand held high, right hand cocked, waiting for the opening.

Like always he moved forward. It was his way. He couldn't remember ever feeling this good. The ring lights were bright and his opponent came charging full speed …

✲ ✲ ✲

As he came around the turn at Rogers Park and moved into Evanston, Buck Stracey opened up his throttle and was about to reach for his thermos when he saw what he could not believe. He sounded his whistle and warning horn. They tore through the night air and blasted.

✲ ✲ ✲

Billy Dumas was a prizefighter who had come upon the moment that he was born to live.

Everything that he had ever wanted, loved and wished for, everything that he had ever learned and knew, everything that he had respected, honored and feared was all compressed into this one micro-instant. He stood poised, ready for this magnificent moment.

✲ ✲ ✲

Jake Flood watched, helpless to do anything, hypnotized by the spectacle that was occurring before him. His hands knotted into useless fists and tears streamed down his cheeks.

✲ ✲ ✲

Buck Stracey was in the eye of the Cyclops. He rode a crazed beast into a mad conflict. There was no believing what he saw in front of him. He hit the brakes with all the strength he possessed and the screeching of metal grating on metal cut through the night.

✡ ✡ ✡

Until this moment the bright lights had blinded him, but now Billy Dumas saw his foe clearly. As the locomotive bore down on top of him there was a horrible squealing and shrieking from the throat of the monster. Billy was set. It was what he was always prepared for. He pushed off his back foot and pivoted from the waist.

✡ ✡ ✡

Jake Flood stared at the macabre sight. The floodlight of the locomotive spotlighted Billy Dumas, causing his shadow to grow to giant proportions, now making it a battle of titan against titan. He watched and listened as the huge engine lurched, brakes screamed shrilly into the night air and an old prizefighter stepped forward.

✡ ✡ ✡

His entire body followed through as Billy Dumas unleashed a mighty blow and smiled with confidence because he believed that … ***he could stop a freight train with his right hand.***

*A kid named Albert "Boomy" Davidoff, who grew up to become the legendary Jewish prizefighter known as Al "Bummy" Davis, typified the spirit and flavor of Brownsville every bit as much as the strident calls of the pushcart peddlers lining its avenues and the odorous mixture of briny sour pickles, knishes and sweet potatoes wafting on every breeze. There was a uniqueness to Brownsville that set it apart from the rest of New York. This kid called Boomy was the personification of what Brownsville was all about.*

*Beware, the following three stories may awaken cravings for some pushcart delicacy from Pitkin Avenue.*

# Boomy And The Cowboys

*Murder!*

That is what Boomy is thinking at this moment. Sitting in the pitch black bathroom of Melvin & Sol's Cut-Rate Store on Belmont Avenue, Boomy is very seriously considering murdering Billy Belch. He knows it is not an easy job for an eleven year old kid to knock off someone who was shaving already and was a foot-and-half taller than he was but he had a whole night to plan it in the dark. He was sure that by now his father and brothers were out looking for him and he would probably get the lukshen strap on his bare ass when he got home which makes him think that maybe being a member of the Cowboys Social Athletic Club wasn't all that it was cracked up to be.

He likes the idea of hanging out with the older guys and being treated like he was one of them, even though that's all he did - hang out. In Brownsville the word is that the Cowboys were like the farm team of Murder, Inc. They were sneak thieves, pickpockets and second-story men practicing their trade with the hopes of making it to the big time.

Lectures and warnings from his mother and father - and his very best friend Shorty - made no impression. Boomy was mad at the way he was treated, blamed for everything by everyone because he was a Davidoff. But so what, he gets mad over a lot of things. That doesn't mean he's going to go out and rob a bank.

He enjoys being a big shot to these guys. They call him the Little Snatcher and being the brother of Big Gangy and Little Gangy, whose reputations will never have them confused with any angels or saints, doesn't hurt, either. Boomy couldn't understand, and he decided he wasn't going to try to figure it out, why, when other people in the neighborhood spit after his brothers walked by, these new friends of his looked up to them like they walked on water. His brothers Willie and Harry were the only ones who are not on his back about being a member of the Cowboys. In fact, they act like they are proud of him. If they only knew that all he did was lay on a couch and read joke books all day.

Almost every Friday night is party night for the Cowboys. Girls, potato chips, soda and even beer and whiskey. Boomy does not stick around for the parties because he does not dance too good and if he did dance his nose would keep hitting boobs because all the girls were older and bigger than he was. The Cowboys did not bother using an interior decorator. Their club room had black walls, a purple ceiling with silver stars painted on it and two lights with red globes which made it very hard to see. Billy Belch said with some of the girls they brought down there you were better off not seeing too good. Boomy wondered how often Billy Belch, who seems to be the head guy with the Cowboys, looked in a mirror.

Boomy likes Billy Belch the same way he likes Milk of Magnesia and enemas. He remembers the first time Billy makes him feel like a jerk which Boomy wishes was also the last time, but it wasn't. The Cowboys clubroom is in the basement of a two-story building on Hinsdale Street. On the other two floors there are girls. Girls who are in business for themselves. They do not wish to work for the mob guys who run everything in Brownsville because they do not wish to share their earnings with anyone and so far nobody bothers them. It seems that everyone is too busy looking over their own shoulders to be concerned with them. The Cowboys give them some sort of protection and cover and in return receive occasional freebies and a clubroom.

One Friday evening, while Poochie, Dizzy and Jumbo are setting up for that night's party, Boomy picks himself up to leave just as Billy Belch comes bouncing down the stairs. He turns to Boomy and laughs, "Where you going, Short-Ass?" and punctuates it with a forced explosion of gas that he draws up from his stomach, channelling it through his throat. This is something that Billy Belch does every three or four sentences which is why he is called what he is. For some reason he finds this both charming and amusing and although Billy Belch does not go to school nor does he have any other talent it is very probable that he does have a future as a volcano.

"How come you're always running away when we got girls coming over, Shrimp?"

"Leave the kid alone, why doncha, Belch?" Poochie counters.

Belch does not listen to Poochie. He feels that Boomy is squirming and he finds this to be very enjoyable. "What'sa matter - you in love with your hand, Boomy?" With which he gives a pumping motion with a clenched fist.

Boomy has no idea what Billy is yakking about. Maybe 'love' is a little strong but he certainly likes his hand - both of them, as a matter of fact. Why shouldn't he? It is beginning to dawn on Boomy that maybe Billy Belch is playing with him so he does not answer but keeps heading for the door.

Billy jumps in front of Boomy and blocks his way, grinning so wide that there is no room on his face for his eyes to stay open. "Hey, whattya think of Flossie, kid? You like her?"

Boomy thought for a second. Flossie was one of the girls upstairs. Whenever Boomy saw her she was wearing a dirty robe with ketchup stains and usually had a headful of curlers. She was fat, had a harelip and little pimples all over her face and always smelled from garlic. "Yeah, sure I like her." Boomy could not figure out why he said that. Poochie, Dizzy and Jumbo stopped setting out the chips and pretzels and turned to look at Boomy now.

"You want her?"

Boomy was having a lot of trouble figuring what Billy was doing. "Naw, I ain't got no room in our house. I got four sisters and two brothers." He knew by the way the four of them were snorting that this probably was not the right answer.

"*B-r-rop*"! Billy belched his loudest belch which got everyone's attention. "Ah, you wouldn't know what to do with a girl if one came up an' bit you on the pecker!"

Boomy knew a challenge when he heard one. "Bullshit!" That was an answer to any challenge that could be made.

"You ever been with a broad, Little Mister Tough Guy?"

Now Boomy understood what Billy was talking about and he knew he was on very shaky ground and would have to bluff his way through. "Whaddya take me for, asshole?" This draws looks of admiration from everyone except Billy Belch but that is exactly the reason why a kid like Boomy Davidoff is accepted as a Cowboy.

"Okay, so you wanna make it with Flossie?"

"She don't even know me."

"Are you kidding me?" Billy lied. "You know how many times she asked about you?"

Boomy couldn't believe it. She had to be at least sixteen, maybe even seventeen. "Aw, go on home, your mudder's calling!" Boomy couldn't stop his face from reddening.

Billy turned towards the three other Cowboys and shrugged. "The kid's chicken. Oh, well, what are you gonna do?"

That was it! There was Boomy, jaw jutting out, balled up fists on hips and eyes glaring at Billy Belch, "Lucky for Flossie I gotta be home for Shobbis or I'd do her right now! Right here!" Four sets of arms folded at the sides of their bodies started flapping, "Cluck! Cluck! Cluck!"

Boomy thought and prayed there was a good chance that Flossie was busy. When you do not go to cheder (Hebrew School) your prayers do not get answered so quickly. Flossie was never busy. When Billy Belch went upstairs muttering, "She is going to be so excited ...", Boomy felt the sweat pouring from every part of his body and he was seriously considering running away as fast as he can and never coming back. Then he felt that little tingle of excitement. He couldn't count how many times he heard his brothers Willie and Harry talking in bed in the middle of the night about how great it was and how they did it to this one and that one and here he was, with an older woman who wanted to do it with him. He was embarrassed because, just thinking about it, he was already stiff and hard and didn't want anyone to see him like this.

Boomy didn't have to worry. As soon as he saw Flossie he wasn't stiff and hard anymore. What a relief! Flossie looked at him and crinkled up her bulb of a nose as though she were smelling him. So, Boomy decided to do likewise and nearly gagged at the intake of garlic. "Hiya doin', kid?" She yawned as she spoke and Boomy noticed that she was able to hide her excitement very well. "Belch tells me you are a real Casanova."

Boomy is stumped momentarily and wonders why Billy would tell her such a thing and decides honesty is the best policy. "Actually I'm Jewish but I ain't so religious."

It is now Flossie's turn to be stumped. But all it takes is a pop of her bubble gum and she is herself again. She tickles him under the chin, which he does not like at all, and says, "Well, you wanna do it?"

The sweat starts pouring again and Boomy can think right off the bat of at least two dozen places he would rather be at this moment of his life. But he knows he is going nowhere because his honor is at stake. "Sure I wanna do it. What do you think I'm here for?" He is sure he sounds good but he does not wish to sound too good. "But if you're tired and wanna wait for another time ..."

Billy Belch did not let Boomy get any further. "Flossie ain't ever tired. She's been looking forward to this. Ain't that right, Flossie? Show the kid how you pant."

Flossie smiled and went, "Huh, huh, huh. I want you so bad."

Boomy did not know how or why, but Flossie was beginning to look better. She was even looking a little beautiful. In a few years all the pimples will be gone; looking at her from the left side you do not even see the harelip; if she stops eating for a few weeks she won't be fat anymore.

The four Cowboys were very disappointed because they wanted to watch but Boomy was a very private person. He was so private that when they went upstairs to Flossie's bedroom Boomy made her pull down the shades and turn off the lights, making the room dark, but not dark enough so Boomy insisted that they get under the covers.

"You always do it this way, kid?"

"Every single time." Boomy could not figure out what it was that Willie and Harry loved so much about doing this.

"You want me to get your weenie hard, kid?"

Boomy and the Cowboys

Boomy felt his face glowing in the dark. "No," he piped with a voice much higher-pitched than he wanted it to be, "it never gets hard. You don't have to worry about that."

Flossie was very puzzled which seemed to make the garlic smell much stronger. "How do you put it in if it ain't hard?"

"Put it in?" Boomy was very upset. He remembered the book, "The Birds and the Bees and Me" that his father stuck on his night table a few months ago and thought that if he was a bee he sure would pollenate Flossie right now. "I just do it, that's all."

"There's no way you can come if it ain't hard."

Boomy tried to remember all the things he heard Willie and Harry talk about - "Sticking it in ... ramming it home ... coming ... " What the hell did it mean 'to come', he wondered?

"Hey, what are you doing?"

"I'm jerking you off."

"Let go of it!"

"See, you're getting hard."

"I'm sorry. It usually don't happen."

"You're sorry? Jesus! Let's get this over with already. Come on, give it to me!"

Boomy had a general idea of how to do it. He just wasn't quite sure of where you put it or what exactly did it mean 'to come'."

"Stick it in already, will you!"

"Ready or not ..."

"Hey, what's going on? Are you some kind of a kiddie pervert?"

"I'm fucking you."

"Through my belly button?"

The four Cowboys were trying very hard to hear the sounds from the bedroom upstairs. It was difficult but now there was some shouting which was easier to hear.

"Oh, God, what are you doing?"

41

Boomy remembered how Willie would describe to Harry how he put it in and then he would come. So he followed it step by step. He stuck it between Flossie's legs and he ... came.

Flossie screamed and shrieked. The Cowboys ran to the rescue. The kid must have gone off his nut. They raced up the stairs and pushed open the bedroom door. Boomy was huddled against the far wall wrapped in a bedsheet and Flossie was cursing, crying and throwing anything at him that she could reach with her right hand. Her left hand was holding her robe, drenched with yellow splotches, away from her body, which was dripping the same yellow liquid that drenched her robe.

"Whatsa matter? Whatsa matter?" Poochie yelled, unable to imagine what could have happened.

"She's crazy," Boomy explained. "We did it an' when I came she goes nuts!"

"Came?" She screamed. "The little momser says to me like he's going to the bathroom" and she mimics, " 'excuse me, I'm coming' and then he does go to the bathroom - he pees all over me."

"I told her I was coming." Boomy grabbed his clothes and put them on as he hopped through the clubroom, then ran for home. He knew he was going to have to ask Willie to explain a little better how a guy comes.

At first Boomy is so embarrassed that he does not think he can show his face in the Cowboys' clubroom again. But instead of the guys treating him like a clown over what happened, suddenly he is a hero. Poochie, Dizzy and Jumbo tell the story like Boomy knows exactly what he is doing when he uses Flossie like she is a fire hydrant and he is something between a bulldog and a Great Dane. Boomy likes their version and after a while he even believes it.

Flossie, meanwhile, wails and moans to everyone that Boomy does this terrible thing to her only she does not say what this terrible thing is because if people hear how she was urinated on by an eleven year old boy she would draw more laughs than Fanny Brice on Second Avenue. So it is no great wonder that among the Cowboys S.A.C.a kid named Boomy Davidoff is transformed into someone who makes Jack the Ripper seem like a Franciscan Monk.

A cat that jumps up on a hot stove and burns its tail and fanny learns its lesson and does not jump up on that hot stove a second time. Boomy was not a cat. Although parliamentary procedure is not observed by the Cowboys, Billy Belch asks for the floor. He lets it be known how proud he is of Boomy and how the little guy should be an official member of the Cowboys. Poochie points out that the kid already is a Cowboy.

"Yeah, but he should be an official member."

"What's an official member?" Dizzy asked. "You're here, you suck on a bottle of beer, you're a member."

"That's for us guys," Billy explained. "We formed the Cowboys. But for a new guy to become an official member he gotta be initiated."

Boomy was not too sure he wanted to be a Cowboy that badly. He remembered Carlie Packman telling him how he got initiated when he joined the Cub Scouts. They whacked him on the bare ass a dozen times with a paddle but Carlie didn't mind because he learned how to make knots. Boomy did not care too much about learning to make knots and he cared even less about getting whacked on the ass with a paddle.

"Naw, don't be a little putz," they assured Boomy. "this is all good, clean fun. They even do it in college. You just do somethin' to prove you're a regular guy and that's it - you're an official Cowboy."

✡ ✡ ✡

As it turns out, Boomy is feeling a lot more like a calf than a Cowboy now since he is tied up with a lasso. He is hoping very much that they do not brand him because he is sure that is a lot more painful than getting paddled across the ass. One thing he is beginning to realize is that an initiation must be a lot more fun for the people initiating than for the people being initiated. They are sitting on a roof on Belmont Avenue and all the guys are laughing and having a good time except Boomy who is wondering *why* he is sitting on the roof in the first place. He is beginning to think that even though he doesn't care about learning how to make knots maybe Carlie Packman's Cub Scout initiation wasn't so bad after all.

Naturally, it was Billy Belch who had planned the initiation. Giving a tug on the rope tied around Boomy's waist to make sure it is secure, he says, "We are going to lower you through this opening all the way to the bottom."

Boomy looked down the two-foot by two-foot opening but could see nothing because it was pitch black. "What is it, a chimney?"

"Why would we put you down a chimey," Billy laughed, "are you Santa Claus? This is an air shaft."

"Where does it go to?"

"It goes to China," Poochie decided to join in.

Boomy looked down the shaft again, then shook his head, "This don't look like such a good idea. I don't think I wanna do it."

to let the contempt that was bottled up inside of him for so long come spilling out. He was there to leave no doubt in the mind of Jim Garrity that it was B.T. Huskins alone who sold him out. And mostly, he was there because he felt so goddam lousy for Billy Dumas.

Jake Flood's world suited him very well. It was simple and uncluttered, made up only of knights and fire-breathing dragons. Being that it was his world, he was the one who designated who were the knights and who were the dragons. Not surprisingly, even though any suit of armor would have made a tight fit, Jake was a knight and by a unanimous vote of 'One', B.T. Huskins was a very credible reptile.

B.T. Huskins also had his own world. It, too, was simple and uncluttered. It consisted of a God (self-appointed, of course) and one commandment – "Thou shalt do the right thing." And the right thing to Huskins was that a rule was a rule. There were no ifs, ands or buts. In fact, there were rules that B.T. Huskins added to the book and these rules were sacred and unchallengeable.

One rule was that anything Jake Flood endorsed was to be unendorsed, not to be granted. Another was that the bottom line governed everything. For Jake Flood, it was much more important to do a good thing than to do the right thing. The two were not always the same. To Jake, it was okay to break or, at least, bend a rule if it made things come out good.

So, when he asked that Huskins have a little compassion ... feeling for a guy who gave everything he had to this game, a guy who fought from bell to bell, not a single tear trickled down Huskins' cheek. He looked Jake squarely in the eye and told him that Dumas was a washed-up has-been. It wasn't that "compassion" was unknown to B.T. Huskins and it wasn't that there was no compassion in his heart. It was simply that it was reserved for himself. He crowed, "You never learn your lesson, do you?" and reminded Jake Flood how "compassion" cost him his license. And Jake Flood corrected him as best he knew how. "Bullshit. You stole my license." The pointless meeting had come to an end.

Jake felt it was a good idea to find Billy.

So Sally went to the fights to see and cheer for Billy Dumas, but there was no Billy Dumas to cheer for. The mimeographed program only cost a dime but, still, Sally felt she was entitled to the correct information. There were eight bouts listed, none with the name Billy Dumas. Sometime during the second four-rounder she questioned an usher who pointed her to someone who he said was the matchmaker and would know. He *did* know. He knew what she already knew - that there was no Billy Dumas fighting on the card. Then he remembered that there had been a Billy Dumas scheduled but there was a last minute change. Sally decided she was not a fight fan and left.

It was almost nine o'clock when she got back to the diner. Her cousin Claire, somewhere between shaken up and confused, told her that Billy had stopped in early in the evening, picked up his suitcase, then hugged her and mumbled something like "Gotta go now, Moll. You'll see, it'll all be good" and left. Sally walked to the back. Billy's few belongings were gone. She was about to leave when she saw on top of the bed, neatly spread out, the old newspaper clipping that she was sure Billy Dumas never was without. Carefully, she tried picking it up but it was so dry and brittle with age it crumbled at her touch.

✡ ✡ ✡

Buck Stracey went over his check-list once more, then uncapped his thermos of hot, black coffee. His train began picking up speed and he smiled as he could never get over the thrill of seeing the lights of Chicago flashing by. He settled back and took a big swallow of the steaming liquid. It looked like another long, dull night but Buck always made sure to stay alert on the job and caffeine was his ally.

✡ ✡ ✡

Billy Dumas got to Grey Park when he tried to remember where he was going. It was always a journey to the next stop, another town, another fight. Suddenly, it all came back to him and he put his suitcase down. This wasn't just another fight. He had something to prove. Billy smiled and sucked in a lungful of air. Suddenly, he was alive and breathing again. Everything was stored in a memory bank and poured out effortlessly. There was nothing to think about, habit and routine took over. It was important to be warm and loose when he climbed into the ring. Fifteen minutes of snapping left jabs, short hooks and an assortment of right crosses and uppercuts had his perspiration running freely. He felt good, relaxed and calm with the juices starting to flow and just the right mixture of excitement and anticipation. He nodded to his trainer, letting him know that he was ready. The Grey Park maintenance man turned away, uncomfortable with the strange guy punching the air by the big oak tree and waving to him like he was a first cousin. He ignored him and continued emptying the waste baskets along the lane.

Billy started the long dressing-room-to-ring shuffle. As he bounced towards the east gate of Grey Park he couldn't believe the turnout. There was Trini Alvarez, all the way from El Paso; Dom DiGiacomo, that plug-ugly son of a gun who broke his nose in Peoria. Joey "The Red" Baron – what a left hook! And even Doug Rafferty! Would you believe it!! All of these mugs coming out to root him on. As the cheers and noise of the crowd cascaded over him, Billy waved his right hand to acknowledge his following and all the trees along the path swayed and bent as the wind whistled through their branches.

✧　✧　✧

Sometimes your gut knows more than your brain. Jake felt that this was one of those times. It was like a baked beans and cabbage syndrome, but the gnawing ache was not indigestion. He had no idea how he was going to ease the hurt that Billy had to be feeling but he knew he had to find him and try.

Actually, even though he wouldn't admit it to anyone, he knew that Huskins was right — Billy Dumas shouldn't be fighting anymore. Huskins may have had the right answer, but he got it with the wrong formula. His bouncing Dumas from the card had nothing to do with the fighter's welfare or to protect him. Nothing noble or anything like that. B.T. Huskins' only reason for shelving Billy Dumas was to stick it to *him* — Jake Flood. Realizing that filled Jake with a strange kind of guilt and a strong sense that he was committed to help Billy. But first he had to find him. He was too fat and out of shape to run, but he ran anyhow.

✧　✧　✧

Billy was calm as he bounced on the balls of his feet, rotating his hips to keep his tone but his jaw was clamped in a tight set of determination. There was no quickening of his pulsebeat, no deep breaths. Just a narrowing of his eyes as he focused his full being on the task confronting him. It should be just another night's work, but it wasn't and he knew that. Why he

Billy Belch was ready for this and knew exactly what to say. "Alright, what do you expect from a little kid? Come on, let's shoot some pool." Nobody moved because the Cowboys were, in many respects, very wise - wise enough to know that at two AM during the week if you are looking for a place to shoot pool, you may look but you will not find.

Boomy knew he was being baited but it doesn't matter. When Boomy gets called - Boomy answers. His feet are already dangling down the shaft and he is resting his elbows on the roof, holding himself up. "I'm just gonna go down an' then you're gonna pull me up, right?"

"Right," Billy answered.

"It sounds dumb to me," Boomy reasoned.

"It is dumb," Billy agreed, "that's what initiations are all about."

They lowered the rope slowly until Boomy was almost at the bottom. "Can you see a window?" He heard Billy ask.

"I can't see nothing."

"Then feel around for it. It's on the left side."

"I think I found it," Boomy called out, "now can you pull me up?"

"Open the window and climb in," Billy ordered.

"What do I wanna do that for?"

"It don't matter what you wanna do or don't wanna do. It's part of the initiation. Now climb in the friggin' window and let's get it over with."

Although at the age of eleven Boomy did not know what a pendulum was, he obviously did know how to swing like one, which he did in order to reach the window. He was wondering, if everyone was so anxious to get it over with, what are they doing it for in the first place? "Jeez, this window's so small! I ain't gonna be able to get through it," he wheezed and grunted, trying to squirm through the small opening.

"You can do it. Just suck it in, kid. Suck it in and push hard."

One of the many books that Boomy had not read was "Alice in Wonderland" so when he came tumbling through the little ventilator window, landing on a toilet bowl then bouncing off it onto a cold tile floor, he had no way of comparing it to Alice's fall through the looking glass. On the roof, all that was heard was, "Owww!"

"Where are you, kid? You o.k.?"

"I'm inna shithouse."

"That's where you're supposed to be," Billy Belch answered softly. "Now untie the rope from around you."

"What am I gonna do that for? Come on, pull me up."

"Will you quit arguing over everything I tell you to do! Now untie the friggin' rope!"

"Okay, it's untied," then very softly so Billy Belch wouldn't hear, "asshole."

"Open the bathroom door. You see next to the counter there's a pile of shopping baskets?"

It was much easier to see in the store than it was in the bathroom with the door closed as the street lamps shone through the large plate glass window. "Uh-huh. Hey, I know this place. It's the Cut-Rate. We get our spaldeens an' kites an' stuff here."

"Well, forget about that shit now. Pick up one of the baskets and fill it with tools. The tools are on the aisle by the wall all the way to the left - you know your left from your right? Then tie it to the rope and we'll pull it up."

"I ain't doin' that."

"Whattya mean you ain't doin' that? Are you a Cowboy or a pussy?" Billy hissed. Boomy knew that the Cowboys sold all kinds of stuff to the pawnshops on Sutter Avenue. It didn't bother him but it wasn't his thing. He sold fruits and vegetables on Blake Avenue - and he paid for everything he sold.

Boomy and Billy never have a chance to enter into a debate. "Vott are you liddle bestids doing on dat roof?" All Boomy can think is uh-oh as he hears the voice, which sounds like it is in an echo chamber as it bounces around the air-shaft. "You don't skeedaddle one, two, t'ree I'm going to call the police who's going to lock you up!"

There is a lot of scrambling around on the roof and Boomy hears moaning and crying gripes of "Oh, shit" and "I told you to keep it down". It is easy enough to figure that one of the neighbors had seen them and in Brownsville when you see someone on a roof you do not immediately think of a chimney cleaner. He yelled, "Hey, you guys, come on and pull me up." At the same time he gave a yank on the rope which was meant to be an attention-getter. It was much more than an attention-getter. It was a rope-getter. Whoever was holding the other end of the rope, wasn't any longer. Boomy had yanked it right out of his hand and now had the whole rope. It was at this moment that Boomy learned it was not always better to have all of something instead of just part of it.

"Hey, you guys can't leave me here like this."

"Take care, Boomy."

"By, kid. Nice knowin' ya."

"They say once you been up the river everyone respects ya."

The rest of the night turned out to be very, very quiet. Boomy spent it sitting in the dark on the toilet bowl because there was no other place to sit. He made the best of what could have been a very bad time by thinking of the various ways he could kill Billy Belch and he decided that no single way, no matter how creative or ingenious, would make him happy. Only killing Billy Belch every which way he could imagine - over and over again - would give him any real pleasure. Also, Boomy realized that this was a moment in time that he should take advantage of and treasure because in his own bathroom he could not sit for more than five minutes without one of his sisters or brothers banging on the door, threatening to break it down.

Taken as a whole, the Cowboys were not guys without compassion or feeling. They were very strongly considering Poochie's suggestion that once Boomy is thrown in the can they take a Greyhound to Elmira and bring the kid things like salami, cheesecake and most important, cigarettes, because every street punk in Brownsville knows that in the cooler cigarettes are not just for smokes - it takes the place of money. Dizzy says maybe they should carve his name into the clubroom wall. Jumbo says that, under the circumstances, maybe they should carve his name on Billy Belch's forehead - the same Billy Belch who is no longer chairman of the now defunct Initiations Committee. It is a very conscience-stricken group of Cowboys who are lounging around their Hinsdale Street clubroom when the door opens and the object of their misery comes staggering in, sagging under the weight of the load of boxes and bags cradled in his arms.

The only thought that rattles around in their heads is that the kid must be on the lam because it is too soon after he is collared for him to be paroled. They cannot think of any other way for Boomy to be there with them.

When Sol turned the key in the lock to open the store for business that morning he was already crossing and uncrossing his legs and almost doing a little Irish jig, that's how bad he had to pee. He kept telling that *fartootsteh* (mixed up) wife of his "one glass of tea in the morning is one glass too much" so what does she do? She keeps filling it up and filling it up like he has a kidney the size of the Betsy Head swimming pool.

Usually Melvin opens up in the morning and Sol closes up at night but today was an auction on Canal Street and Melvin is the one who goes to the auctions because he doesn't have high blood pressure like Sol who gets very excited by things like someone bidding against him for a job lot that he wants. Sol gets excited by auctions, by noodgy customers, by not being able to find an item he's looking for, Sol gets excited by a lot of things. Melvin and Sol's Cut Rate Store is almost an institution on Belmont Avenue. It is like a pushcart under a roof. They buy up job lots from places going out of business or with overstocked inventory and they sell nothing for the price it's marked for. Every sale is made with jabbing fingers, raised voices and finally, somehow, a meeting of the minds. To Melvin, with the slicked-back jet black hair and always smelling from Bay Rum, every day is a pleasureable adventure from which he departs with a smile on his face and a song in his heart. To Sol, with the freckles that are now being overrun by liver spots, and the few remaining bedraggled strands of faded red hair that hang as a wilted fringe to the thin white dome of scalp capping his always perspiring head, each day is like a war from which he retreats in exhaustion to his refuge in East Flatbush where he regathers his strength to return to the next day's combat. For him, each Shobbis is truly a blessing.

As he pushed the door open he prayed to himself, "Please, God, no customers for two minutes." Then he thought to himself that if there are no customers for two minutes it will be a very slow start for the day - a truly bad omen! But the call of Nature was loud and strong. Sol closed the door, locked it from the inside and danced through the empty aisles to the bathroom door at the right side rear of the store.

Mendel the Baker, whose store was right next to Melvin and Sol's just missed burning his foot but good when he dropped a tray of freshly baked rolls he just took from the oven because never in his life did he hear such a scream - or was it two screams - like he just heard coming from the

Cut-Rate. He always knew that when you run a business where your customers fight you on price over every item, somewhere down the line someone is going to be very dissatisfied. At a time like this he decided it was best to pay attention to baking another tray of rolls and minding his own business.

In certain things Sol was very well coordinated. His fly was already unbuttoned as he flung the bathroom door open and prepared to deflate his bloated bladder. Fortunately the store was lighted by ordinary incandescent bulbs and plain tin fixtures because what came forth from him was a "Yeeowl!" that was shrill enough and loud enough to have shattered a crystal chandelier. Sol was not a solo performer. He quickly became a duet. He expected to enter a small four by five room whose main attraction was a toilet bowl, and at this moment there was nothing that Sol desired more. He was not prepared to see a little boy who was not supposed to be there, be there. Sol was never one to handle the unexpected very well. On the other hand Boomy had been sound asleep and there are various ways to react to being awakened by a scream that can awaken the dead, let alone a sleeping boy on a toilet. Boomy did not choose his response. It just happened. When he was jolted from his sleep by such a nerve-shattering scream, he, in turn, screamed just as piercingly and shrilly as the offending howl. For Sol, the emergency was over. He no longer had to pee. That happened already, somewhere during his shriek. Later he would have to confiscate a pair of overalls from the menswear counter. When, finally, the scream rippled off into the far reaches of wherever sound travels to, Sol felt the blood in his veins banging and knocking like little triphammers. Boomy never had a chance to say a word.

"God in heaven! What are you doing here little boy? Mein Gott, Mein Gott, don't tell me. You got locked in overnight!" He slapped his hand to his head. Boomy sat on the toilet bowl, staring at him in wide-eyed disbelief. "Who closed up last night? Oy vay, it was me, it was me! I didn't check! I didn't know! They must got the police looking for you by now. Vay ist mir. Soon a kidnaper I'm going to be called." He clasped his hands together and closed his eyes to the world. Boomy felt very sorry for this strange person who, a few minutes ago scared him half to death.

"Listen, mein kind, you tell your momma and poppa it was all a mistake, that nobody meant for you to be locked up." In a way, Boomy felt slightly cheated. He had spent half the night thinking up stories to tell when they found him in the bathroom but nothing he came up with was close to the story this guy had made up for him. "Come, I'll give you a little something so you'll show people how good you're treated at Melvin and Sol's, a place where nobody would ever hurt a hair on your head." Sol didn't know where to start and where to stop. He loaded Boomy down with games, binoculars, skates, magazines and books, toothpaste, soap and a whole carton of fireworks. Boomy thought that he was as nice a person as he had ever met - it was too bad he smelled so bad from *pischachs*.

In Brownsville, it seems leaders were not seated upon sturdy thrones. When Boomy comes in with a haul which was a lot more than they ever dreamt of pulling off with Billy Belch calling the shots the guys start having some very serious second thoughts which brings them to the conclusion that if Billy Belch's brain was put into a cow we may all have to forget about drinking milk anymore. So it is no longer necessary for Boomy to consider murdering Billy when Poochie takes over as leader of the Cowboys and his first rule is that anyone passing gas, regardless of point of emission, must say "Excuse me."

Boomy donates all of his loot from Melvin and Sol's Cut-Rate to the Cowboys only because he does not know what else to do with it. He knew he couldn't take it home because his brother Willie never got such a third degree at the 75th Precinct as Boomy would get from his parents if he walked in with all that stuff. There was no way they would believe his story, and he could not blame them. He had a hard enough time trying to explain why his bed wasn't slept in that night. Even though he had three or four well-rehearsed stories, he cannot convince them. So Boomy Davidoff becomes a philanthropist as well as the Cowboys youngest living legend and is very instrumental, without pulling a trigger or even throwing a punch, in bringing about a changing of the guard. His was not a widely employed method.

# MOUSEY COHEN'S NEW HOUSE

To Boomy Davidoff, Brownsville is Paradise. He loves Brownsville and cannot understand why anyone would choose to live anywhere else. So when his own brother Willie gets married and moves to Flatbush Boomy is shocked. But at least Willie only sleeps in Flatbush. All the rest of his time he spends in Brownsville.

How everyone does not see that Brownsville is better than anywhere else, Boomy cannot figure. What other place has pushcarts on one block, fancy stores on the next? Movies like the Supreme, the Oriole and the Pitkin ? No other place has all the good kinds of food that Brownsville has and you don't even have to go to a restaurant to get it; there are wagons on almost every corner selling every kind of food a guy could want. And you got all kinds of parks like Lincoln Terrace, Betsy Head and all the schoolyards and playgrounds. Boomy is also sure that no place has as many candy stores to hang out like Brownsville. Then you got the guys. Where are you gonna find a great bunch of guys - and even some of the girls - to pal around with like the ones you got in Brownsville? As far as Al "Boomy" Davidoff is concerned there is only one Brownsville and it cannot be replaced.

So when his good friend Mousey tells Boomy one morning while they are pitching pennies in front of Shorty's house, that he is moving to East Flatbush because his father says it is a better neighborhood Boomy cannot believe what he is hearing. The first thing Boomy points out is that Mousey's father has a butcher shop on Belmont Avenue.

"That's okay," Mousey answers. "He's gonna take the Church Avenue trolley and get a transfer at Rockaway Avenue. He says it's only a half hour."

"Yeah, sure," Boomy points out "It's okay for him but what about you?" When he sees that the look on Mousey's face is not one of joy he stops.

All the guys know that when someone is really down the best thing to do is eat a lot of candy and drink a lot of soda so there's Boomy, along with Shorty, Snake and Mousey, all getting rid of the blues in Max Davidoff's candy store nibbling on pretzels, JuJubes and chocolate babies, trying very hard to save their friend from what Boomy considered, a fate worse than death.

"It ain't the end of the world," Mousey kept saying, as though it were a line drummed into him. "Lenox Road and East Fifty-third Street - my old man says it's tree miles at the most."

"I hope they get you a turtle or something," Snake offers, "because I hear they ain't got no decent kids to hang out with there."

"Who needs anyone to hang out with there?" Mousey is very much on the defensive now. "I'll be here every day. It ain't no big deal."

"Leave him alone and just wish him luck," Max interrupts from behind the counter. "I'll bet it's a real nice house and he'll love it there."

"It is, Mr. Davidoff. It's really nice, an' I got my own bedroom with a closet just for my stuff."

Being a pretty fair-minded bunch of guys they decide not to decide. At least not until they check out where Mousey is moving to. If it is an okay house and everything meets with their standards, then Mousey moves. If not ... well, probably Mousey moves anyhow, just not with their approval. This is the general feeling. Only Boomy is against it. He simply cannot see anyone, especially a friend, leaving Brownsville.

So, the plan is that all the guys will join Mousey and make an inspection of the house and the neighborhood. It seems that Mousey's father, Mr. Cohen the butcher, has made this unbelievable deal on a handshake with his shelving and counter supplier, Bernard Swerdloff of Swerdloff and Co., who was moving his business to Philadelphia and had to sell his completely detached brick house on Lenox Road for a steal. Cohen and his wife took one look and they knew it was meant to be. While Swerdloff was away in Philadelphia setting up his new showroom and his wife was setting up their new house in a fancy neighborhood called Oxford Circle, he left the key with Cohen so they could take measurements and check things without losing any time.

Why not, they have been doing business for years.

Cohen had no idea that Mousey even knew about the key, let alone that he knew it was hidden away in the cabinet next to the Yahrzeit candles, so why would he bother to warn him not to touch it and being that Mousey was never warned not to touch it, there was no reason for him not to touch it ... or borrow it for a very short while.

Once they got to the large intersection of Kings Highway, Remsen Avenue and Linden Boulevard, it was like another universe. The trees and lawns looked different, sounds like horns and even the way cars whizzed by, sounded different. Boomy sensed that even the air smelled strange; maybe there wasn't enough oxygen in it. But mostly, the way Boomy saw it, things just looked too ordinary - too normal. Maybe he wasn't giving it a fair shake but so far, he didn't trust this place at all.

Lenox Road was just a short block off the intersection but the traffic was coming from all directions and there were so many traffic lights that they were totally confused, which did not slow them down in the least as Snake put up his hand and gave a loud shrill whistle as the four of them shoved their hands in their pockets and walked casually into the traffic, horns blaring loudly, tires screeching and drivers cursing. After all, they were from Brownsville.

Walking down Lenox Road, Shorty wanted to know where all the people were. "What is this, a ghost town?" There were no kids playing skelly or potsy on the street. No peddlers haggling with housewives at the curb. In fact there weren't even any stores on Lenox Road. They looked at Mousey, wondering how their poor friend would survive in such a strange place. But when they stood in front of the house, Snake and Shorty couldn't help admiring how impressive it was to them. 'Would you look at that, a real garden," Shorty said, looking at the weed-filled patch of scruffy grass that served as a small lawn just beneath the porch. Boomy smirked, unimpressed and somewhat unnerved by the relative quietness of the neighborhood.

Mousey got the front door to open with the first turn of the key and motioned for his friends to follow him. They entered a small vestibule and then a narrow center hallway. To the left of the hallway was a living room and to the right was a stairway that led up to the bedrooms. Directly behind the living room was a dining room to the right of which was a full size, eat-in kitchen.

Snake's head was bobbing up and down in approval. "Wow, what a house! Your old man musta sure struck it big!"

"Some house, ain't it, Boomy?" Shorty echoed, nudging his friend with his elbow. Boomy grumbled a half-hearted approval, "It's okay. Plenty nice houses in Brownsville, too."

"Jeez, take a look at this here ice box," Snake exclaimed as he popped his head into the kitchen.

"It's not an ice box," Mousey explained, with a real sense of pride as the three of them walked into the kitchen and gathered around the GE refrigerator, "it's a 'frigerator."

"What's a frigerator?" Snake wanted to know, opening the door and looking inside.

"Same as an ice box, only you don't use no ice. It works from electric."

Snake touched some of the food and bottles on the shelves and then fingered thewalls of the refrigerator to make sure they were cold. "Ain't no way to be cold inside with no ice."

Mousey was now a little offended at being questioned. "You see for yourself, there's no ice."

"There's gotta be ice," Snake repeated. "It's probably behind the walls – real thin sheets of ice."

As Snake pulled out from his pants pocket a Swedish pocket knife and inserted the screwdriver blade into the head of one of the screws fastening the top molding strip of the interior right side panel, Shorty, who had no interest in what made a refrigerator cold, walked off on his own while Boomy and Mousey looked on, Boomy with great interest, Mousey with more than a bit of anxiety.

"Hey, Snake," Mousey warned, "I don't think you should do that. It ain't my house yet. In fact we ain't even supposed to be here."

"Will you quit bein' such a pain-in-the-ass already," Snake grimaced as he worked on the screw. "I just wanna prove to you there's ice in here."

"Ain't you interested in learning at all, Mousey?" Boomy joined in.

Snake removed the last screw and pried the knife inside the thin wall, slowly peeling it back, exposing coils and wires, when they hear Shorty's muffled shout, "Boy! You guys oughta see this!"

"I don"t believe it - no ice." Snake steps back, with his hands on his hips, staring at exposed innards of the refrigerator. "What the hell is Shorty yellin' about?"

"I told you. You shoulda just listened to me," Mousey says, still offended, but now vindicated. "We better see what's with Shorty."

Turning and heading to the stairway at the front of the kitchen, Snake is still mumbling, "It don't make no sense. There gotta be ice."

When they reached the bottom of the stairway they were standing in a large wood-panelled room with a pinewood plank floor. Shorty was standing in the center of the room, looking around in near wonder. "Wouldja give a look. What a house! Ain't this somethin' ?"

The guys looked around. Shorty was right. It was something. It was a large, musty but neat rectangular room, about twenty by forty feet, with four small windows, two on each side, a couple of cushioned chairs and a small sofa. "Would you believe it?" Shorty's enthusiasm was not to be dimmed.

Mousey looks at him like he is missing some very major point. "Believe what?" Boomy and Snake are also awaiting the great revelation.

"Would this be the greatest indoor punchball court you ever saw?" Shorty is almost appealing to them to see it the way he is.

"The way you go over the lead line, you'd bump into the front wall before you ever hit the ball," Snake heckles him.

"What kinda punchball court?" Mousey asks. "It's a finished basement."

Boomy just shakes his head in an expression of 'What's the big deal!' while Snake is ready to listen after not coming out too good with the ice that wasn't in the refrigerator.

You don't even know what a great house this is," Shorty answers. "Come on, gimme a hand." He then enlists the help of his three buddies to move the pieces of furniture into the small room behind the finished basement where the coal furnace and fuses were.

Standing in the center of the now-empty basement, Shorty keeps mumbling, "Boy, what a house," as he fishes around in his pocket and finally pulls out a few broken sticks of chalk, a very useful commodity on city streets when it comes to making bases and boundaries for punchball and stickball games, skelly courts, hopscotch and potsy courts and naturally, to keep score for any street game.

"Will you cut it out already with this 'what a house' crap," Boomy pleads. "What do we live in, stables?"

"What're you doin' with the chalk?" Mousey wants to know, getting more nervous with every passing second.

"You'll see in a minute," Shorty promises.

It takes a little more than a minute, in which time, only because it is a physical impossibility, Mousey almost has kittens. When he has finished, Shorty has constructed the most complete indoor punchball court any of them had ever laid eyes on. At the rear wall, there is home plate, then a diagonal line to the midpoint of the right side wall where first base is drawn. He continues to map out the whole court, complete with a lead line, which Snake immediately makes him move back a foot. The bases are not just outlines but are completely filled in, a true work of art they all agree - even Mousey, although there are mixed feelings on his part.

For the next hour or so they test out the court by playing a punchball game with the spaldeen that Shorty, who has very deep pockets, has brought along also. It is a hard-nosed, hotly contested game with a lot of cheering, back-slapping and more than a few arguments, like every time Shorty was up and would inch over the lead line, but all things considered, it was a lot of fun. They all agree that some changes will have to be made and ground rules worked on, especially when the ball smashes into and breaks one of the side windows but they decide that they will play punchball there all winter when Mousey moves in, which they are all now heartily in favor of - all except Boomy, that is, whose attitude has softened a bit but is still 'wait and see'.

Some waits are longer than others.

When Sam Underberg finished taking the order for one new scale and two display trays he moistened the pencil with his tongue, totaled up the bill, then turned back to the phone, "You have an account with us, Cohen?"

"No. But I want to open one. From now on I'll be buying my equipment from you."

"Who were you buying from up to now?"

"Swerdloff."

"I hear he's moving to Philly. I'll get a reference from him and you immediately have an account here."

"Forget it. I'll pay cash. Don't ask him about me. The man is a lunatic."

"Swerdloff? I never heard bad things. What kind of lunatic?"

"The man is absolutely meshuggah. If I didn't have a good disposition he could have ruined my life."

"He overcharged you? He gave you defective merchandise?"

60

"You wouldn't believe it. I'm buying his house from him. The deal is all set. My wife even bought new bedroom and living room furniture on Rockaway Avenue - paid in full."

"Nu, so what happened?"

"The crazy goniff comes back from Philadelphia and calls me up like a madman, yelling I ruined his house, calling me every name under the sun and telling me I should be locked up for destroying property and kept away from normal people. This from a man I've done business with for twenty years."

"What happened to make him act like that?"

"What happened? What do you think happened? Nothing happened. Someone obviously came along and offered the schnorrer another fifty dollars. A lunatic of the first order!"

"I'm telling you, every day you live and learn."

"I got to tell you something, Underberg. Me, I'm a grown man. I can take heartache and disappointment. But when that call came to my house from Swerdloff, when he gives me that bobbemyseh about ruining his house my kleine boychik is standing next to me and it was like somebody sucked the blood from his body - that's how white he becomes. You know what? We'll all survive. He's already playing and laughing with his friends. And me, If that's how the hoi polloi from a good neighborhood act, I'll stay in Brownsville."

So, Sam Underberg had a new customer. Bernard Swerdloff sold his house on Lenox Road after he scraped and shellacked the basement floor, repaired a broken basement window and replaced the refrigerator. Cohen the Butcher decided his kind of people were the people who lived in Brownsville.

Boomy Davidoff could have told him that all along.

# THE SKELLY CHAMP

There are skelly players and there are skelly players. Just as when one thinks of baseball the name of Babe Ruth immediately comes to mind, so it was that with the skelly-playing community of Brownsville the name Bitsy Beckerman would stand out like an icon, the symbol of a standard of excellence that others could not dare even dream of attaining. Bitsy, although well past what is considered the age where a skelly player reaches his peak, showed no signs of diminshing ability. On the contrary, he seemingly continually improved with experience and became a legend to his peers - well, not exactly his peers, but more to Boomy's peers.

Skelly was a game born on the streets of New York City. White chalk, which worked very well on a black macadam background, would mark off a framed course, not unlike many board games, where the object was to get to a position at the core of the course, routing your opponents en route with your weapon-vehicle - a soda bottle cap. It was a very popular game in Brownsville as well as many other parts of the borough and city because, besides it being a most competitive game that could be played by as little as two people, the equipment needed, a piece of chalk and a soda cap, was relatively easy to come by and inexpensive and best of all it was played on the street, amidst varying amounts of traffic, in defiance of the pleadings and warnings of all mothers.

The starting average age of a skelly player was usually about five, with the peak years being eight to ten. For Bitsy those years were a distant memory but the peak was not. Word had it that Bitsy Beckerman was almost bar mitzvah - he would have been except he stood up his parents and family at the shul because of a big skelly game - more than two years ago. But you wouldn't know Bitsy's age by looking at him. He was a freckle-faced, elfin featured carrot-top whose hair was always uncombed and laces were always untied. Forever wide-eyed and open-mouthed you almost expected to see him fly off with Peter Pan.

To Bitsy skelly was a way of life. His arsenal of soda caps were of museum quality. He used only perfect caps, none that were bent or marred by being gruffly pried from a bottle. Very often he would go to one of the local soda and seltzer distributors in order to obtain virgin caps, getting them before they were placed on a bottle. Then he would spend hours scraping off all the paint and polishing the caps to a high silvery shine after which he would very carefully weight and balance the inside of the caps with his secret filling, said to be a mixture of wax and bubble gum. No one, before or since Bitsy has ever raised skelly to such a high art form.

Wherever he went young kids were in awe of him and some fantasized the day they would topple him from his throne. One of these daydreamers was Boomy Davidoff.

Boomy loved competition in any form. It probably grew out of learning to survive the antics of his brothers Willie and Harry and carried over to all the street games he played as well as his current role of a lookout. He couldn't believe how Lady Luck chose to smile upon him when, while carrying out a carton of empty soda bottles from his father's candy store he was stopped by the one and only Bitsy Beckerman who asked him if there were any bottle caps mixed in with the bottles.

Boomy did not answer at first. He just stood there open-mouthed, holding the carton of discards, momentarily struck dumb at the realization of who confronted him. Finally, regaining control of all his faculties he seized at an opportunity that he knew may never again present itself and arranged a most equitable deal with Bitsy. He challenged him to play skelly with the promise that win or lose, he, Boomy, would turn over to Bitsy Beckerman all the soda bottle caps in the carton - and there were plenty. As soon as he proffered the challenge he turned a beet red upon recognizing his audacity at even mentioning the possibility that he could dare think of defeating Bitsy.

Bitsy, cool veteran that he was, smiled and withdrew from his jacket pocket the bag of soda caps that he carried with him at all times. He had caps to use for any type of surface he might encounter. After the first few flicks of Bitsy's tapered magical middle finger, that which propelled his cap with unerring accuracy into action, it became obvious to Boomy that what he was getting on this day was an education - nothing more. Victory was no longer even a thought, but that didn't bother Boomy in the least. It was an honor just to be shooting caps against the master. He was so focused upon studying Bitsy's technique that he was oblivious to all else around him. This, unfortunately, made him quite vulnerable in his role as a lookout.

It was only due to a stroke of good fortune, a Bitsy bomb-shell sending Boomy's cap skittering to the curb and Boomy chasing after it, that enabled Boomy to see the approaching gumshoe soles just yards away. Leaving the soda bottle-cap legend squatting on his haunches in the middle of the street, Boomy hissed, "I quit! You win!" and without another look back, darted for the door of his father's candy store. There are certain very distinct qualities, Boomy knew, that separated lawmen from the rest of the populace. Starting from the ground up you did not have to go very far. Nobody wore shoes like a cop. Maybe because nobody would dream of paying for such unstylish brogans. Also, maybe because it was a carryover from pounding a beat, their shoes had thick, cushiony soles. Another easy thing that Boomy learned to pick up on was the way cops had this strange way of trying to make you think they were looking somewhere else when they were looking right at you or the thing they were looking for. Their faces had no expression; their mouths were one straight line, no smile, no nothing. Boomy enjoyed picking out cops. It was something that he was very good at doing. Except this one time when his mind was in a totally different place.

Bitsy yelled after him as he dashed madly to the candy store, "Hey, kid, my bottle caps!"

"Take them! They're yours," Boomy shouted breathlessly as he bolted through the door. "In the carton by the alley."

His father was standing on a step ladder arranging cartons of cigarettes on a shelf behind the soda counter when Boomy, it seemed, vaulted over the counter rather than taking the time of going around it and cried in a frightened whisper, "Poppa, chickie, the fuzz!"

Max didn't panic. This was not the first time they had been visited and searched by the feds and he was sure it wouldn't be the last. They had their routine down pretty good. Boomy was able to pick out a cop just as easily as you could pick out

a lemon in a bushel of apples. Max, not knowing that Boomy had fallen asleep on the job this time, figured they had at least a half minute before the feds arrived.

"Okay, take it easy, I'm coming down."

"No, Poppa, there's no time. Stay there," Boomy warned hoarsely. The words were hardly out of his mouth when the door opened and closed as the two agents entered. "Come on down from there, please, Mr. Davidoff. We'd like to have a little look around if you don't mind."

From the corner of his eye Max stole a glance at Boomy who was crawling on his stomach and sliding open the door under the counter where the two bottles were hidden. "Mind? Why should I mind? But what do you need me for?" Boomy had now stuffed both bottles under his shirt and, unable to crawl on his stomach, turned over and was crawling on his back to the rear screen door. "By now you guys know this place as good as I do."

Looking around, one of the agents asked, "Where's the kid who just came in here?"

"What kid?" Max asked, as he climbed slowly down the ladder. "Now you seeing kids? You sure you guys aren't drinking on the job?" Then, pointing to the rear of the store, "I didn't see no kid but I'm up here. If a kid came in, try the back room." As the two officers turned towards the rear of the store Boomy leaped to his feet, shoved open the screen door and bolted for the alley as quickly as he could run. He scooted out the alley and ran down Blake Avenue holding the two bottles in place. Turning around, he saw the two feds chasing, about a half block behind. He was very frightened thinking about whether they would dare shoot him in the back and started running zig-zag like he saw the soldiers do it in the war movies he saw at the Supreme.

He darted across Pennsylvania Avenue and compounded this taboo by not even bothering to look. He ran up sidestreets all the way to Sutter Avenue then cut over to the next street, coming back around from Sutter Avenue to Blake, afraid to look around but praying silently that he had lost the fuzz. At Hopkinson Avenue, he turned and once again headed towards Sutter. His lungs were on fire when, suddenly, something hit his ankle and sent him sprawling to the sidewalk. The two bottles fell free of his shirt and splattered across the cement surface. He heard somebody laughing like a horse who was frightened by a truck, then more laughing joined in.

Boomy couldn't believe it. After all he had gone through the two bottles, which in Boomy's mind, represented a small fortune to his father, was now gone. He was furious with himself, with circumstances, with fate. Enraged, he cried and banged his fists into the sidewalk until his knuckles were raw and bleeding. Then the laughing stopped.

"Hey, Shit-ass, look what a mess you made. Clean it up." Boomy looked up. He was in front of the candy store that was across the street from the H.E.S. Community Center where his sisters hung out. Looking up he saw Kozzy Itzkowitz and the guy who was telling him to clean up the sidewalk, Porky Kramer, together with a gang of about four or five other guys. Even though everyone called Kozzy a real jerk Boomy felt sorry for him because of what happened to his father. One of the reasons he was called a jerk was because he had friends like this fat slob, Porky. "Okay, you did enough," Kozzy whined. "Leave the kid alone already." That's when Boomy realized that Porky had intentionally tripped him.

"Whatsa matter with you?" Porky asked, giving Kozzy a wake-up shove. "This brat is Little Gangy's brother. After what they did to your old man you're tellin' me to leave him alone?"

"It was Reles and Bugsy. Little Gangy had nothin' to do with it," Kozzy shot back.

"Bullshit! Birds of a feather ... ," then turning to Boomy who was trying to get up, he kicked him with his foot, sending him sprawling back on the sidewalk.

"You guys think we should send a message back to those yellow bastards for what they did to poor Itzik?"

With fists pumping bravely in the air, Porky, who needed no urging at all, was urged on by a chorus of cheers by the group of candy store jockeys. Boomy saw a much larger crowd gathering now. People spilled out of all the neighboring stores and houses, hearing the commotion. From the corner of his eye he saw Bitsy Beckerman and thought, "What's he doing here?" Strangely, Boomy wasn't frightened at all. He was too angry to be frightened. He saw the huge figure of Porky standing right over him. It reminded him of last year when he snuck into a high school football game between Jefferson and Lafayette. Porky was playing right tackle for Jefferson - he quit school shortly after that - and there was a pileup after the Lafayette quarterback fumbled the football. The play was near the sideline, almost directly in front of where Boomy was sitting and he remembered how shocked he was when, with the play already whistled dead and everyone unwinding to get up, Porky, viciously and intentionally, smashed the heel of his right hand onto the bridge of the nose of the Lafayette quarterback, shattering it.

"Go on, lick it up, you little fucker," Porky shouted, ramming his shoe into Boomy's side, sending a hot flash of pain ripping through his body.

"After you squeeze your pimples, you fat tub of lard," Boomy sang out, each word causing the pain to stab out at his hurting ribs, "or maybe you're afraid you'll drown in your puss." This caused a wave of snickers through the crowd while Porky's buddies urged him on even more enthusiastically.

Porky reached down, grabbed Boomy by the hair and slapped him hard across the face. The sting was like an electric shock and brought new, involuntary tears to Boomy's eyes. All the colors of the rainbrow and a flash of light tore through his head. From somewhere he heard Kozzy's voice, "Come on, he's just a kid. Cut it out." In the crowd he saw Bitsy jumping up and down, cheering for what or for whom Boomy wasn't sure.

Another kick from Porky, followed by an "Ooh" from the crowd and some calls of "Leave the kid alone."

Porky was snorting now. He wanted everyone to be behind him and not everyone was. And here he was, avenging what those gangsters did to that schmuck Kozzy's father. He leaned down and this time threw a closed-fist punch at Boomy, which by ducking, the youngster caught on top of the head. Boomy tried very hard to keep out the clouds that were filling up his head. He remembered a lesson that his brother Willie had taught him. "When you're fightin' down an' dirty, go for the balls, kid. That's the weak spot of any and every guy you'll ever be up against."

Boomy felt his head wrenched up as Porky virtually lifted him from the ground by his hair. Still, there was no fear in Boomy but the anger was now uncontrollable. As Porky started to bring the heel of his hand down the same way Boomy remembered it from the football game, the young boy gave out with a cry of rage that pierced through everyone like a knife. So shocking was this scream that Porky's fist stopped in mid-air. It was as though time had frozen for a moment and everyone was a statue except for Boomy. His hand shot out and up, aiming for Porky's crotch. He grabbed at the pants and next was holding firmly and squeezing what felt like a pouch with two marbles. Another cry tore through the air. It was different though. This was a cry of fear and pain. Porky screamed and flailed arms that had no coordination or strength. Boomy was not going to let up. He squeezed tighter and tighter. Now Porky's knees buckled and he was swaying, not knowing whether to permit himself to collapse in shame or to try remaining on his feet. Boomy's anger wasn't abated at all. He started kicking at Porky's shins and increasing the pressure on his scrotum. A couple of Porky's buddies jumped in and started pounding Boomy but before more than two or three punches landed, people in the crowd came to Boomy's aid, pulled them off, grabbed hold of Porky, who had no strength left in his body anyhow and gave Boomy the chance to get away.

Boomy felt the blood running from his nose. He looked at Kozzy and still felt sorry for him. But people were right - he was a jerk. As he turned to leave Bitsy Beckerman came up to him and put his arm around Boomy's shoulder. "Hey, kid, you were great. But what about my soda caps? I couldn't find the carton." Boomy couldn't believe that an hour ago this guy was a hero to him. What a schmuck, he thought. He didn't bother answering Bitsy. He turned and hurried toward home. He was hurting, but much more than the hurt done to him physically was the hurt he was feeling because he was just learning to understand that his brothers were gangsters and in some way that affected him. He also learned that sometimes you had to pay very heavily for making a mistake and mistakes came in many shapes and forms. He reached into his pocket and pulled out a shiny soda cap which he casually flipped away. He wasn't ever going to play skelly again.

# THE PEDDLER FROM NORFOLK STREET

*- Ron Ross*

Kaminsky the Peddler removed the last few balls of yarn from his pushcart, placed them into the large burlap bag that he dragged to and from his home each day and was about to cover the cart when he stopped and looked at the black Packard taxicab that turned from Delancey Street onto Norfolk. It was the fourth time since the moon started to rise and replace the sun about fifteen minutes ago that the car had driven slowly down the street. He turned and looked away because he did not want to stare. He already saw that the Bulvon and the Brain were in the cab. At them you don't stare, When they pass you can go "Ptooey!" and spit, but you don't stare at them.

It was October 15, 1927 and Boruch Kaminsky had been working from this spot on Norfolk Street for more than seventeen years and except for the goniff protectors who became partners with no investment it wasn't so bad. For Kaminsky, the moon coming up was a love-hate sort of thing. It meant the work day was over, time to cover up his pushcart, which also meant he wasn't going to make any more money that day. That was the "hate" part. However, it also meant that he could drag his bone-weary body home, flop on the deep-cushion easy chair in the foyer-dining-room-living room until his wife Ettie put his dinner on the table. That is what made him love the moon.

Now that the Packard was a safe distance down the street he turned and looked. The Bulvon and the Brain. "Ptooey!" It was thirteen years ago, 1914, but he never forgot. Then, too, he was closing up after a day's work – a day's work that didn't exactly fill his pockets, but it was six dollars and eighty-two cents that he worked and sweated for in a twelve hour day. That's when he met the two of them. He could have made the introduction; they didn't even know each other. The skinny one, the Brain, Lepke, he got up behind him maybe five seconds sooner. Kaminsky was going to give this pisher who was maybe sixteen years old and dressed in rags, the back of his hand, but feeling what could have been a switchblade against his back he gave him the money instead. That's when the Bulvon, Gurrah, comes from the other direction, grunting that he got there first when he definitely came in second. Kaminsky had no intention of being a referee. What he hoped was that they would both choke on his six dollars and eighty-two cents. They didn't and Kaminsky berated himself for not being a more pious person whose prayers might then have been answered.

Maybe God had no intention of intervening; maybe he was too tied up with the war going on over in Europe but, whatever, Louis "Lepke" Buchalter, who was seventeen the day he pressed a shoe horn against Boruch Kaminsky's back and Jake "Gurrah" Shapiro, who was a barrel-shaped fifteen year-old both managed to grow up. Much of their growing up nourishment came at the expense of others. It didn't matter who - neighbors, shopkeepers, peddlers, even friends of their parents. And even though Kaminsky was not invited to any of their birthday parties, he was there to watch as they grew and gave them presents anyhow. They were not gift-wrapped and it wasn't out of the goodness of his heart.

From that first meeting on Norfolk Street, Lepke and Shapiro became a team. Lepke, a shrewd, analytical planner and plotter, recognized that he found his counterpart, the physical enforcer necessary to implement the schemes of a brilliantly diabolical mind. They refined their pillaging of the pushcart community by turning it into a business, with ledger books and even "thank you's" upon receiving payment – which was a foregone conclusion. Delinquencies? There was no such thing. Not as long as Jacob "Gurrah" Shapiro made the weekly collections for the protection service that provided the peddlers protection mainly from their Collectors, Lepke and Gurrah.

As time passed, their protection-extortion racket of the pushcart peddlers spread – and so did their reputations and renown. But to Kaminsky they remained the schmendricks, the pishers, especially since right around the corner on Delancey was where a real big time schlammer hung his hat. Jake "Little Augie" Orgen, one of the top head-bashers on the Lower East Side, with "Legs" Diamond as his right hand man, had his own cartel which was a penthouse operation compared to the street-sweeping operation of Lepke and Gurrah. "Little Augie" started his career as a strike breaker, at which he displayed a great talent, mainly due to his proficiency at breaking legs and an occasional head of some poor working slobs carrying placards on a picket line asking for a better deal from their bosses before they would return to work. It didn't take Orgen long to realize that it was much more profitable to control the unions, so loyalty never being his strong suit, he switched sides but he continued with his same unique talent, only now he was he was bashing the skulls of union chiefs.

Little Augie was always searching to recruit new talent. He didn't have to search very far to find Lepke and Gurrah. For a while, Kaminsky had slept like a baby at night. He would have this dream about how the big shots, Jake Orgen and Legs Diamond, would walk down Norfolk Street, give a good, swift kick in the behind of the two paskyudniks, telling them they don't want any riff-raff in their neighborhood and Lepke and Gurrah almost wet their pants as they run away and never come back. Such a dream had to be too good to be true. And that's just what it was! Instead, what happens? Lepke and Gurrah are invited to join up with Little Augie's gang.

For Kaminsky, to see these two trombeniks who robbed from him his six dollars and eighty-two cents that took him a whole day to earn being turned into big shots with neckties and fedoras and helpers who now made their collections for them, it was enough to almost make him believe that the devil was stronger than God.

If Boruch Kaminsky stopped dreaming, Louis Buchalter did not. And he dreamt on a grandiose scale. Whether, at that stage of his life, he envisioned that some day he would be sitting at the head of the table setting the rules and agenda for all of organized crime, no one will ever know. But getting to the head of that table took more than just dreaming.

Kaminsky was just about finished closing up his cart for the night when he looked up. There was the black Packard cab again, driving even slower now. He wondered why Lepke and Gurrah Shapiro simply didn't stop and pick up Little Augie. He was sure that's why they were here. He looked at the car as it drove past him to begin its circle of the block again. He turned away, not wanting to stare as he saw Lepke looking at him from the front passenger seat.

Kaminsky was walking towards Rivington Street with the bag of yarn slung over his shoulder when he had this feeling that he shouldn't turn around. So he did. Jacob "Little Augie" Orgen and Jack "Legs" Diamond had just turned the corner of Delancey Street and were walking briskly on Norfolk now, looking more like a couple of guys on their way for a sandwich and a cup of coffee than waiting for a cab. The Packard wasn't driving slowly now. It pulled to the curb with a screech. Jake "Gurrah" Shapiro jumped out with a machine gun spitting loud and fast. At his side was another "loyal" Orgen soldier, "Little Hymie" Holtz, with two pistols blazing. Louis "Lepke" Buchalter sat in the Packard, smiling and staring down the street at the lone pedestrian, Boruch Kaminsky. "Little Augie" was cut nearly in half by the fusillade of blazing flame from Gurrah's tommy gun. "Legs" Diamond took his bullets but faithful to his reputation, dodged the Grim Reaper. On that night Boruch Kaminsky did not dream because he did not sleep and Louis "Lepke" Buchalter began his ascent to the top of the crime world.

The police came around and spoke to everyone in the neighborhood, from tenement dwellers to shop owners to peddlers. No one saw anything.

About a week passed when Boruch Kaminsky was stocking his pushcart for a new day of business when he received a not unexpected visitor. Lepke looked at him and his lips did something that resembled a smile. "Business is good, Kaminsky?"

Kaminsky looked over at what he used to call a pisher, now dressed in a navy blue suit with a red and white striped tie and a snap-brimmed fedora. "Good, but not as good as yours."

"So we can make it a little better." Lepke held out his hand. There was a roll of bills. The top one was a hundred. Maybe the rest were also.

Kaminsky looked and shook his head "No."

Lepke responded with a shake of his own head. "This is just my way of showing that I think you're a good person – and a good person deserves to be shown he's appreciated."

Again Kaminsky shook his head.

Lepke's smile faded and was replaced by a puzzled look. "How can I show you my appreciation? If this isn't enough, you name it."

"Six dollars and eighty-two cents."

Louis "Lepke" Buchalter blinked. He heard it, but wasn't sure he heard it correctly. "You're joking, right?"

"Six dollars and eighty-two cents. Not a penny more. Not a penny less."

Lepke opened his hand holding the roll of bills and let it unfold. All hundreds.

For the third time Boruch Kaminsky shook his head.

Lepke sighed. He put the bills in his left pants pocket and reached into his right pocket. He came out with a few crumpled bills and held them out. Carefully, Kaminsky reached and removed a five and two singles. With his other hand, he reached into his own pocket, pulling out a handful of coins. He placed a nickel, a dime and three pennies in Lepke's hand and turned without saying another word, not even "Thank you."

Lepke, with a puzzled look on his face, turned and walked away.

Boruch Kaminsky waited about a half minute before turning around and looking at the retreating figure of the new crime lord of the Lower East Side. "Ptooey!"

# THE CASHAYFELOPE MAN

*By Ron Ross*

Dovie Mendelson was six going on six-and-a-half when he concluded that this world he lived in was a truly magical place with strange and wondrous things occurring all around him. Yesterday the streets were blanketed by a fresh early spring snow. What he saw today from his third floor bedroom window was a clean, dry asphalt universe bathed in sunshine and not a sign of the whiteness that had so excited him just a day before. He heaved his little boy sigh of disappointment, recognizing that the brand new Flexible Flyer that his father had placed in the cellar storage bin last month would now remain there until next winter when he would be seven and 1936 would become 1937. Maybe he would be able to do belly wops better on his sled when he was seven than he could now, he consoled himself.

He was just about to retreat and get dressed when, still at the window pane, he stared with wide, unblinking blue eyes at Mischa the Fruit Peddler's horse which suddenly had five legs. Mischa came around with his wagon at least twice a week and Dovie was absolutely certain that his horse, like all other horses he had ever seen previously, was the good old-fashioned, four-legged kind. Could Mischa's horse have grown another leg since last he saw him or maybe Mischa went out and bought a new horse. Dovie had learned recently that they made glue from old horses and he wanted to cry if that is what happened to Mischa's old horse - that is if Mischa got a new horse.

Hurriedly, Dovie pulled on his gray corduroy knickers and his long-sleeved Katzenjammer Kids sweat shirt, raced for the front door and out, ignoring his mother's wail, "Your Cream of Wheat, it's gonna get cold, Dovedel!"

Dovie bounded down the staircase from the third floor to the second, hurdling two to three steps at a time, in spite of the continual and ever-present objections of his parents, landed like an out-of-synch gymnast executing a graceless dismount, then raced to and pounded upon the door to Apartment 2C.

The door opened and Sollie, who was almost a year older than Dovie and about a head taller, was busily indulged in his favorite pasttime, scratching his head. Dovie associated this act with being extremely intelligent. Even though Dovie got better grades on all his tests, still, Sollie seemed to know about everything and, if he didn't know, you believed by the way he acted, that he did. Dovie was not the only one who believed that Solly was the wisest kid around. Sollie also expressed this belief - to anyone and everyone who would listen. Yanking at Sollie's sleeve Dovie blurted out the tale of Mischa's five-legged horse to which Sollie smirked and gave as condescending a wave of his hand as a seven year old could. But with an unrelenting assault ranging from pleading to menacing, little Dovie, obviously energized by a more than abundant flow of adrenalin half-dragged and half-carried a none too enthusiatic Sollie to the street.

The sight that greeted Dovie deflated him but did not totally humble him. Mischa's horse, concentrating on a feedbag that the considerate fruit peddler had recently placed under his snout, now seemed to be the possessor of only four-and-a-half legs. Sollie gave Dovie a whack on the back of the head. "That's five legs? That's a horse with a big schmeckel." Being so bright that he may even skip 2A and go straight to 2B in P.S. 232, Dovie immediately knew that a schmeckel was a penis, which he, his father, every male that he knew, even dogs and cats - and let us not forget horses - used for making pee-pee - and Mischa's horse did not have five legs ... But who ever heard of such a big schmeckel? This is the question that he posed to Sollie.

In less than two minutes, which is about how long it took Sollie to enlighten Dovie in a not-quite-textbook manner how the schmeckel is used in making babies, little Dovie's entire world crumbled around him just like a set of building blocks. "My papa uses his schmeckel just for pee-pee. I see it all the time. He lets me watch," Dovie cried, ready to swing out at Sollie in defense of his father's honor. "And it's little! It's very, very little. I swear to God!"

Sollie lowered his face, almost up against Dovie's and taunted, "Well, it grows and grows till it's like a snake - it's called a hot-on because it gets very hot - then when your mother is sleeping at night it opens up her belly-button and it crawls into her stomach and spits out a tiny little baby into her."

The tears were squirting out of Dovie's eyes now. "You're crazy, Sollie, you know? You're crazy! My momma and poppa would never do anything like that!"

"Oh, no? How do you think you got here? You really think the stork brought you?"

Just then there was the loud sound of splashing, and turning, they saw Mischa's troublemaking horse release a yellow torrent of steaming urine bouncing off the street beneath him and as he did so his appendage in question receded in size until it was reduced to relatively normal proportions, considering, of course, that he was still a horse. Dovie laughed frantically and with forced relief, "See? See all that pee? What happens to the teenie babies that come out with the pee, smarty-pants?" The urine slithered along the contour of the street to the curb where it settled in a puddle. Sollie took stock of the situation, then remarked very sagely, in a low confidential voice, "How do you think orphans are born?"

Dovie sat in the fire passage alley of the apartment building on the other side of and down the street from his own, cradling his tear-stained face in his arms. He had no idea how long he'd been there but he did know that he was probably in a lot of trouble because it was a long time ago that his mother gave up calling out his name from their window to come home for lunch, after which she came down, trudging back and forth on both sides of the street, now wailing his name in anguish while he crouched in malevolent silence. As her voice drew closer, Dovie, crawling and sliding, made his way to the scarred metal cellar door, pushed it open and entered a grayish darkness heavy with coal dust and soundless save for the pulsating and throbbing growls of the mammoth furnace whose red eyes glared at him as some monster-master guarding its lair. Fear of this alien place squashed Dovie into a corner yet he felt a sort of serenity being safely out of his mother's range.

Lunch in the Mendelson household was no small thing. Dairy lunches like bananas and cream or a peanut butter and jelly sandwich were frowned upon by Mrs. Mendelson. Dovie was force-fed three hot meals a day. Lunch would usually be something simple like lamb chops with peas and carrots and mashed potatos, thick slabs of rye bread and warm apple strudel for dessert. Dinner, of course, was much more elaborate.

So, to miss a meal, any meal in the Mendelson home was a violation of major proportions. To make matters worse, today was Sunday, which meant Poppa Mendelson gets off from work at three o'clock and gets home about four with much more strength than on the other days of the week when he gets home late at night, barely with enough energy to make it to the living-room easy chair which was really "home" to him. Today is the one day he is able to deal with recalcitrant youth. But Dovie didn't care. He might not ever be able to face either of his parents again. He could not believe that they had deceived him so all these years. It was then that he heard the bell and the booming voice of the Cashayfelope Man, which even the cellar walls could not muffle, as the sound first wafted then reverberated, making its way from the street to the alleyway and came to a halt as the cellar door creaked.

The Cashayfelope Man was part of Dovie's magical world. Dovie could fathom no reason for his existence or why he came around almost daily ringing his large hand-held bell and bellowing that meaningless, to Dovie at least, cry of "Cashayfelope" - that is the sound that reached Dovie's ear anyhow. All of those people who were not part of Dovie's everyday world as he was unable to relate to or understand them, were merged and delegated to his magical world. He looked upon them with awe and admiration but also with some degree of fear. Beside the Cashayfelope Man, there was Mr. DaGinny, the Organ Grinder with his large waxed handlebar mustache and his little monkey who was dressed in the same clothes as Johnny, the "Call for Phillip Morris" bellhop. Dovie really believed his name to be Mr. DaGinny, because whenever he came around and ground out his same three pieces, "Sorrento", a Tarentella, and "The Sidewalks of New York", Momma would always carefully wrap two pennies in a torn-off piece of newspaper, place it in Dovie's palm and say, "Go, Doveleh, we'll give a couple cents to the Guinea." Then

Dovie would run down three flights of stairs, unwrap the pennies so everyone could hear them jingle when they landed in the monkey's tin cup and know how generous his mother was. Momma could have thrown the wrapped up pennies out the window with a "Yoo-hoo!" to the Organ Grinder just as she did to Yitzhak, the Fiddle Player, but she knew how Dovie loved to play with the monkey. Yitzhak, Dovie realized, was very smart, because whereas the Organ Grinder entertained from the street and could only be appreciated and rewarded by those tenants facing front, the Fiddle Player always gave his recital from the courtyard, surrounded by a three-sided audience. Dovie would hang over the sill and always listen attentively because a show was a show, but truthfully, he enjoyed the Organ Grinder more. Therefore, he could not understand Momma's "Oy-yoy-yoys", her clasping of her hands in front of her and constantly sighing every time Yitzhak would play "Belz". As his violin cried out the wistful strains, Yitzhak would sing along, "Belz, mine shtetele Belz ..." and Momma would moan and cry, eyes brimming over with tears, lamenting, "Oy, a canary, the man is a canary". Dovie expected Yitzhak to fly but he never did, in spite of the fact that Momma would occasionally lavish him with as much as a nickel, much to Dovie's displeasure.

None of Dovie's magical world characters fascinated him as much as did the Cashayfelope Man, however, nor was he as apprehensive of any of them as he was of this near-mystic being. Much of Dovie's fear was based upon Sollie's lurid warning that they should steer clear of this bell-ringing eccentric as Sollie had overheard from reliable but confidential sources, mainly his father, Maxwell London, whom can best be described as the block that Sollie was the chip off, that he made off with little children in the bag that he carried upon his back. And as Dovie saw it, Sollie's father was probably the very wisest man he had ever come across.

He never spent the hours at work that all the other fathers did and he had answers and opinions for everything and seemed to know everything that was going on anywhere in their building or around the world. Not like his father who would give a wave of his hand, a shrug of his shoulders and say nothing.

So when he heard the ringing of the bell draw nearer and nearer, then heard the footsteps clop-clopping down the steps to the passageway and the opening and closing of the cellar door, he sucked in his breath and curled into a little ball, trying to become invisible. He froze as a hand prodded and shook his shoulder.

"Nu, what have we here, a monster?"

Hesitantly, Dovie raised his head and in a choked stammer, answered, "I'm ... I'm not a monster. I'm a ... a little kid."

"Oh, a kleine kind ... a little child," retorted the man, placing the bag that was slung over his shoulder on the ground and then gently raised Dovie to a standing position. "But, still, what are you doing here?"

Trying to muster up some bravado, Dovie sputterd, "I'm ... I'm running away from home. What are you doing here?"

"Running away from home? Vay iz mir! I am here because I live here," he waved his hand, encompassing the cellar. "And where, may I ask is your home that you are running away from?"

"Across the street near the corner ... Number Eighty-Seven," little Dovie half-sobbed. "How can you live here?" asked Dovie. "It's a cellar. I'm not even allowed to go to our cellar by myself."

"It's a good question. Maybe I should be the one running away from home."

Taking a quick look around the cellar, Dovie saw the large mattress on a wooden platform and the row of 3 upright orange crates that was used as storage cabinets in the separate rear section where the meters were. He wanted to ask where the bathroom was but he didn't want to sound like a nosey-body. Just like a mind-reader, the Cashayfelope Man waved his hand, pointing to the rear of the cellar, hidden away in the shadows, "We even have a private toilet and a small ice box. Could you live much better?"

Dovie did his best to suppress the fear that felt like a frog in his throat. "You don't live here alone?"

Without changing his expression, the man answered, "When I am here by myself, it is 'me' but when I have company, which is not very often but right now you are my company, it is 'we'."

He had never seen him at a close distance before and as he looked at the round-bellied smallish man whose face was mottled with soft gray hair that never quite made it to becoming whiskers he sensed that there was no reason to be afraid. The man's eyelids seemed to droop limply which made him look so sad that Dovie had an overwhelming desire to reach out and stroke his face in spite of Sollie's fearful admonition. Once he regained the ability to again speak normally, Dovie told of his travail - this great deception foisted upon him by his parents because of which he would never again be able to face them or anyone else for that matter. How could they permit him to be born in such a way!

"First, what is your name, boychik?"

"Dovie. Dovie Mendelson."

"Who told you such a mishagos, Dovie?" He asked, rumpling Dovie's hair.

"My best friend, Sollie London."

"Aha!" exclaimed the Cashayfelope Man. "And such a wise person who tries to disclose the Lord's secrets, how old might such a wise person be?"

"Sollie? He's not very old but he's more than seven."

"He's not very old, and you know what? He's not very wise, either."

Dovie's eyes lit up. "You mean it's a lie? That's not how I was born?"

The Cashayfelope Man shook his head. "Tsk, tsk. What is this, how you was born? Nobody else counts?"

"I didn't mean ..."

The Cashayfelope Man held up his hand to stop Dovie. "Sha! Still! Next, I don't call anybody a liar ... bu-u-ut ... what he told you, it ain't so. In the beginning God would pick up some clay from the earth, shape it and breathe into it – and you had Adam. Then he pulls a rib from Adam – and now you had Eve. How do you like that way for making babies?"

Dovie shrugged. "I guess it's okay."

"Don't you think maybe it hurts a little to pull off a rib?"

"Probably."

"You better believe it, boychik. It got to hurt a lot. Also, God has a lot more to do than make people from clay and bones. So God makes a rule, from then on babies could only be made from love. You know what love is, Dovie?"

"Love is to like a lot."

"You're probably a lot wiser than your friend Sollie," he beamed at Dovie.

"But where does the baby come from?" a still bemused Dovie inquires.

"Enough learning for one day. When you're six or seven your kupf, your head, is not made to hold so much, which is probably why Sollie gets so mixed up. You know what happens if you have a balloon and you fill it up with air? You put in a little too much - it goes Pop! - Right?"

Wide-eyed, Dovie nodded his head in agreement.

"Okay, young man, so now that you understand that your parents are good people who love you very much, I think you should go home because they are probably worried sick."

Dovie pulled back, almost shrinking into the wall, and whispered in a choked, frail voice,"I can't go home. I'm in a lot of trouble."

"What kind of trouble? The only kind of trouble is maybe they'll hug you and kiss you to death."

"No, I'm not allowed to stay out without telling my mother where I am. And if she calls me I'm supposed to answer right away ... that's because what happened to the Limberg baby and especially after what happened to Mrs. Peschkin's baby." As Dovie spoke he couldn't restrain the cold blade that ran the length of his spine as he thought of the contents of the Cashayfelope Man's bag.

The old man's eyes moistened and he gently pried Dovie from the wall and hugged him tenderly. "The Lindbergh baby," he mused, "such a heartache. And with the Peschkins', a double heartache. Who could blame a person for being worried. Come, mein kind, I'll take you home and explain to your Momma that you lost track of time helping me sort out my rags."

As he walked across the street to his building with the Cashayfelope Man, Dovie was well aware that he had been put off - that he was given no clear-cut answer but he was able to accept such treatment because he felt that he could really trust this person. His parents never spoke to him in such a way but, then again, nobody's parents did, except, maybe for Sollie's father. But he was different. Besides seeing him as being very wise, he also thought of him as being very different. Dovie couldn't figure out how he was different, but he just knew that he was. Dovie reconciled himself to the fact that he might have to wait until he was ten to learn the truth about how babies were born. It was the same as learning about Geometry. He was watching his cousin Milty doing his homework and it looked like a lot of fun, working with circles and squares and triangles. When he asked Milty to show him how to do this Geometry homework, Milty told him that first he had to learn simple arithmetic and then when he was ten or eleven, he could learn Geometry. There were things that a six year old kid just had to wait to learn.

In time, Dovie found it in his heart to forgive his parents for their possible transgression. It still was not clear to him whether they actually were guilty, but what was clear to him was whatever method they employed was obviously being used by everyone else also. Beside which, in his parents' case it would have been just a one-time sin. Look at the Gluckman's on the first floor - ten children. Everytime Dovie passed Mr. or Mrs. Gluckman in the building or on the street now, he was not able to control a snicker and a second look over his shoulder.

His mother answered the opening of the door with a screeching yowl, a crushing hug to her bosom, a wet kiss on the forehead and a slap to the face. This was much better than Dovie anticipated but he forced himself to give an oblig-atory, expected cry. This happened so quickly and unexpect-edly, although not by Dovie, that the Cashayfelope Man was unable to intercede until after the fact - or the slap. At that instant he stepped between them acting as a calming, reassur-ing peacemaker, although such a role was no longer neces-sary as the slap got all the frustration out of Momma's system and she was now cradling and stroking Dovie's head while he continued, with much difficulty, to affect a soft staccato of whimpering and sniffling. They spoke softly in Yiddish, which Dovie resented, because he felt that he should not be precluded from any talk that was about him. He fantasized about the day that he would be able to taste revenge by being the best student imaginable when he studied Spanish in high school.  Then, whenever an important discussion arose, he would speak to his parents only in this foreign tongue.  The more important the topic, the purer the Castillian.

Before he left,  Mrs. Mendelson invited the Cashayfelope Man, whose name Dovie now learned was Mottel,  to stay for a glazele te - a glass of tea, but he thanked her and excused himself,  explaining he had several chores that he still had to take care of.  Dovie appreciated that, as he left, he gave another friendly rumple to his hair.  He knew that Sollie was mistaken about what was in the bag that he carried over his shoulder - especially  when he learned that what he cried out when ringing his bell was a sing-song, thickly accented "Cash f ' your ol' clothes!"  "Cash f' your ol' clothes!"  It only sounded to Dovie like "Cashayfelope!"  When Poppa returned from work late that afternoon, Momma recounted how Dovie disobediently missed lunch and did not respond  to her calls, causing her nearly to faint and almost to call the police,  she did not remember in which order.  "The rag-picker brings him home.  Could you believe?"  She finishes off with great theatrics. Poppa moved his hands in a little circle, then opened his mouth but nothing came out.  Again he moved his hands in a circle - it was as though he had to crank himself up before his mouth worked.  Finally, "How come you don't listen to what you're told?"

Momma stood, hands on hips.  "Questions he don't need! A strap on the behind he'll understand!"  Dovie felt this was a perfect time for another good cry, a cry in fear of the unknown. The strap was his mother's ever-available threat of severe punishment – a threat never yet carried out by the reluctant executioner, his father. But still, it warranted a defense to assure that threat would always remain in the realm of the unknown. So, a carefully crafted  cry and whine developed into an art form for Dovie. "How come I get blamed for everything?

If Limberg lost his baby and Peschkin lost her baby, it's my fault?" It worked like a charm.  Instead of a spanking he sat and listened to another lecture from Momma accompanied by nods from Poppa about how much they loved him and how careful everyone had to be with their children since the kidnapping of Colonel Lindberg's baby and then the disappearance of the Peschkin's baby right on their own block. The only one who got into a little trouble was Poppa, who Momma said was so much like Charlie McCarthy that she was beginning to think she was Edgar Bergen.

It was understandable to Dovie that his parents as well as all other parents should obsess over these two events.  After all, even though it was four years now since the two kidnappings, every night they listened as Walter Winchell and Gabriel Heatter still spoke about it on the radio more than anything else except maybe how terrible the Great Depression was and President Roosevelt's New Deal. Even though Dovie only read the comics he knew it was also in the newspapers almost every day because whenever he accidentally looked at page one, two or three he saw Lindberg's picture.  It was so important that they even talked about it and kids brought in stories and pictures from the papers for "Show and Tell" in school.  He couldn't figure out why anybody would want to take somebody else's baby, especially Mrs. Peschkin's, because it cried all the time.  She was always screaming and hollering at the baby, who his Momma said was collicky - you could hear her from all the way across the street.  Mrs. Mendelson used to call her a nervous halailya and Dovie recalled that nobody used to like her - not even Mr. Peschkin because the two of them were always yelling at each other.  But as soon as she lost her little boy, who would be old enough to go to kindergarten in another year or so, just a little more than a month after the Lindberg kidnapping, everyone felt sorry for her and stopped saying bad things about her. Dovie felt especially sorry for her because just before Mrs. Peschkin got the new baby, her daughter Miriam moved out to live with relatives in Connecticut. Mrs. Peschkin explained to his mother in the appetizing store that the classes were smaller there and she would get more personal attention. Dovie wasn't even three then but he remembers how he felt bad because Miriam used to baby-sit for him and he liked her and he thought how lonely it must be for the Peschkins to have no children. So, even though, when Mrs. Peschkin got the new baby, it cried a lot, Dovie was still very happy for them. That's what made it so much sadder and more terrible when their baby was stolen right after the Lindberg's baby.

Actually, Dovie did not really feel that bad about all the rules and restrictions imposed upon him due to these dual tragedies because he was so young when all this evolved that he actually knew no other way and over-protectiveness was very natural to him. He was merely echoing the complaints of the older kids and, of course, Sollie. In fact, Sollie, rather than listen to Dovie's description of the Cashayfelope Man being a rag-buyer and a really nice man solemnly reiterated his statement that he abducted little children and carried them off in his large canvas bag and emphasized his disappointment in Dovie by calling him both a putz and a schmuck. What really bothered Dovie, beside not being certain what either word meant, other than their not being complimentary, was that he called him a little putz and a little schmuck. Remembering from the relay races in the schoolyard that he was much faster than Sollie he measured off and quickly dispatched a quick kick to each shin, then ran like hell.

As the small, young elms that had been planted a couple years before, two in front of each apartment building, began budding their leaves, and the sparrows began pecking in the sidewalk cracks, and to Dovie's revulsion, sometimes feasting on the small piles of horse manure that dotted the street,

Dovie realized that Spring was his favorite time of the year. Having had the experience of five prior Springs to fall back on, this to be his sixth, this realization was a measured, calculated call based on a vast well of knowledge and experience. Along with the budding plants and trees and the beckoning warmth and glow of the sunshine came the return of the Charlotte Russe man with his glass-enclosed double-shelved cart bearing the smaller whipped cream cakes on the bottom for three cents and the super-sized cherry-topped ones on the upper shelf for a nickel. He would position his wagon right at the entrance to the schoolyard and was joined by the "Mom's Knish" man with his white tin cart with the enclosed oven. When it came to the mouth-watering good smell department he won hands down. Then parked at the curb were the Good Humor, Bungalow Bar and Eskimo Pie ice cream trucks. This line-up guaranteed an almost 100% attendance record. It was also the reason why so many kids, Dovie included, did not walk out of school at the three o'clock bell - they skipped! Their hearts abounded with joy at the sugar-coated buffet awaiting them each afternoon.

On this day there was no skipping for Dovie. He was weighted down with the regret of yesterday's assault upon Sollie's shins and walked the walk of a zayda. Retribution by Sollie was near at hand - of this he was certain. History does not have to be stretched over eons to leave its indelible stamp; six years can be more than sufficient. He did not fear Sollie in a physical sense because Sollie had this technique of fighting with his eyes screwed tightly shut which afforded his opponent, even if he happened to be a very little kid, a wide latitude in mapping out a plan of battle.

As Sollie realized that his style of fighting was somewhat lacking he depended more upon cunning and slyness at which he was much more effective and was the cause of Dovie's current regret. With his face pressed against the glass showcase window of the Charlotte Russe wagon Dovie recalled how several months ago, then also being in Sollie's disfavor over a somewhat similar disagreement heightened by a somewhat similar act of defense-of-honor he was apprehended not by Sollie but, it seemed, everyone else but Sollie. And this after an apparent truce was entered into cemented by Sollie's reassuring slap on the back together with, "Forget it, Dovie. We're friends no matter what." How was an innocent, trusting soul such as Dovie to know that with that slap on the back came a handwritten loose-leaf page pasted to the rear of his shirt inviting one and all to - "KICK ME PUNCH ME SLAP ME"?

Dovie, acting like Neville Chamberlain before Neville Chamberlain acted like Neville Chamberlain, decided that there would be peace in our time. Through the wagon's display window he saw Sollie exiting the schoolyard and reached into his pocket, extracting all its contents - four pennies, which gave him the leverage to purchase the large, cherry-topped nickel size Charlotte Russe, requesting, as a steady customer, a penny's credit. Although reluctant, the Charlotte Russe Man, obviously sensing the direness of the situation, agreed and the deal was consummated. When Dovie called Sollie over and made his peace offering, "My treat, Sollie," Sollie smirked his lopsided smile and beamed, "I wasn't even mad at you," emphasizing it with a friendship-cementing slap on the back. Sollie was greatly puzzled, as was the Charlotte Russe Man, at Dovie's sudden removing of his jacket and shirt to check the backs of each.

Not that the truce was an uneasy one, but Dovie was still upset at Sollie's depiction of the Cashayfelope Man. Even his mother, whom Dovie never heard praise anyone except President Roosevelt, seemed to like Mottel. But his upset was somewhat muted by his recognizing, in his youthful wisdom, that his friend Sollie parroted his father.

Maxwell London's favorite and most frequently used statement was, "Believe me, I know what I'm telling you." And if anyone should dare to question what he was talking about, then came his second most favorite statement, "What's the matter? You don't like to hear what I'm saying?" To which Dovie's mother would always respond, "Gott zie danken - Thank you God for making radios with knobs. How come you forgot to make knobs for Max London?" Which, for quite a while, Dovie believed to be words of praise as he liked radios very much and if his mother was comparing Sollie's father to a radio, she must think very highly of him.

He was a large man, at least in comparison to Dovie's father, with a bald pate surrounded by bushy, tightly curled locks of hair and was always chomping on a large unlighted Havana cigar, which Momma swore was always the same cigar, one that he didn't even pay for but was given to him by Mr. Gluckman when his wife gave birth to their first son. Also, Dovie noticed that he didn't wear a belt to hold up his pants like his father did but instead held them up with his bulging stomach assisted by a pair of suspenders to which his thumbs were always hooked. Dovie was not sure whether his thumbs helped the suspenders in holding up his pants or did the suspenders hold his thumbs in place? This was the same pose that Dovie was accustomed to seeing Sollie strike. Solomon London's suspenders elevated him to a level of near-stardom as he was the only kid in their school that wore suspenders.

Dovie couldn't quite understand how come his own father worked such long hours that he hardly had any time to spend with his family whereas Sollie's father never seemed to work and was always home. One day Dovie noticed Max London in front of the building, just studying it from early morning until the dusk hours when Dovie was called in for dinner. After dinner Momma went down with Dovie because she had to pick something up at the grocery store and Mr. London was still standing there, studying the building. When they returned Poppa was just getting home from work and they arrived at the entrance door together. "Label," Max called over to Mr. Mendelson, "what's the matter? Only half a day today?" Label Mendelson tried to ignore him, hoping a smile would suffice but he was too tired to smile. Dovie noticed that Momma gave Mr. London the same kind of look she gives after scrubbing the kitchen floor and then still finding a spot of dirt on it. Undaunted, Max London poked Label on the arm and asked, "Tell me, Label, you got any idea how many bricks they used to make this house?" It registered immediately upon Dovie that this represented the sum total of Max London's workday and he was looking to capitalize on such an accomplishment.

Before Poppa was able to respond in any way, Momma shushed him, gave him a nudge and staring right through Mr. London, said, "Label, don't tell him. Let him count if he wants to know" - and immediately proceeded to drag him upstairs, leaving Max London staring at their departing figures and mumbling, "I got news for you - I already did count them." His day's workload had been reduced to naught.

Dovie was in awe that the London apartment was always cluttered with pots and pans, encyclopedias, carpet sweepers and whatever else Sollie's father happened to be selling - or, rather, was supposed to be selling. Maxwell London was a salesman but selling was beneath his dignity. From his samples his family had the latest of everything and when it came to borrowing or establishing store credit, he was second to none, so the Londons seemed to get along pretty well. Another talent that Max London had was barking like a dog - a big dog, not a little one. This ability was not inherited or instinctive but was born of necessity. The steady flow of process servers that was constantly knocking on the London apartment door would invariably run for their lives rather than face the perceived monster behind the bark. Dovie, duly impressed, would ask, "Shouldn't he go on the Major Bowes' Amateur Hour?" And Momma, with a disparaging shake of her head, would answer, "Him? Not him - it's too much like work."

If Max London had a problem it was that he was not meant to be a salesman. He would have been very happy with a microphone in his hand or at the very least, a soapbox. In fact, without any encouragement at all, Max had something to say about everyone and everything and not too much of what he had to say was complimentary unless, of course, he was talking about himself, which was another thing that he spent a great deal of time doing. He was fortunate in not dislocating his elbow and shoulder in the process of patting himself on the back for not knuckling under to, what he called, Roosevelt's communist regime and becoming a union puppet like Dovie's father and so many other working men from the neighborhood. With a great deal of finger-pointing and chest-pounding, he proclaimed as true American heroes those who made the ultimate sacrifice and remained in the ranks of the unemployed, a movement of which he was at the forefront. Besides the "communist working class" Max London bunched everyone different than he was in the enemy camp. Dovie often found himself without a playmate when, bounding down from his apartment he would see Max and Sollie London strutting side by side along the length of the street, thumbs tucked under armpits and suspenders, casting judicious glances in every direction.

It wasn't that Dovie believed Sollie's father was perfect. There were times that he would wonder about his doing things that his own father would never do, but then he would listen to his friend who always explained it in such a way that all Dovie could do would be to shake his head in amazement.

There was the time that the blind man who sold pencils on the street corner ran after Max London, shouting "Stop!

Thief!" When a crowd gathered around, Sollie explained that Max was just exposing a phony. And when he barked like a dog, that was a very special talent.

Dovie didn't mind being by himself, especially when it was spring and there was so much to learn and discover. That's when he thought of visiting his friend Mottel, the Cashayfelope Man. The warnings of his parents – "Stay away from the cellars!" didn't apply here. This was the home of his friend.

He mixed together walking fast and skipping, making sure not to step on the cracks. Who wants rain? He smiled, thinking how surprised Mottel would be to see him waiting for him.

Mottel wasn't surprised. Dovie was. He was just about to bound down the steps to the fire passage when he stopped at the top step. He held his breath as he watched Mrs. Schwedde, the super's wife, take the sleeping child from Mottel and whisper something softly to him. Dovie turned and ran. He was tucked tightly up against an entrance door of a neighboring building as the Cashayfelope Man walked down the street in the other direction, calling out in his sing-song voice, "Cash f' your ol' clothes!"

Dovie thought that he should have felt frightened. He wanted to cry but it wasn't from fear. He was so disappointed. Not because maybe Sollie was right and he was wrong. That didn't matter to him. How could somebody who was so nice to him steal little kids and be such a scary person?

He waited until Mottel turned the corner and he couldn't hear the bell anymore. Dovie needed someone to turn to for help and advice. He knew who he shouldn't turn to. That was easy. Whenever he would question either of his parents about something that someone else did, they never failed him with their answer which he knew before the question. "Mind your own business." It was plain, simple and to the point – and it always stopped Dovie in his tracks. That's not what he wanted to hear, so hoping that this time it would be different he told them of his anguish over seeing the Cashayfelope Man and the little boy he was carrying into the cellar. It was different this time.

"You like mystery stories and all kinds of scary people?" his father replied, digging his hand into his pants pocket. "Here, here's two cents. Go to the candy store and buy a Daily News and read Dick Tracy. There you'll find plenty scary people and mysterious things."

It was different this time but it was really the same. That left only Sollie.

☆   ☆   ☆

Dovie appreciated the advantages of being six and almost three-quarters, realizing that was an age at which making mistakes was still forgivable. But he was still very upset. Standing on his tiptoes he stared at himself in the bathroom medicine cabinet mirror. "Big fat troublemaker!"

There was no response from the image staring back, but there was a look of chagrin. Dovie turned away, but not before smirking, "Serves you right!"

As soon as he told Sollie what he had seen he was sorry. "Come on," Sollie screeched, eyes bulging. "Let's wait till we hear him coming back and you'll show me. Betcha there'll be some reward!"

"I don't think we should do that. Let's just tell a grown-up and they can ask Mrs. Schwedde."

"Maybe I shouldn't hang out with such a fraidy-cat baby ..."

That was the ultimate insult. Dovie was locked in but it turned out that he wasn't the only fraidy-cat baby.

When the clanging of the bell sounded a short while later, Dovie followed Sollie as they raced across the street, through the fire passage and past the cellar door that was the entrance to the Cashayfelope man's quarters, then to the rear court-yard where they ducked behind a row of garbage pails and waited. It wasn't a long wait and it happened just as Dovie knew it would.

Mrs. Schwedde's back was turned as she walked towards the front entrance, while coming towards them and the cel-lar door holding a small boy in his arms was the Cashayfelope Man.

"Yikes!! Let's get outta here!" Dovie turned as he heard the frightened, muffled cry at his side. He never would have believed that his friend Sollie London was that fast. He did feel bad for him later that evening as Mr. Marcus, the phar-macist in the drug store around the corner plucked the splin-ters from his tush that he got from trying to climb over the fence separating the courtyard they were hiding in from the next building's courtyard.

As they walked back to their building with Sollie's jacket tied around his waist hiding the shredded rear of his pants from the world, Sollie turned to him and said, "See what I told you. I knew it! I knew it."

"You don't know what you're talkin' about, Sollie." Dovie knew he was on shaky ground but he couldn't let himself believe that someone who seemed so nice that Momma even wanted to give him tea and cake was really a scary person who stole little kids.

That night Dovie didn't sleep as well as he did the night before or almost any night that he could remember. Considering that Saturday was the one day that everyone was able to sleep late in the Mendelson apartment – Poppa didn't work on shobbis – made it feel even worse. As he tossed and turned in his bed all the time thinking of a burlap bag and what might, okay, or might not, be in it he found himself first stiffening to attention then trying to burrow his way under the bed sheets as first he heard his mother's voice after the doorbell rang, "Shh, listen. Usually this isn't early, but it's shobbis, the one day we sleep a little late." Then he heard that voice and he dug his way deeper under the sheets.

"Please, I'm sorry. But for a minute if I can speak with your sweet, young child … It's important or I wouldn't ask."

Dovie closed his eyes tightly as he heard his Momma sigh and say, "Let me see if I can wake him up."

It was just a few seconds later that Dovie felt the bedding being pulled away and there was Momma standing over him and there was that look. He didn't know what she thought he was guilty of but he knew as she stood above him, glaring, that he had to defend himself.

"Nu, what now, Mr. Rascal?

"What for are you mad at me? I didn't do anything."

"If I wake up your father he'll first give you a what's for!"

As Dovie followed his mother into the kitchen – actually, he didn't follow her; he was in front of her being pushed – he was doubly frightened. He was afraid for his mother to wake up his father and order him to use the lukshen strap on his bare behind without him doing anything wrong and he was even more frightened to find out what brought the Cashayfelope Man here this morning.

When he saw the man standing with his back to the kitchen door, holding his hat in his hands he wasn't frightened for himself anymore. Grown-ups usually didn't cry – except in the movies – and there weren't any tears coming from his eyes but to Dovie it looked like this man, who he really felt was his friend, was crying. No tears, but he was crying. Dovie tried to smile. It wasn't a very good smile but maybe, he thought, it looked okay to someone else.

"My little friend Dovele," Momma stepped back as she listened to him speak. She sensed this was going to be a lot different than she had expected. "I know that you and your friend – the one you think is so smart just because he's seven – I know you were playing by the building where I live and saw something I didn't want you, or anyone, to see."

Now Dovie wished he were back in his bed and able to pull the sheets over his head again. His mother put her arms around him and drew his body up against hers. She clasped her hands over his chest. It made him feel better even than hiding in bed.

"He's a good boy. Sometimes he does what he shouldn't but not because …"

"No, no," Mottel stopped her, "the boy did nothing wrong." He reached out his hand to pat Dovie's cheek and Dovie felt ashamed because he pulled back without meaning to. He wanted to say he was sorry, but shook his head instead.

"What you and your friend saw was my little boy. My little boy who I love like your Momma and Poppa love you. Only he's a sick little boy and I can't let him play with other children till he gets all better."

Dovie stammered, "I'll play with him when he gets better. I get sick sometimes. I get colds and I even had chicken pots once, so I know. I can't play with anyone or go to school till I'm all better." His mother put her hand over his mouth, but very gently, then asked, "Your wife, she takes care of him, right?"

He lowered his head as he answered very softly. "She never set foot here. She died from consumption on the boat coming over. She was such an angel, my Ada, that she was needed more in heaven than here with us."

Dovie watched as his mother kept clasping and unclasping her hands as she said,

"Such a heartache," Dovie looked up as his mother spoke in a sing-song, breaking voice. "But the boys, my Dovie and his friend Sollie? What did they do? Because I'll make sure that, for my Dovie, at least, whatever he did, it won't happen again!"

"I said, the boys did nothing. They're boys. They were playing. You know, there's games where you hide or explore, that's what they were probably playing when they saw my little boy. Understand, they did nothing wrong. If there was wrong, it was me.

This time when Mrs. Mendelson offered him a glass of tea, Mottel gratefully accepted and sat down at the kitchen table. Dovie watched as he lifted the glass to his mouth with both his hands and the hot liquid seemed to melt away the nervousness. Nobody spoke a word until the glass was drained. He slid the chair back, got up and walked over to Dovie and placed his hands on his shoulders. Even though he spoke very softly Dovie realized it was a very serious moment.

"It's not just that I think of you as a little friend, but also because I know you are a very good and kind boy, that I ask you, please, not to say anything to anyone about what you saw. They must not take my little boy from the only world that he knows. And for your friend who is seven and so smart – if he is your friend he must be s good boy, too. If you can just say to him how I plead not to tell anyone … I know you can't talk or do for someone else. All I ask is you try."

Dovie didn't say a word but both he and the Cashayfelope Man knew that his silence was as strong as a solemn promise. Then there was Sollie …

There was a very good chance, Dovie thought, that when his best friend Sollie became eight, he would be a little nicer – at least, he hoped so. That's why, the day after the Cashayfelope Man came to his apartment, Dovie ran to the

Candy store on the corner to buy a Milky Way candy bar, for Solomon London's eighth birthday.

When he got back to his building Sollie was standing outside, a year older and hopefully, nicer. Running up to him, he pulled him into the vestibule and standing on tiptoes so that he could speak very confidentially into Sollie's ear he related the pleading request of the worried peddler the night before and how he and his mother felt so bad for him and his sick little baby boy. "So we can't say anything about the baby to anyone!"

Sollie looked at him and shook his head, "Aw, you'd believe Chicken Little if he told you the sky was falling. That's what I get for hangin' around babies."

"Yeah, well my mother believed him and felt bad for him, too, and she's old – real old. She's more than thirty-five, Smarty-Pants!"

"Well, I know the whole truth, because Max told me. The rag picker is part of the same gang that stole the Lindberg baby and Max won't let him get away with it."

Flustered and confused, Dovie asked, "Who's Max?"

"Jeez, what're you, kidding me? Max is my father!"

Dovie just shook his head, not comprehending why Sollie didn't call his father, Dad or Poppa like every other kid that he knew. Another thing that he knew was that being eight didn't make his best friend any nicer so he turned and skipped away, taking the Milky Way that he had placed in his pocket for Sollie's birthday present and ate it himself.

It was the day after Sollie's birthday and two days after the Cashayfelope Man's visit to the Mendelson apartment that Dovie thought it must be the most important day there ever was the way everyone was talking about how somebody named Bruno Hauptman went to the electric chair for kidnapping and killing the Lindberg baby.

They wouldn't let Dovie's class talk about it in school, not even for Show and Tell. Mrs. Pearlman, his teacher, said that they were too young to discuss such a topic, but after school that's what everyone was talking about in front of all the buildings and in all the stores on the street. Everyone was very happy about it. But when his father came home from work that night, he wasn't so happy. He turned from one news station to another and then shook his head as he got up from the table and said to his wife who was too busy washing the dishes to be concerned with kidnappers and electric chairs, "It wasn't right. They never proved he did it and when a man is offered his life if he says he did it and he refuses ... I don't know." He looked around at Dovie. "This is not for your ears. Go, play in your room."

Usually Dovie woke up either to the sound of garbage cans clanging or his mother pulling the blanket from him. This time he woke up to a very different sound, people talking and shouting, a siren and the feeling that this was a very different day. He pulled his pants on over his pajamas, slid his feet into his bedroom slippers and raced to the door. There was no shout of reprimand because as he soon found out, his mother was already downstairs with almost everyone else in the building and all the other buildings on the street.

Dovie was sure that never before was there people from the newspapers and radio on his block. Further down the street there were two police cars and an ambulance. He looked at his mother who was huddled together near the front door of the building with Mrs. Peschkin and Mrs. Gluckman, watching in wonder as a voice rose from the crowd.

"Excuse me, please. I see you're from the newspaper, is that right?" It was Maxwell London, waving his finger in the air. The young man with pencil and pad in hand, turned and stared at Max questioningly, then walked over to get a closer look. "It's me what called. I recognized my duty as a citizen.

When I saw with my own eyes the kidnapper and his victim –
actually, it's my boy here, Solomon, Solomon London – eight,
just eight years old - who uncovered the plot."

The reporter squinted as though he was studying him
under a microscope but wasn't sure of what he was looking at.
Hesitating for a moment, he scribbled a few notes on the pad,
still not saying a word. He didn't have to. Maxwell London
had center stage.

"My boy, Solomon, who learned from me to be very obser-
vant, caught this foreign rag-picker red-handed, taking the
poor, helpless little baby from the burlap bag he carries
around – mostly, I assure you to steal and kidnap - and lock
him away in a dirty, filthy, rat-infested cellar." Sollie smiled
proudly as his father patted him on the head.

As an officer approached, the reporter turned to Sollie.
"Is this what you saw, young man?"

Sollie shook his head.

"Were you alone?"

"Sort of. I was with a little kid who got all scared when he
saw him pull the baby from the bag and he ran away." Dovie
bristled and wanted very badly to kick Sollie in the shins again,
but this time as hard as he could. He turned and watched as
his mother and Mrs. Gluckman brought a chair over for Mrs.
Peschkin to sit on and the janitor brought her a glass of water.

The reporter spoke to the policeman for a minute or so,
with Max and Sollie both looking on very proudly, both with
their thumbs tucked into their suspenders. Then the officer
spoke with Max and when he finished he turned and headed
back to the building where Mottel lived. Maxwell called after
him, "Look, I want you should know – I did this as my duty as
a good citizen. I did it because that's exactly what he did with
the baby of my poor sweet neighbors, the Peschkins. In fact,
this may very well be her child, God should only be so good.
I didn't do it for no reward or anything – but if anything

is coming … I'd probably give it to charity, anyhow." Sollie stared at his father, wide-eyed and spellbound.

The shouting, pleading cry reverberated through the alleys and between the buildings. "What are you doing? Are you crazy? You can't take this child. I am caring for him. He needs my attention. His father is out working!!" A policeman was escorting two Emergency Medical men, one carrying a small, crying child wrapped in a blanket. Mrs Schwedde, the super's wife, was walking after them, pleading. The officer, not overly enthusiastic in carrying out the job at hand, restrained her, but very gently, as the ambulance workers carried the child, whose crying was now intermingled with a wracking cough, into the ambulance and with siren wailing shrilly, they drove off with the little boy's screams blotting out all other sounds.

Maxwell London was still holding court and there was now a group of reporters scribbling away when the bell clanged down the street. Dovie held his breath, then closed his eyes as after a moment's silence there was a wail of anguish that tore into the hearts of all that heard it.

Mottel, the Cashayfelope Man cried, trying to explain that his little boy was sickly and was never away from him a night in his life, that he had to take his medicine three times every day and before he went to sleep at night. He cried and pleaded. The policemen listened and cared; they even made a phone call. They tried calming the cash-for-your-old-clothes man by telling him that if it was his boy and the child had no highly contagious disease he would be returned tomorrow. Then they looked towards Max London and it was not a look of affection.

Maxwell London never skipped a beat. "Cunning, shrewd like his compatriot Hauptman. Birds of a feather …" The reporters were no longer taking notes. Sollie looked at his father and smiled. Dovie looked at his friend and no longer shared his awe of Maxwell London. Mrs. Peschkin came over, looked at him, shook her head and walked away with the help of her neighbors.

Dovie didn't get up early. He never really slept. He kept thinking of Mottel, wondering what he was doing and wondering about the little boy who was never away from his father before. These thoughts kept him from sleeping and he was sure he wasn't the only one. Therefore, hardly anyone was pulled from a sound sleep when the most pitiful crying and wailing imaginable shattered the early pre-dawn silence. Windows opened and all anyone could do was watch as Mottel stumbled from the grasp of the police officer and someone in a white uniform, obviously a doctor. They were kind and considerate – and apologetic, hoping to calm him and help him through the pain and agony, not leave it to a phone call. They came to tell him that the little boy had coughed, cried and spit up throughout the night and even though around-the-clock nurses cleaned him and kept an eye on him, he choked on his own sputum. He literally cried himself to death.

Mottel stumbled and ran, crying and screaming at the world. He kept falling, getting up and running through traffic, down side streets, over fences and through alleys and backyards. They searched for him but couldn't find the Cashayfelope Man. They tried but it was as though the very earth had swallowed him up.

People drifted out of all the buildings. Going to work, school and tending to daily chores suddenly seemed meaningless. Only for Maxwell London was it business as usual. The reporters were back and now their pencils were poised.

Sollie stood by his father, resolute in his belief of his near-infallibility. He was listening, as was everyone else, but it was as though they were tuned into a different wavelength as Maxwell London tried twisting tragedy to triumph. "Sure, we all feel bad. We should feel bad. A poor innocent little child died. He died because of this terrible person who stole him away from his parents. He died from a broken heart. We should feel sorry for the child and his parents, right here - the Peschkins, who lost their little angel to this monster." Sollie's eyes were lighting up and he looked up at his father.

"Plotka-macher, troublemaker, liar! I've taken enough!" Mrs. Peschkin moved to confront Max London in front of all their neighbors, a crew of reporters and a few shocked policemen.

Sollie's mother, who was usually next to invisible in the shadow of her husband, stepped forward to put a protective arm around her son. He shrugged it off and took a step back.

Tears were spilling from Mrs. Peschkin's eyes as she pointed her finger at Max. "My Miriam got pregnant when she was sixteen – she was a good little girl but she was in love and made a mistake - and this piece of garbage who – God should only help me – lives next door to me," still pointing a trembling finger at Max, "and listens with his ears to the walls, knows everything about everybody else's business. He tells me and my husband what a disgrace we are and what a terrible reputation we're giving to the building. We were so stupid because we were frightened – frightened mostly for our Miriam - that, instead of slamming the door in his face we try our best to make him like us and win his friendship. First we bought everything – from pots and pans to tools and encyclopedias – that this fahrshtunkener salesman couldn't sell to anyone else because he's too busy minding everyone else's business. Then – and I will regret it till the day I die – we sent our Miriam to live with my sister in Connecticut. And you know my biggest sin? When she gave birth I kept the baby here and said it was mine. Then, a blessing – my Miriam married her boyfriend, the baby's father and they came back and took the baby back to Connecticut with them. But let me tell you something – this terrible lying troublemaker knew all of this. Still, he made up the whole story of the Cash-For Clothes peddler stealing the child and I know that I'll have to answer to God some day – I was afraid to tell the truth. And look what it caused!"

Maxwell London was almost at a loss for words. Almost, but not quite. After all, he was Maxwell London. "Look, Peschkin – everybody, listen! Whose baby he stole doesn't matter. What I was doing was uncovering another demon – one just like Hauptman – who goes around stealing children …"

Mr. Peschkin held his wife in his arms and spit at Maxwell London. Sollie looked at his father, started to cry and tried to shove Mr. Peschkin, but his mother grabbed him, clasped him tightly as he buried his face inside her protective arms and Dovie watched in anguish as his friend's body shook with uncontrollable sobs.

Max London moved away with his wife and Sollie the very next day. They piled into a taxi with a few cartons and a couple of battered suitcases stuffed with as much of their clothes, dishes and important personal items as they could carry. There were no goodbyes and no looking at any of their neighbors. A couple days later he returned by himself with a small rental three-wheel pedal-wagon and cleared out the rest of their belongings. Nobody in the neighborhood was going to miss Maxwell London. In two days, Dovie Mendelson's world changed as he lost his two best friends.

Dovie sulked and moped until a couple weeks later when Label Mendelson felt it would be best for his boy to find new friends in a new neighborhood, so he bought a small house about a mile away, which seemed like a different world.

✳   ✳   ✳

David Mendelson was twenty-six and a half going on twenty-seven when, looking from his bedroom window he heard his mother call, "Dov, is everything alright, sweetheart?" and he decided that as long as this planet was still rotating on its axis and revolving around the sun, what was there to complain about? "Everything is fine, Ma."

"So come down already. Breakfast is ready!"

"Ma, I just had breakfast less than twenty minutes ago. I'm stuffed."

"You're nothing but skin and bones. What kind of an army we got that starves its own soldiers?"

David smiled as he looked at the framed sheepskin diplomas hanging on his bedroom wall. He had a Master's from Brooklyn College and a Doctorate from Columbia but he still couldn't win an argument from his mother so he walked down to the kitchen and permitted himself to be force-fed breakfast number two under the adoring gaze of his mother. He was wearing his khaki uniform with the single PFC stipe because his mother liked it – she felt it made him look so important. In her mind, a PFC was the army equivalent of a PHD and there was no way of dissuading her. "And in less than two years. Such an impression you must have made on them."

After his two years of military service, most of it in Korea and Japan, home was no longer the comfort zone it had always been before. True, it was by default as, except for his stint in the army, it was the only place that he ever put his head down on a pillow at night. Even his college years were a "remaining in the cocoon" experience, Brooklyn College being a bus ride away and Columbia a bit more worldly, requiring a bus and subway. Living on-campus was never even a consideration. He leaned back on his chair, smiling as he thought that despite all the thoughts of getting out and seeing this and doing that, how warm and wonderful it was to be with his parents again.

He was just about to butter a thick slab of pumpernickel bread when he saw the open newspaper next to his setting where his father had finished his breakfast earlier, then left for work. It was open to page seventeen – nothing ever earth-jarring on page seventeen - so he wondered whether his father had left it open for him to see or that was just the page he was up to when he finished his breakfast.

Ordinarily, an article about a local candidate for a city council seat holding a rally in his district wouldn't be of much interest to David, who would skip right to the sport section. If the name hadn't been in the headline he undoubtedly would never have paused to read further. But "Solomon London" reached out from the Daily News and stopped his old friend Dovie Mendelson from checking the box scores at the back of the paper – which was pretty major with a Yankee-Dodger World Series taking place.

He couldn't suppress the twinge of excitement as he got off the bus three blocks from where he was born and thought, Sollie London, a politician, then smiled to himself, realizing that, actually, how appropriate. "First" friends never fade from memory.

According to the newspaper article, his friend Sollie never left Brooklyn and David wondered why neither of them ever bothered looking up the other. It was twenty years since the heart-wrenching Cashayfelope Man incident but for David Mendelson hardly a day would go by without some fleeting thought or memory of the lovable old peddler and his agonizing cry for his child. He wondered whether that had anything to do with he and Sollie never searching each other out.

He put the thought from his mind and felt the excitement, the surge of anticipation of – after all these years - seeing his childhood friend again. Without realizing it, David broke into a trot in his anxiety to get there. He stopped in front of Resnick's candy store on the corner of the street where he grew up. He was sure Resnick was no longer there but was still tempted to go in for his old favorite, an egg cream with a frozen twist. He passed it up when he saw the small crowd gathered just around the corner and walked over to join them.

At first, he thought it was Maxwell London and he hadn't aged at all. In fact, he looked even younger … then David realized that it was not Max London and it was not a clone. It was his friend Sollie – and, then again, maybe he was a clone because even Maxwell London never looked more like Maxwell London than the person kibitzing with a few of the people at the front edge of the crowd.

David was going to wait until after the talk but didn't want to put off meeting his old friend any longer. He had no problem weaving his way through the small gathering – Sollie should know better than to try bucking a Yankee-Dodger World Series – and there he was, an arm's length from his once-upon-a-time very best friend.

"Sollie," he smiled.

"Look, the United States Army is here," Sollie waved to the crowd. Then turning back to David and hooking his thumbs onto his suspenders, squinted at him and said, "If you know me, I must know you."

"The last charlotte russe you ate at this school yard was on my charge account."

Sollie's eyes widened. He moved closer to David, staring, then, beginning in a whisper and rising in crescendo as the words tumbled out, "Dovie? Dovie Mendelson? I don't believe it! You're all grown up!"

"I don't think you get in the movies for children's price anymore, either."

Sollie stepped back and studied him. "What's with the monkey suit?"

David just smiled.

"Don't tell me you're in the army!"

Again David simply smiled. He didn't bother explaining that he just got his discharge.

"Don't you have better things to do with your life then taking a chance of getting shot at, maybe killed? And at the least wasting two, three years of your life. Max pulled a few strings and kept me out. A couple doctors' letters on top of which I was a conscientious objector … you know," and he winked, "Like I object to getting up early in the morning, and marching and crawling on my stomach. Did you try to get out, at least?"

David wasn't enjoying the conversation. Shaking his head, he explained, "No, in fact I volunteered for the draft. It was sort of like paying back a debt that I felt I owed."

"Dovie, Dovie! Oy, still such a putz!"

Now floodgates of memory opened up.

"Anyhow," Sollie continued, not noticing the mood change in David, "what are you going to be when you grow up?"

Better to ignore it, David thought to himself, but Sollie was still oblivious to David's reaction. "Look, if you ever want a job when you get out, look me up. I still owe you for helping me and Max rid the world of that pervert, foreigner peddler."

David had the choice of answering him or vomiting. He chose neither. Slowly, he backed off and turned away.

"Hey," Sollie called out, "What's wrong?"

"Wrong?" David shrugged. "Your suspenders, they make you look like a schmuck! A great big schmuck."

"Come on, we're friends. Aren't you going to stay for my talk? You're gonna vote for me, aren't you?"

"No, I don't think so." David felt much better and he was smiling as he turned, deciding to walk down the block and look at the building where he had lived. But he slowed down as he came to the alleyway of the apartment building where he hid from his mother and met Mottel – his Cashayfelope Man.

As he stood there looking at the passage leading to the cellar door that was still emblazoned in his mind all these long years, a voice called to him, "Can I help you, young man?"

David turned and stared at the pleasant weathered face of the white-haired woman standing at the entrance to the building. "Mrs. Schwedde?" He didn't mean for his voice to come out so high-pitched.

She walked towards him, scrutinizing him carefully as she approached. "You are familiar, but … were you a tenant?"

He shook his head but never had to answer.

"Oh, good lord!! Mottel's little friend?"

David smiled.

"Wait here a minute, better yet, come with me."

He followed her into the building and into her apartment on the first floor. He stood, hands behind his back, not knowing what to expect. Then he gasped. There from a shelf in the foyer, she uncovered a brass bell on a long wooden handle.

"You were always his favorite. I know that he would have been happy for you to have this."

It was hard for David to see clearly. His eyes were misted. "Was there ever any word of what happened to him? Did you ever hear anything?"

She shook her head, smiling sweetly. "Nothing. He only wanted to be with the little one. And he made sure that happened." She wrapped the bell in a towel, handed it to David and gently kissed him on the cheek.

There was no longer any crowd on the street. Not much of a gathering, not much of an event. He decided to walk home rather than take the bus. After a couple blocks, he unwrapped the bell and caressed the smooth brass surface. As he walked towards home he raised the bell, shaking it gently. He smiled through his tears and as the bell rang out with its long-ago familiar peal, he called out "Cash for your clothes …" and thought of sweet, gentle Mottel, his Cashayfelope Man.

*I wrote "AN ENTREPRENEURIAL ACT" in 1992. It is a story based on the life of a person that never was, a media distortion/creation of the much maligned, misrepresented courageous Brownsville prizefighter, Al 'Bummy" Davis. Accepting the written word of some highly regarded sport writers as gospel I created what turned out to be the totally fictitious anti-hero, Monk. Although a work of fiction, I was so disappointed at being caught up in the hype, that once learning the true qualities of the based-on Davis, I took a silent pledge to set the record straight and let the world know about a tough street kid with a seemingly inborn sense of morality who was devoted to his family, friends and neighbors and refused to be pushed around – by anyone.*

*I placed the manuscript of "AN ENTREPRENEURIAL ACT" on my file closet shelf where it has been abandoned for nearly twenty years. In that time I wrote about the real, the true Al Davis as told to me by his friends, neighbors, ring opponents, street peddlers and even those who he stood up against, toe-to-toe, jaw-to-jaw, and in so doing earned, if not their love, at least their everlasting respect. It is now time to let the story of a completely fictitious character of a guy named Monk be told, bearing in mind that any similarities to persons living or dead is purely coincidental.*

# AN ENTREPRENEURIAL ACT

*- Ron Ross*

When Monk says, "Show me a guy who wantsa be a hero an' I show you one dumb fuck," I am truly offended because I think it is in very poor taste to voice such an opinion especially considering the time an' the circumstance. But you do not say to a guy like Monk that you think he is wrong as he very often takes criticism quite poorly. So I try most tactfully to point out to him that when a very dear friend meets a most untimely demise by comin' to someone's aid, it is usually appropriate to say nice things about him, especially if you are at such friend's funeral, which is exactly where we are at this time.

I make an impression of sorts on Monk, who gives it much thought before reconsiderin' and respondin', "Okay, in Hymie's case he is one very nice, very dead dumb fuck."

Now, I got a lotta respect for Monk so I listen when he talks. Monk earns this respect, not just from me, but from just about everyone in Brownsville, because you can never be too sure about the degree of his sanity on top of which there ain't too many guys around who are tougher an' have a shorter fuse than him, which, considering the crowd makes him very tough with a very short fuse. There is no question in my mind that if the army takes him, World War Two woulda been over before it started. I know they do not take guys with flat feet, but if what comes back to me is true, Monk is the only guy that is 4-F because of a flat nose which is because he is a prizefighter who throws as many punches with his face as he does with his fists.

When we leave I.J. Morris, which is where we all wind up some day to take a ride in the back of a big, black Caddy, I mention to Monk how guys who do what Hymie did wind up on page three in the Daily Mirror and are called a hero an' other very nice things – nobody makes fun of such a person. Monk points out to me that beside page three in the Mirror they also usually wind up on a cold slab in the morgue. "I do not know you to be such a cynical person," I say to him as we walk down Pitkin Avenue munchin' on two hot sweet potatoes that Monk picks off Mendel's wagon an' I pay for, when Monk puts on the brakes an' gives me a look that makes me think I may wind up gettin' a nose similar to his. I immediately realize that not only is a clarification in order but it is most necessary so I very quickly give him the dictionary definition of 'cynical' at which he nods his head then gives with a small smile an' we are both much relieved.

"In this world every slob gotta take care of himself. An entrepreneur gotta protect his own interests."

"A 'who?' A 'what?'" I ask with a burst of new found respect for a guy who, I gotta admit, never ceases to surprise.

"You know, an entrepreneur, a businessman. But forget it. It don't matter 'who' or 'what'. It's an across the board thing. Everybody gotta look out for himself – and only himself. Like Big Turk always tells me, 'A clean nose leads to a long life.'"

I do not enjoy my knees rattlin' in public, but it is a condition I cannot control whenever the name of Monk's older brother comes up.

Monk is my friend – true, not by choice, but because we grow up together – an' he is by far, the class act in his family. When he is just eight years old, while the rest of us are playin' punchball, he is playin' lookout at his ol' man's speakeasy on Stone Avenue where Big Turk starts buildin' his reputation as a head-buster supreme. What I am pointin' out is Monk grows up in spite of, not because of the teachings of Big Turk, and I am only sorry that to him, his brother, who is not one of history's prominent philosophers, is some sort of guru. But even though he looks up to him, Monk does not choose t' follow in his footsteps, which in my book earns Monk many kudos.

However, it is pointless to try to change Monk's mind or give lectures about people standin' up for one another, which is a shame because I cannot think of anyone who I'd rather have standin' up for me than Monk. Unfortunately, it is not always the guys you wanna count on that you can count on because it is usually the wrong guys in this world who wind up with the moxie.

So, even though we are on different wavelengths, Monk is still my friend, an' because he is my friend I like him. Well, maybe I do not exactly like him but I accept him. Ain't that what friendship is all about? That does not mean that the rest of the world gotta like him. In fact, much of the rest of the world that knows Monk doesn't like him because he is not the easiest kinda guy t' like. Even bein' a sport celebrity of sorts does not change the situation. He is the guy who is always getting' booed while the guy in the other corner gets all the cheers. The only one who gets treated worse by the press is Adolph Hitler. This is understandable if you ever watch Monk fight. Sir Galahad he ain't. God supplies him with two thumbs, two elbows an' two knees — there is no reason in Monk's mind he cannot use all this equipment when he fights. It is only the promoters, besides his friends, who love him an' that is because promoters see dollar signs dancing before their eyes as there are so many people that hate Monk an' are willin' t' cough up their dough in the hopes they see him get his butt kicked in.

Actually, I feel a little sorry for Monk. We are not kids anymore an' his career is definitely windin' down. While the rest of us are gettin' married, myself included, an' startin' t' raise families, Monk, who never learned how t' treat a girl, spends most of his time hangin' out alone in candy stores an' bars. Knowin' his days as a fighter are numbered an' not cut out for Big Turk's line of work, he tells me it is time t' start lookin' to invest in something that'll give him security in his old age.

"Ya know, some business of my own."

I smile at my friend whose face now resembles a roadmap with train tracks zig-zagging across the terrain. "Ya mean you wanna be an entrepreneur?"

Monk smiles back at my remembering. "I got news for you – this whole world ain't made up of ditch-diggers and pugs. Yeah, I wanna be an entrepreneur. I wanna be a guy who uses his gray matter and invests his money in a business or a store which will support him and give him a comfortable life as long as he watches over and takes care of it. Hey, I'm savin' my chips because you don't think I'm gonna be climbin' through those ropes forever, do ya? I know the path I'm gonna take. Only ya don't get nowhere if ya start lookin' to help this one an' that one. I told ya, a guy gotta look out for himself – Numero Uno – an' only himself and what is his. Take care of and mind your own business an' let the next guy take care of his. I may not walk the walk with Big Turk but when he talks it pays t' listen. All I wanna do is be able to take care of myself."

I get the chills because these words I never think I will hear spillin' from Monk's mouth. It is very difficult t' believe Monk c'n have feelin's that for other people are normal.

After the birth of our second kid, like everyone else in our crowd, we desert Brownsville an' make the big move t' East Flatbush. When Monk takes a wallopin' like I never seen no human bein' take before, in a non-title fight at the Garden against the welterweight champ, he hangs up the gloves an' I do not see or hear from him in quite a while. Now that I am a guy with a nine t' five job, a potbelly an' a recedin' hairline I guess I do not have too much in common with a *trumbanick* like Monk anymore. But there is always a soft spot for some-one you grow up with.

That is why, when I get the call from Heshy Four-Eyes, I take the day off from work even though it may cost me my job. Once again, I am together with all my Brownsville buddies an' all we can do is shake our heads an' say how we cannot believe it. When Big Turk storms in I think the walls of I.J Morris are gonna col-lapse, he bangs his head against them so hard, bawlin', "I teach the kid — I beg him, I plead with him — Watch your own frig-gin' pot! Don't put your nose where it don't belong! Ay! Ay! My baby brother! Why don't you listen to me? Why?"

Who'd've believed Monk goes outta here in such a way?

Reporters who always tore him apart in their columns wrote, "In one last glorious act of selfless heroism he has redeemed himself in the eyes of all."

It seems Monk is sittin' by himself in this bar on Ralph Avenue when four mugs with rods walk in an' announce a heist. They start musclin' some of the guys around the bar out of the way. Nobody argues or talks back t' guys waving rods around. But as soon as they move t' the cash register Monk pounces like a tiger. He breaks a couple of jaws, but it is fists against bullets — no contest. He takes his final breath chasin' the getaway car down the street.

In the chapel I meet the owner of the bar who comes t' pay his respects an' I learn somethin' that sorta puts it all together. He is really the *former* owner as he tells me that Monk, only a week ago signs a contract to buy the place from him. He then relates that Monk comes in every day t' check an' make sure everything was okay, that the place is kept clean and business is goin' on as usual. It was on the morning of the holdup day that Monk finalizes the deal and becomes the new owner of record. He sits around until the place opens for business, then he watches as the bartender measures out the shots, keeps **count** of people comin' and goin', even checks the bathroom t' make sure the place is mopped and there is enough toilet paper.

"I go home right after he gives me the cash, which he delivers in a brown paper bag and I sign the place over to him," the old owner says, "but then I come back because I gotta give another look. It's not just that I had some good feelings for the place — after all, it was my home away from home. But never before do I see a guy kvell over a business like it is a newborn infant. I only thank God I left before it all happened. I simply can't understand. There was maybe twenty dollars in the register. Go figure what a person will fight for."

I did figure. I knew Monk and I had the answer.

When the Rabbi recites his eulogy explainin' how Monk earns eternal rest in Heaven by aiding his fellow man, defending the other patrons in the establishment even though he probably didn't even know them, there is quite a bit of snifflin' and nose blowin' goin' on. It dawns on me that for once the whole house is in Monk's corner as the Rabbi finishes by saying, "There is no greater act of devotion than a man laying down his life for others."

I smile but it is a sad smile because I know that is not Monk's style. His was purely an entrepreneurial act.

# The Glory Days

Every once in a great while he would sit back and think of those glory days. He didn't permit himself the luxury of doing it too often because Clee was a realist and what good would it do anyhow except make him feel bad about what could have been – but there were those dreary times when he felt that he needed a lift and that's when Clee would let himself dream. He'd think about how it was when the Golden Gloves was his stage and people besides the ones who lived on 138th Street would turn and say, "Hey, that's Clevon Nance, the kid who won the Gloves." It was good, probably the best thing Clee had to remember from his whole life.

All the rest of the time Clee spent thinking about what had to be done at that moment and maybe what had to be done five or ten minutes later. He'd get up early every morning, like five, five-thirty, wash and put on his work clothes, then carefully put together his paint brushes and tools and after having a hot cup of tea and a bowl of oatmeal – Clee hadn't changed his breakfast in more than thirty years – he'd go to wherever that day's work would happen to be. He'd come back home usually around eight o'clock, right after having dinner at one of the fast food places on the block, when he would take a long, relaxing shower – if there was hot water, which was a hit or miss thing in Clee's building – or else he'd spend the better part of an hour heating up enough pots of water to fill the tub. Usually, that was the favorite part of Clee's day, that hot shower or bath – and those were the times when he would close his eyes and let himself drift back over the years and hear the crowd shout out his name and stamp their feet as he'd climb into the ring and salute them with upraised gloves. And whenever he'd let himself go back like that, those were the only times that his face would crease into something like a smile. After cleaning up, Clee would read the Daily News which he bought every morning and carried around with him to read at night. He'd finish up his day by watching about a half hour of television and then if his one-and-a-half room apartment needed any straightening up, that's when he would do it. But as Clee didn't have much to straighten up anyhow, that never took much time. Usually it meant rinsing out one teacup and one bowl from the morning, an occasional dusting and a little Lysol in the bathroom that had no window or vent. Every day was the same except Sunday when he would go to church in the morning and spend the afternoon either at a movie or watching a baseball or football game on television. Clee wasn't a religious person but his daddy had always lectured him that to lead the good life you had to honor and respect God and your church. The only other entertainment that Clee would permit himself was to go to see any fight card within a subway ride away. And also, if he happened to be working in the vicinity of any of the local gyms, after work he would stop in and watch the young kids work out for about an hour before going home. That's all there was to Clee's life until one day he met Connie Green.

Clee kept a small ad running in the local Pennysaver and also posted notices on bulletin boards of some of the small shops listing his services as a painter and handyman. That's how he got most of his work, the rest coming from referrals. Sometimes he'd take on a job where he'd have to hire one or two young men to work with him. He was always able to find help by asking either at the paint supply shop or the hardware store. That's how he came upon Connie. He took on a job to paint a loft just off the F.D.R. Drive and 125th Street. It was really a job that required more than two men, but Clee hardly ever hired more than one person to work with him. First, he priced his jobs cheaply and the only way he could do it was by keeping his overhead low. And, also, Clee never felt comfortable in the role of a boss and working with more than one man made him feel like a boss. So it happened that Charlie, the paint store manager, sent him this kid Connie who was looking for work. The kid admitted to him right off that his painting experience was limited to graffiti and as he was never paid, he was strictly an amateur, but he added that he was a quick learner and was sure he could handle it. Clee liked the kid's honesty, because most of the time a kid would try to bluff his way through just so he could get the job. Anyhow, he took the kid on and they worked together for the better part of two weeks. During this time Connie, though he was happy and thankful for the job, told Clee how he really wanted to make something of himself – that spending his life being a painter in Harlem wasn't what he was willing to settle for. And Clee thought wryly to himself, "Who is, kid? Who is?" Then Clee thought of the things that make a young man settle – like having to put bread on the table, having doors slammed in your face so many times that you just can't go back and knock anymore, and like in his own case, having a daddy who set the ground rules and there was no way to say "No".

Without skipping a stroke with his paint brush, Connie kept talking about the black fighters like Ali and Frazier who were making millions and how a black kid who had athletic ability had to be crazy if he didn't work hard and take a shot at that pot of gold. Clee didn't pay him that much mind because mouth action was the easiest work of all. He thought back to that night over thirty years ago when he won the Golden Gloves lightweight championship and he remembered how he wished he could stop the whole world at that moment when they were cheering him, just freeze it in time forever. And afterwards the newspapers predicted what a great future he had, how he and this other kid, Ray Robinson, who lived less than a mile from him on 119th Street, and had won the featherweight championship, were the twin toasts of Harlem and with the right breaks should both go on to win world championships.

Clee thought he would never come down from that cloud he was on until he got home and described to his daddy how unbelievable the whole thing was and how people knew him and respected him and how he knew now that he wanted to be a fighter. His daddy hadn't gone to any of the Golden Gloves shows because, as he put it, "Sportin' is foolishness and a waste of a man's time."

When Clee finished relating to his daddy what a wonderful thing it was that happened to him his daddy responded, "That's very nice, Clevon. What did you get for all of this?"

Clevon opened the copy of the Daily News sitting on the kitchen table and smiled as he pointed to his picture and the results of the championship round. The smile faded when his Daddy said something about how "in another day or so all that paper will be good for is wrapping fish." Then Clee opened his shirt and proudly displayed the championship Golden Gloves award hanging from his neck.

His daddy stared at the medal for a long, heart-stopping moment, then, speaking softly but as firmly as a man could, "This part of your life is in the past, Clevon. Man was not meant to fritter. Man was meant to work. Starting tomorrow, you'll be going with me to earn your keep and learn a respectable trade. I suggest you go to bed early. We'll be up at five and on the job, painting, by seven."

So, at the age of nineteen, Clevon Nance terminated his embryo career as a prizefighter and watched his neighborhood rival win world championships in two divisions. But Clee accepted his lot as part of life and if he resented it at all, he never showed it. That's not to say that Clee didn't have feelings and didn't have a hurt deep down inside over not being able to do the thing he did best and loved the most in life. In fact, on that first day at work with his daddy, Clee, who wasn't too much at expressing how he felt about things, tried explaining how important fighting was to him and how there was so much money to be made if you were good at it, like he was sure he was. "See what Joe Louis is makin'? He's a millionaire, Daddy."

His father listened to him but never missed a stroke with his paint brush until he turned, looking hard into Clee's eyes. Clee could never quite figure what that look was but he always believed that mixed in there somewhere with the sternness and one-mindedness was a shred of love.

"Clevon," his father said, "when a colored boy sits down at a table with a hunk o' bread on it, he better take that hunk o' bread an' eat it up 'stead of waitin' to see if maybe they's gonna set a platter o' meat 'n taters on that table cause if he waits, he may be one hungry colored boy. Son, you got the bread right here – don't go dreamin' 'bout no meat 'n taters."

After that, Clee never brought up the subject of his being a fighter again. Instead of hope and ambition he settled for a dream – a memory.

When they finished the job at the loft Clee paid Connie and slipped him an extra ten dollars, telling him he was a quick learner – just like he said - and a good worker. "If you'd like some more work, son, just tell me where I can reach you."

"Really 'preciate it, Clee, but I wasn't jivin' ya, man. I wanna be a fighter. I don' want no crutch to fall back on. If I get to be a fat cat painter, ain't gonna be no incentive for me to bust my hump in no gym. I gotta be mean an' hungry, Clee."

That was the first time that Clee realized the kid was serious. "Don't you have no folks who may feel differently?"

"Hey, I got only me, man. Ain't no one I answer to but myself!"

Connie was just eighteen, about a year younger than Clee was when his daddy aborted his career some thirty-odd years ago. Clee didn't want to let loose the thoughts that were going through his head at that moment but suddenly it seemed almost possible to bring part of a dream back to life. He found himself reaching back through the years, restringing simple memories and pleasures that he had buried from a place where time had stopped. That night, from beneath his bed he slid out a carton and carefully lifted out an album which he dusted off before opening the cover. On the first page was a photograph of him at the age of seventeen in a classic boxing pose. The following pages contained newspaper articles of his journey through the Golden Gloves. The beginning articles were small with maybe a couple of sentences describing his bout in a rundown of the evening's results. As he progressed the articles became larger and more detailed, some containing action shots of his fight. Then the final articles, full page stories of Clevon Nance, the winner of the Golden Gloves lightweight title. He permitted a small smile to brighten his face and, almost lovingly, smoothed that page, closed the cover and returned the album to the carton which he replaced under his bed. The smile stayed as Clevon slept through a dream-filled night.

As so often happens with dreams, when he awakened the next morning, it was gone and Clee did what he always did. He had his breakfast, went downstairs, bought the morning edition of the Daily News which he stuffed into his back pocket and walked to the hardware store where his brushes sat in jars of turpentine in the cellar. Like so many of the other local painters, he kept all his equipment there with Charlie because most landlords said it was dangerous to store in residential buildings. It was a good trade-off for the painters and for Charlie.

Charlie knew that Clee had another large job lined up, the painting of six apartments in a newly-renovated building so he asked him if he wanted a helper or two. Clee didn't have to think. He said 'no'. For the next week-and-a-half he buried himself in his work. He had no room for dreams. Hard work brought sound sleep and kept him in a world that he was familiar with and Clee had convinced himself that it was the only world he wanted to know. Well, he tried convincing himself of that. But whenever those glory days came back into his head he would allow himself to believe there was nothing wrong with dreaming. You can't stop a dream from happening. They just come to you and that was okay, as long as you don't go chasing after it.

Clee was in his mid-thirties when his daddy died of emphysema. Until then he would follow his father's word, but as a reluctant subject. Now that his father was gone he had become infallible and Clee went from a reluctant subject to a devoted disciple. Suddenly, all his daddy's preachings and admonishments became irrefutable and Clee truly became his father's son. He continued the painting business and narrowed his horizons so that work, sleep, church and TV became his routine. His was a life of true contentment. Clee believed that.

He was a loner. Not a hermit or a recluse. He didn't lock himself away from the world. Just did things his own way – by himself – and went his own way. That's how it was from the day that his daddy took him on as an apprentice. That's when his life changed. He drifted apart from his boyhood friends. Dances, dates, clubroom parties and street games all became part of another life. His socializing was limited to whatever conversation was necessary on his jobs and his solitary visits to an occasional movie house, gym, fight club and his Sunday mornings in church. He never married and had no family. Over the years he did not permit many temptations to test his resolve.

Maybe Clee would have been better off if things just kept going along the way they were and, actually, Clee never did anything to change that. At least, not consciously.

☆  ☆  ☆

"Hey, what you doin' here, Clee? Don' tell me you're gonna be paintin' this gym!"

Clee couldn't believe the rush of excitement that quick-ened his pulse. There was no reason for it, he told himself. It probably wasn't noticeable to anyone, but Clee was smil-ing. A quite small smile by ordinary standards but for Clevon Nance it had to be a knee-slapper. He studied the lean, finely muscled copperskin body of Connie Green that was bounc-ing around in front of him like a scarecrow on a pogo-stick. "I ain't paintin' any gym, son. Just a stop-off place for an hour's entertainment when I'm nearby. So I see you meant what you said about bein' a fighter."

"Bein' you're here, hang around about a half-hour. I'll be sparring a couple of rounds an' you will see why the painter's union has lost a major brush pusher." He turned and bounced over to the ceiling-to-floor mirror where he slashed punches at his image without any fear of being hit back. Clee leaned back against the wall and watched as Connie showboated his way through his floor exercises, rope-skipping and work on the heavy bag. Nothing was by the book and Clee wondered if the kid ever considered vaudeville. But he did have fast hands and that, Clee knew, you had to be born with.

It was that hand speed and the kid's cocksure attitude that had Clee move up to the ring and rest his elbows on the apron to get a better view of his sparring session. He watched Connie strut and prance around the ring for three rounds, mixing in a few sweet jabs and hooks with a whole bunch of clowning, off-balance punches. The kid he was working out with looked lost in there, like he wound up in the ring while looking for the subway. Connie was having a party, but he was the only one enjoying and appreciating it.

Clee shrugged uncomfortably as Pop Chambers came over and spoke with him. Pop was the senior trainer there and he was the only one still around from the "old" days. Clee always liked Pop – it's just that he always felt uneasy when he wasn't lost in the shadows – especially with people from a world he was no longer part of. Pop touched palms with Clee and asked him how things were going.

"Same as always," Clee answered. "Nothin' to complain about. How about you, Pop? Still climbin' in the ring with those water buckets?"

"Ain't as heavy as a paint bucket." Then, nodding in the direction of the ring, "You know that peacock, Connie?"

"He did some paintin' work for me."

"Lots of natural ability. Good power, real fast hands. Needs some tutorin', though. If the boy learns his p's 'n q's he'll do better'n okay."

Clee nodded his head. He agreed with Pop. Connie Green was a diamond in the rough.

The kid bounced down from the ring with a smile so big it looked like his face was broke in half. "Now don't go bustin' your hands applaudin' me, Clee. Did you see a flash of Ali and a touch of Kid Gavilan in there?"

"I saw a lot more Abbott and Costello."

"You gotta be kiddin' me! Hey, just because you're a painter don't mean you shouldn't appreciate artistic talent in another field. I knew nothin' about paintin' but now I appreciate when I look at a wall and see it's smooth, no brush marks, paint blisters – smooth, man, smooth … an' I appreciate it."

"Don't get me wrong. I appreciate things, Connie. Remember the first thing I told you about painting? You don't just take a brush and smear the paint. First you gotta prepare the wall by scrapin' and spacklin'. Then you use a primer. You do all of the basics before applyin' the good stuff. Same thing up in there. Before Ali or Kid Gavilan throws those showy punches, the bolos an' such and doin' mambo steps an' the Ali shuffle they do the basics. When you know how to jab and hook properly, when you throw a cross with your body behind it, when you know how to cut off the ring, tie up your man, when you know all your fundamentals, then, maybe, you can do some fancy stuff."

"Hey, the whole world ain't about paintin' houses, Clee. You gotta try an' understand – there are other things in life."

"You're right, Connie. That's it. I think like a house-painter."

About three or four days after Clee's visit to the gym, Pop Chambers called Connie into his office. As offices go, Pop's would not be considered top of the line. It was an alcove to which someone slapped a few plywood panels, cut out a three-by-seven opening and attached a three-by-six hollow core door with a couple of hinges, a slide bolt and handle, leaving a one foot open-air transom at the top. The furnishings consisted of a battered, lumpy-cushioned easy chair with a hassock that was transformed into an emergency bed for Pop as long as he folded himself like an accordion, a bridge table that served as a desk and two Sheffield milk boxes that made very adequate chairs for company. The three original walls were circled with a shelf that was filled with trophies and awards and the walls were decorated with newspaper articles and photographs of the gym's stars of the past.

Entry to Pop's office was a "by-invitation-only" event and it was Connie's first visit. Pop told him he was calling him in as he had to change his locker. Connie walked out with a new key … and an education.

What Clee liked best about a fast food place like McDonald's was that he was able to sit at a small table and be by himself as he ate and read his newspaper, not like at a diner or restaurant where he had to rub elbows at a counter as there were only large tables or booths. Clee enjoyed his privacy. Loneliness and being alone were not one and the same to him. So he wasn't annoyed – just surprised – when someone sat down at the chair opposite his at his "private" table. He looked up and was suddenly glad to no longer be alone.

There was no invitation or offer but it didn't matter. Connie reached over, picked up some French fries from Clee's tray and dipped them into the little paper cup of ketchup next to Clee's elbow. "You don't look nothing like Garry Moore, so what're you doing playing this 'I've Got A Secret' game, Clee?"

Clee ignored the question and smiled. "What about a burger to go along with my fries? My treat."

"Clevon Nance," Connie leaned forward, ignoring the offer, "I respected you all over the place … as a painter, man. Where do you come off tryin' to fool a fast-thinkin' dude like me?"

Clee smiled a soft smile – the kind that covers a baby lie – and shrugged. "Don't know what you're talkin' about, son." But that smile said he knew.

"Your picture all over Pop's office. Stories, headlines. Man, you was a Golden Gloves champ and you let me run at the mouth about how I'm a combination Muhammad Ali, Joe Louis and Superman."

"If we stuff your mouth with that burger there won't be nothing else coming out of it." Clee got up and walked to the counter.

"Not that thirty-nine cent bird feed. Double cheeseburger with the works. You owe me big time, Clee!"

It wasn't until he finished the strawberry shake and wiped his mouth with the back of his hand that Connie began turning back Clevon Nance's clock. "Pop Chambers says the only thing you know more about than house-painting is boxing. He says you coulda been the best, Clee."

All Clee  could do was listen. He was afraid to speak. Too many things were going on inside of him – things that he tried shutting out years ago.

"You taught me good about painting and you know I'm a good learner. How about bein' my teacher again?"

"You're workin' with Pop Chambers, in his gym. He's the man who's going to teach you."

"You know how many kids Pop is working with? My weight alone, 147, he got four guys. It was Pop who suggested I team up with you. Clee, he says you're smart, that you know what it's about. I need someone to work with me, just me."

"I can't do that, Connie. I got a full-time business. Anyhow, I ain't no professional trainer."

"According to Pop, you got the sharpest eye in the gym. He said you point things out to him before it pops into his head."

"Pop never stopped being in my corner. He's been tryin' to get me back in that gym as long as I can remember." Clee smiled. "I think he's looking to take over my painting business."

"I'll listen to you, Clee. You know that."

"Ain't no percentage for you to hook up with someone who got no track record and it don't make sense for me to give up my bread and butter to work a one-fighter stable where I get my cut out of zero, which is the wages of an amateur."

"Listen to me, Clee, listen. You don't have to give up your business. I do my roadwork and stuff in the morning anyhow and I can work with you at night after you finish up. Anyhow, I ain't looking for no amateur career. I want to jump in with the big boys as soon as I can."

"You don't do no jumping until you're ready to jump. You hear me?"

Connie's smile was bigger than Ronald McDonald's, who was grinning down at them from a poster on the wall. "That mean we're a team, Clee?"

"I'm beginning to think Connie's short for Con-Artist. I didn't say that."

The kid placed both hands on Clee's shoulders and stared at him like a cocker spaniel that needed desperately to be petted. "Will you sleep on it?"

Clevon Nance, the once upon a time Golden Glove champion from 138th Street, did not sleep very well. But he did dream. New dreams and old dreams. He dreamt of those "glory days," the days that were and the days that could have been. Those dreams he dreamt before. Then there were the days that still could be. These were the new dreams, the dreams that made his pulse race, the dreams that pulled him from his sleep but continued as his waking dreams. Fortunately, Clee was a guy who did not need much sleep.

A few days after their meeting at McDonald's, Clee found himself standing in front of the medicine cabinet mirror in his bathroom. He wasn't checking how well his clothes fit. Didn't matter that much when you're wearing overalls and a denim work shirt. He had struck a boxing pose and was gently flicking out a left jab. That's when he realized that the dream was no longer just a dream. He stared at the image in the mirror. Strangely, it wasn't his reflection but that of a serious-faced Connie Green. The cocky, face-splitting grin was gone, but the look of confidence was still there, now with eyes narrowed and focused, as his hands moved at Clee's commands. Clee sat down on the edge of the bathtub, rubbing his eyes but decided not to open them. At least, not just yet. He skipped breakfast that morning so that he could leave earlier and walked the entire distance to his workplace. It was a long early morning walk on a cold, winter day. When he returned late that same night there was no more dream. It had become real life.

At first, he tried convincing himself that what he always believed was a life of satisfaction and contentment – the good life - was really a life of wasted opportunities. Then he told himself that it was the path his daddy set him on and not the course his life was meant to take. That made it a little easier but he felt a sense of guilt and shame, as though he had to blame someone for where and who he was. Then Clee made a realization. There were no regrets. There was no blame. Life was good to him. It's just that it could even be better. Now it was his choice.

It was not a simple task to change direction.

He stole a look at the clock on the bank building across from Mattie Jean's four-story apartment building and quickly began cleaning up and packing his equipment. Six-thirty. He told Connie he'd be at the gym between six and six-thirty. He had the key to the apartment and if he got there and finished up early tomorrow morning …

"Clevon, where you going?" He didn't hear Mattie Jean walk in. "You promised to finish this unit today."

"Somethin's come up. I'll be back before the milkman's horse wakes up in the morning and have this place finished by nine."

"Tomorrow is the first. My new tenant is moving in. Paint ain't going to be dry in time."

"Then I'll come back later tonight. It'll be finished with enough time to dry." He had done work for Mattie Jean for more than twenty-five years. The main reason his long-time customers stayed with him wasn't just because of the quality of his work or that his price was always fair – there were plenty decent workmen out there and to stay in business, your price had to be competitive – it was his reliability.

He didn't give her a chance to say anything else and he avoided looking at her as he ran out the door and headed for the gym. He didn't feel good about what he just did, but it was happening a lot lately. His business was not a nine-to-five operation so it did not exactly mesh with his schedule of being at the gym. Clevon Nance was troubled. He wanted to do things the right way and he knew that wasn't happening.

And it wasn't happening in his working with Connie either. Clee had been a pretty decent student years back before his days as an apprentice painter but he was first learning that two half-jobs don't add up to one full job and Clevon Nance was not a half-way person.

Later that night, after finishing his session at the gym with Connie, instead of stopping to have dinner at McDonald's, he picked up a ham and cheese sandwich at the local deli and rushed home. Usually a disciplined eater who chewed his food carefully and ate slowly, Clee broke the rules and swallowed his dinner in eight chomping bites, washing it down with a bottle of ginger ale and finishing off with a rebellious belch. With no dishes to wash as he ate right out of the brown paper bag, Clee went directly to the chest of drawers where he kept his underwear, shirts, sox and assorted knick knacks and pulled out his bank book from under the paper lining of his underwear drawer.

The fact that Clevon Nance was a frugal, thrifty guy who did not splurge on shiny baubles and treated himself only to life's basic needs was now going to pay dividends. He smiled as he scratched away with his yellow Ticonderoga No. 2 pencil on the napkin that he had barely used with his dinner. After double checking he was certain that he had enough in his savings account to carry himself for two full years – and that took into account buying some new clothes more in keeping with his new profession, paying the gym dues for Connie and even shelling out a few bucks here and there to help the kid out while getting his education during his amateur career.

Charlie did a double-take. It just dawned on him that in all the years he had known Clevon Nance – and it went way back to when Clee was a boy working with his father – he had never before seen him in anything but work clothes. Not that a cardigan sweater and an open-neck button-down shirt was exactly formal wear but for Charlie it had a near- traumatic effect. Clee was a benchmark in Charlie's life. They had grayed together, traveled from youth to post-maturity in tandem. Charlie looked at the jars holding the paint brushes that Clee had just brought in. Very few days were different from any other day in either of their lives. Their routines were as regular as the beat of a metronome, but Charlie had a sense that a change had already begun. It started with Clee coming in a bit later in the mornings to pick up his painting equipment and finishing up a bit earlier. Charlie had been wanting to say something about how a couple of Clee's long-time regulars had called the store asking for referrals for painters for upcoming jobs but he felt uncomfortable. He didn't have to say anything.

"Can't even figure out why I came in with these paint brushes," Clee said with a sheepish grin. "Guess it's force of habit. I coulda just thrown them in a dumpster. I'm sure you noticed that I've been cuttin' back a bit. Charlie, believe it or not, I'm gonna be changing my whole life. New horizons. Whoever says you can't teach an old horse new tricks is all wrong." Then Clee held up his hand, stopping himself as though making a great realization. "Actually, here it's gonna be a case of an old horse teaching a new horse old tricks."

Charlie couldn't remember seeing a smile that big creasing Clevon Nance's face ever before.

Clee was about to leave when he turned back to Charlie. "Why am I leaving these brushes with you. Here, let me take them and toss them in the garbage."

Charlie shook his head. "No. I'll just store them. It's not a problem. One never knows …" He watched as Clee turned and left and silently wished him luck, knowing he would need it in abundance.

Clee's hours didn't change that much. They were just spent differently. He'd still get up before the sun peeked over the roofs of the buildings across from his. Still had his oatmeal and cup of tea, but before that he'd place his wake-up call to Connie. Only it wasn't a wake-up call anymore. It was at first but now he'd get a wide-awake, rarin'-to-go answer from his caterpillar-turned-butterfly pupil as they'd get ready for Connie's daily run in the park after about fifteen minutes of stretching and limbering up. Then Clee would take Connie back to his apartment and make him a better, healthier breakfast than he'd be able to get in any local diner or fast food restaurant – and you couldn't beat the price. From there the kid would go to work at whatever his job was at the time – stockboy in a clothing store, messenger, window washer or delivery boy while Clee spent the late morning and early afternoon hours prepping himself for his new career as a trainer by working with Pop Chambers in the gym. He had saved up enough "mattress money" as well as putting away a few dollars in the bank each week so that he didn't have to worry about no money coming in for a while – not forever, but for a fairly good while. The benefits of being a bachelor-hermit.

Clevon Nance was in love with life! He couldn't wait for late morning and midday to fade into late afternoon when he would be in the gym again working with Connie. The kid was true to his word. He listened to everything that his trainer told him. Connie was conscientious and hungry. The jive and prancing was still part of him, but not in the ring. He was the obedient student who listened to and respected his teacher.

Pop Chambers stood at the ring apron, his lips pursed and his head nodding in silent approval. Seeing potential in a boy was one thing; seeing the precision fighting machine that was dazzling this roomful of hardened ring rats – that was something of a much higher order. He looked over at Clee, who was standing next to the steps going up to Connie Green's corner, his eyes never moving from the figure gliding smoothly around the ring. Clee didn't shout instructions to his boy like the other trainers did. He spoke to him, somewhere between a husky whisper and a conversational pitch. It was as though they were transmitting and receiving on the same wavelength.

It was just a few days after the Daily News came out with the entry forms for the Golden Gloves that Clee figured it would be so much easier if the kid lived with him. It was a small apartment but there was more than enough room for one more cot or mattress. "It makes good sense," he told Connie, wondering why it was so difficult to say it out loud. The kid agreed. In fact, he thought it was a great idea. Clee couldn't understand why that made him as happy as it did. Clee wasn't very big on asking questions. Anything beyond "How are you?" was prying in his mind. More than thirty years of being a loner had conditioned Clee to relish his privacy and, in turn, to respect the privacy of others, never considering the remote possibility that much of the rest of the world did not share his penchant for solitude.

He knew that Connie didn't live with his family but never asked him where he did live. When he went with Connie to help him move – no help was really needed – they wound up in the cellar of an apartment building.

Connie shrugged. "My friend's old man is the janitor. Nice an' warm in the winter. I got the furnace right next door to me," he smiled. Then he pointed to a large covered sewer drain. "My own private john. I just raise the cover and answer Nature's call. And the rest of my bathroom …" he raised a coiled garden hose. Clee looked at the youngster. He wanted to say something, and to hug him. He remained silent and did nothing.

It took about a minute and a half to pack and leave. His clothes were in a burlap duffle bag and his few toilet articles in a plastic bag. Connie offered to drag along the battered, soiled mattress resting on a sheet of plywood that served as his bed. Clee waved him off. They stopped at an Army-Navy store a block from Clee's buiding and picked up a roll-out cot and folding mattress. Clee beamed at the look of excitement lighting up Connie's face. Next to Clee, he was the happiest guy around.

Conversation comes much more easily when you're under the same roof with someone. It was a few days after Connie moved in with him that Clee learned that the kid had no family. They were sitting on the couch, when some movie they were watching on television triggered Connie. He told Clee how his father took off shortly after Connie was born and was never heard from again. His mother needed dreams and thought she could buy them in nickel packets of crack. Connie hadn't hit his teens yet when his mother OD'd. Maybe she went out with a dream. If so, it was her last one. Connie chose the streets over an orphanage. Clee had stopped watching the movie as soon as Connie began talking. He told Connie that he could feel free to bring over any friends. This was his home now. The kid shrugged and explained that there were no friends. He was too busy scrabbling to earn some money and the rest of his time was spent in the gym. No one to pal around with, no real social life - no buddies, no girl friends. Clee thought, all that bluster and jive talkin' ... just like a coat that came off and went in the closet when he got home. He placed his arm around Connie's shoulder and gave him a reassuring pat on the back.

They worked tirelessly, day after day, preparing for the Golden Gloves tournament. Clee stressed the basics – balance, punching properly, never letting your guard down and getting used to the ring like it was your backyard. He wanted to make sure that before Connie answered that first bell he was totally prepared. Connie felt that he already was.

The toughest part of Clee's job was convincing Connie that being a prizefighter was a 24-hour-a-day, 7 days a week fulltime job. At first Connie followed the rules, but when he finished kindergarten he thought he was ready for graduate school. Bolos, peacock prancing, shuffle steps – "Here's my chin, hit it if you can!" Clee would stay calm, rein the boy in and bring him back to the basics. Each day was pretty much like the day before, but Clee would smile because each day the kid was better than the day before. They would usually finish off by watching an hour or so of television after dinner and then get a good night's sleep. Connie begged off going to church with Clee on Sunday mornings but would meet him afterwards when they would go to a local movie house.

Here Clee always gave in. Connie didn't share his taste of westerns or who-dunits so it became a steady diet of fraternity hi-jinx or school kids getting eaten up by some weird monsters on some exotic island. Clee's movies all had happy endings; not so with Connie's. That bothered Clee who was used to an orderly and predictable world.

Other things bothered Clee, too. But they were about himself. He didn't understand the strange feelings – how he'd wake up at night and walk over to look down at Connie, sound asleep - and feel such a warm glow. He couldn't remember feeling that way ever before. Clevon Nance never had a brother or sister, maybe that's why this was all new … he shrugged it off, telling himself it didn't matter. He just knew it made him feel good having Connie there with him. It felt more than good. Life had become filled with anticipation, looking forward to each day and each moment as a new and wonderful experience. He felt ridiculous even thinking it, but Clee had the urge to just bounce up and whirl around the room. He couldn't believe that life could be so beautiful.

What did worry him, though, was wondering if these feelings fit in with training a prize fighter. Connie was coming along fine so far but Clee kept the reins on him. He did not want to see the boy get hurt – and fighters get hurt. Lucky for Clee though, all he had to do was squeeze his eyes shut hard …blot everything out … it was something he learned to do as a boy when he would be painting with his daddy and wanted to think of – and be in - a different world.

The Gloves was a little over a month away but Connie was ready no matter when that bell would ring. Whenever the kid climbed into the ring the sing-song thwacking whistle of ropes hitting hardwood floor, the rat-a-tatting chorus of speed bags and all the grunting and snorting of a living, breathing fight gym would come to a noticeable slow-down. All eyes would turn towards the ring as this kid Connie Green, who had never even fought a round in a sanctioned bout, had already shown them that he was something special. Pop Chambers would lean against the wall separating his alcove office from the rest of the gym, smile, then sigh as he marveled at how Clevon Nance had reconstructed Connie Green. It was like taking a jumble of random notes from a musical scale and turning out a symphony. And even Pop didn't know that the kid hadn't opened up on all cylinders yet.

Clee got the letter two days before but that was a Saturday so he couldn't do anything until today, Monday. Clee's mailbox was not the most popular stop on the postman's beat, that Clee was sure of. Once a month an electric bill and a gas bill and an occasional notice about a super sale at the A&P. He got more mail addressed to the wrong party than he received for himself so when he got this very official looking letter notifying him that he was to report for jury duty, Clee felt like he was hit by the crosstown bus. It was a weekend of misery, worry and a bit of deceit as he tried to act calm and hide his anxiety from Connie. He told Connie that he had something to attend to and would be a little late on Monday morning; that Connie should work on the heavy bag, rope skipping and calisthenics but not to do any sparring until he got there.

It was early afternoon when Clee strode down Lenox Avenue whistling a happy tune and waving to everyone he passed; a few of them he even knew. He was embarrassed that he hadn't read the fine print – he was entitled to one postponement! Still, he was glad that he went because when he explained to the administrative clerk that he would be busy until after the Golden Gloves, it was arranged that he would not be contacted before then. And looking at his watch, he saw that it was so early that he might even get to the gym before Connie.

on Nance started rebuilding his business. He was
rjoyed nor despondent. He simply went with the
alendar. He didn't watch as many ball games or go
es but he still went to church on Sunday. He slept
g for dreamless peace but was unable to keep out
images and hurt that he tried so hard to suppress.
ing link to the world was to read the Daily News
ng. That's how he saw that Lester Duke was pro-
how in Atlantic City with his "hot new prospect,
onrad Green in an eight round semi-final."
uldn't believe what he was reading. No amateur
onal experience and he was being put in an eight
fessional fight?!? He knew that they had a board-
benches in Atlantic City and he'd never been that
New York City ever, so Clevon Nance treated him-
very first vacation of his entire life – a two hour bus
eft early Saturday morning. It rained so he didn't
nch on the boardwalk. He sat in a hotel lobby and
til 7 PM, then walked to the Convention Center and
e lowest priced ticket. A five dollar tip to an usher
pretty close to the ring. He was sorry he made the
ht because from his original third tier seat he would
seen Connie do all the aping and copycat moves
nothing but useless fluff but he probably would have
d the agony of seeing him throw the wide right hand
ked more like it came from an arthritic outfielder
izefighter as it missed its mark by about half a foot –
his opponent keeled over and listened very carefully
he referee say "Ten" before getting up, running over
ie and congratulating him – or maybe he was just
g him. Clee caught the bus home right after the fight
ed his eyes, but he couldn't sleep. The look that he
Connie's face as he watched his opponent crumble
e phantom punch that whistled through the air – it

Clee bounced up the stairs and stopped whistling.
Perfection had unraveled. Some of the regulars looked at
him as he entered the gym, then turned away uncomfortably.
Connie was in the ring bouncing around like a Raggedy Ann
doll, taunting, teasing and peppering a kid who looked as at
home in the ring as a polar bear in the Sahara desert.

"That is the kind of razzle-dazzle the crowds love, Conrad!"
The voice boomed across the gym. The trademark cloak and
top hat caused Clee to draw a deep breath as he walked slowly
but purposefully to the ring. Lester Duke, self-appointed ruler
of the boxing world, felt that any cookie jar was there for him
to dip into, but here was a cookie that wasn't even half baked
yet. "Come on, son," Duke continued, making sure that he
was heard by all. "Let's see some more of that magic!"

Clee walked to the side of the ring that was adjacent to
where the Duke was putting on his show and waited for the
bell to sound. Then he found himself squeezing his eyes shut
hard again and sucked up a deep breath when Connie walked
down the ring steps, and without hesitating bounded over
to where the Duke was holding court, not even looking in
Clee's direction. On legs that weren't as steady as they should
have been, he walked to where Connie was doing his peacock
prance, placed his hand on his shoulder as Lester Duke let
out a "Whooee! My boy, you do have the goods!" Clee tried
erasing Duke's bellowing voice, at least from his own mind.
Wanting to sound calm and in command, he gently turned
Connie's shoulder so that he faced him. "Didn't I ask you not
to get in the ring until I got here?"

Connie made no effort to pull away. He simply moved his
head so that he and Clee never made eye contact. A hole
opening under his feet and swallowing him would have been
a welcome comfort zone to Clee who was feeling as though
he might have been invisible the way Lester Duke and Connie
ignored him as they carried on a two-way conversation. "I can

go out today", blared the Duke, "and get those light bulbs ready to put your name up on the marquee! You are ready for the Big Time – and Big Time is what I work with. Just give me the keys and I'll take you for the ride!"

"The boy's got learning to do," Clee cut in, trying desperately to keep his voice steady. "His first step is the Golden Gloves." From the corner of his eyes he saw a fuming Pop Chambers heading towards them from his office.

"Golden Gloves?" Duke forced a laugh. "Conrad, are you looking for some prize that looks like it's from a Cracker Jack box instead of the Pot of Gold just sitting there for you?"

Pop Chambers had seen and heard enough. "This place isn't a chicken coop where the foxes can break in …." Clee wanted to grab Pop around and thank him. Instead, he held up his hand to stop him.

"All due respect, Mr. Duke – Connie gotta crawl before he can walk."

Lester Duke took a step back and stared at Clee as though examining some strange insect through a magnifying glass. Then he turned to Connie, "This guy, him," and he pointed at Clee with his thumb as though he were hitching a ride, "is he with you? I mean, like a manager or something … with a contract?"

Clevon Nance moved his head ever so slightly. He didn't want to stare at Connie, but he did want to see and hear this young man who had become the most important person in his life. Clee was not breathing at all.

Connie did not look at Clee. It was strange, but all Clee was able to think about was how it was so very quiet in the gym.

"Him?" Connie hesitated. He didn't stammer but there was a hesitancy as he spoke. "My manager?" Now he did turn towards Clee. He smiled what Clee felt – or, maybe, wanted

to feel - was a warm smile – ɛ Nance – a house-painter."

✶

Pop Chambers asked Clee to v with him, helping him with hi: "no" to Pop but he suddenly fɛ that he was no longer part of. sharing his time between lying the couch, trying to blot out all was not to think at all.

Connie never came back to his things. He didn't have to wit to pay his way. Clee washed and f put them in a pile on the shelf of ɪ est part was opening doors he tho Making oatmeal became a chore an appetite anyhow - so he changɛ cold cereal. The solitude – no, the at a fast food restaurant was once a as though his overalls and work shi

Clee thought it would be easy g tine. After all, it was just returning tɪ his return trip to the paint supply sɪ

It was much easier for Charlie tɔ and customer when he walked in the trade. Clee smiled and without ɡ Charlie, "Goin' back to work, Charli new supplies and brushes."

Charlie's smile was bigger than Cl ing about? I told you I was going to keɛ

Slowly, Clev neither ove clock and c to the movi a lot, strivir the painful His remair each eveni moting a Cunning (

Clee c or professi round pr walk and far out of self to the ride. He sit on a bɛ waited un bought tl got him investmeɪ still have that was been save that loo than a p but still to hear to Conɪ thankin and clos saw on from tl

was one of surprise, not joy. Clee wasn't sure but that's what he wanted to believe.

Clee was glad that he was afforded so much "think" time on his job. He told himself that he wanted to forget about Connie Green but he knew that he was lying to himself. Instead of thinking of where to place his drop cloths and blending his colors properly all he could think of was how the kid was getting along and what he was doing at that moment. He went up to the gym, telling himself that it was just to drop in to say hello to Pop Chambers but he knew the real reason. Pop knew the real reason too and told him that the Duke had moved the kid to a more upscale Times Square location. Pop Chambers grumbled about what an ingrate the kid was, dropping Clee after all he had done for him not just as a fighter but taking him in as family. "Talk about bitin' the hand that feeds you! You turned an organ grinder's monkey into a prizefighter! When I see him in the ring now, I have to blink. I'm not seeing Conrad Green, I'm seeing Clevon Nance in there."

Clee shook his head as he walked Pop back to his office. "Maybe the boy has a dream, Pop, an' he's chasing after it the best way he knows how." He turned and walked slowly towards the exit door as Pop Chambers just stopped and looked after him. As Clee walked down the stairs he thought of another young boy who, more than thirty years ago, also had a dream – but he didn't chase after it.

The next day after work, Clee walked to the subway. He was supposed to take the uptown train two stops to get home – a trip he had made so often, he should have been able to do it with a blindfold. Instead he went to the downtown side. Clee told himself it was just a mistake, he wasn't paying attention. He didn't mind deceiving himself. When he got off the train at 42nd Street he paced back and forth about three or four times on the block where the gym was before sucking up a deep breath and going inside. A boxing gym was a place where he had always felt at home. Not now, though. He felt like a stranger, an interloper. But he also felt that he had to be there, that he was drawn to the place as though a magnet had pulled him.

From the back of the gym he watched Connie work out. Everything he had worked to teach him – the basics, the fundamentals – all stored away like a discarded textbook. Connie was in the ring going through his entire routine like an auditioning vaudevillian. Actually, to a casual observer – someone who would read the front of a newspaper before the sport section – the kid probably looked great – as long as he was in there with a perfect foil, which is exactly what the situation was. It was difficult, but Clee forced himself to stay in the back and remain quiet – almost as quiet as the kid's trainer who seemed to know only four words – "Good show!" and "Nice work!"

Clee turned to leave as soon as the kid's sparring session was over but before he reached the door, "Clee, wait a sec, man." He knew that Connie had seen him but he didn't think the time was right. "Hey, it's good seeing you, Clee."

"Good seein' you too, Connie."

The kid held out his hands. He was still wearing his gloves. "You okay with … I mean … you don't feel …"

"An' if I did feel? Sure I feel bad, mostly about the way you left."

"Hey, Clee, I'm really sorry. It's just that … well, the Duke feels with my natural style he can take me right to the top. He believes in me just the way I am and he can move me now."

"Then let me wish you good luck, son. That's about all I can do – but I wish it from the bottom of my heart." Clee turned, not knowing whether the hurt he was feeling was more for himself or Connie, and headed for the door.

He didn't break stride as Connie called out softly after him, "Maybe dinner or a movie some night, Clee…"

"Some night, maybe." He never looked back as he left the gym.

Clee didn't call Connie and Connie didn't call Clee. It was three weeks later that Clee read about Connie fighting in Cleveland against Chuck Malone, a guy who was considered a "top ten" before Connie learned how to walk and hung around for an occasional pay-day. Clee stayed up later than usual that night switching channels and radio stations to listen to the latest sports news. It was close to midnight when he finally heard on a sports channel that Connie stopped Malone with a left hook to the body. There was no film coverage of the fight but Clee had conjured up a good picture image of a not-very-battered Malone on a knee counting floating dollar signs for ten seconds. He felt a bit ashamed of his cynicism as he headed for his day's job.

Clevon Nance had pretty much rebuilt his business. He poured all his time and energy into it. There was nothing else. He didn't want anything else. There were days that he took on two jobs – a day job and another one at night. He thought he was very successful at shutting off the rest of the world. He was.  His major link to the world was his telephone ringing and that was almost always an inquiry about a paint job or a wrong number.  When the phone rang one night while he was soaking in a hot tub, still his favorite form of relaxing, Clee grabbed a towel and made a mad dash to answer it. Maybe it was instinct, a sixth sense … or was it anticipation? It just seemed to Clee that the ring had a different sound to it.

The towel had nothing to do with modesty. There was no one to cover up for. He was soaking wet! But for Clevon Nance the telephone ringing was like a clarion sounding the call to battle.

He tried to control the deep breaths that swelled his chest when he heard Connie's voice. "I gotta meet with you and tell you what's happening. Connie Green did not try to hide his excitement. "We're a team again, Clee!" It was contagious! Clee's first thought – no, it was a wish, maybe a prayer – was that Connie had split with Lester Duke."

Twenty-four hours later Clee was tossing around in his bed, unable to sleep after turning down two offers that he could have, and maybe should have said "yes" to but didn't. When Mattie Jean Williams walked in while he was painting a three room apartment in one of her buildings on West 133rd Street, he sensed it was a different than usual kind of visit. He knew Mattie Jean almost as long as he could remember. His Daddy worked for her Daddy, painting apartments for him just as Clee was doing for Mattie. He also knew her from school, but not very well as she was three years behind him. She was a handsome enough woman but what Clee admired most was her head for business. And that's the way he always thought of Mattie Jean – strictly business.

After standing in the doorway watching him paint for more than a half hour without saying a word she came up behind him as he continued gliding his brush in neat, vertical strokes. "You really do good work."

Clee thought to himself, "That's the left jab," but didn't answer as he forced a smile.

He sensed what was coming next- the knockout punch! "You know, Clevon, I've been thinking ... we'd make a great team. We've known each other a long time. Friends, business partners ... there's so much more we can share together."

He wanted to say it the right way, no bruised feelings, no hurt. Instead, he did it all wrong. He wanted to be tactful and say that after all the years of being a bachelor he was just too set in his ways, that he had become a creature of habits – habits unsuitable for a family way of life. But when he opened his mouth he flubbed it and stammered, "It just won't work, Mattie Jean. I don't think of you that way." He had counter-punched without intending to.

"Just thought it could be a nice partnership." Her voice was barely above a whisper – and she was gone. He stayed until the paint job was finished and when he left he wondered whether it was his last job for Mattie Jean.

He knew that he was slouching, whether from weariness or a reflection of his mood he didn't know, but he straight-ened his shoulders and concentrated on standing erect and tall as he approached the drug store next to the gym that Connie had selected as their meeting place. Holding his gym bag in his left hand, Connie broke into a face-splitting smile and thrust his right hand in a high-five greeting. Before Clee had a chance to return the greeting with even a simple hello, Connie's excitement spilled over.

"Listen, my manger – you know - the Duke, he comes to me with the news that he has me lined up as number one choice to fight Grillo for the title. You hear that – the title!"

Clee wanted to share the boy's enthusiasm. He wanted to but he couldn't, not just yet. "Grillo is his boy, though."

"So? He'll still have the champ, only his name will be Connie Green, not Buck Grillo."

"Connie, listen to me. I ain't putting no damper on any-thing. You got the equipment, boy, but you got to learn to use it."

Connie dropped his gym bag and placed both his hands on Clee's shoulders. "Okay, Professor, I ain't saying 'No.' I want to be back with you, Clee. I want you in my corner. I need you. And I told the Duke that."

Clee looked Connie in the eye. "And the Big Man said …?"

Clevon Nance heard first hand what Lester Duke said. They went up to the gym where the Duke was holding court.

He was all smiles, which was the only way he was ever seen in public. They shook hands and the Duke welcomed Clevon Nance to join the team, as long as he trained Connie the way Lester Duke wanted his fighter trained – as a flamboyant, showboating crowd-pleaser. And when Clevon began suggesting that Conrad Green was not yet ready for a Buck Grillo, the Duke, as though commanding a not-yet-broken-in horse, bellowed, "Whoa! That is not in your discretionary province! You will do things my way!"

"I'm sorry. I only know one way."

As he walked back down the stairs to the street, Clevon Nance was aware that his shoulders were slouched again. He couldn't help it and he didn't really care. It was far from his best day. He consoled himself by knowing that he had done the right thing but he silently berated himself for cutting himself off from what he realized he loved the most. It was a long walk from the gym in Times Square to his home but that was the option he chose. He wanted to think, clear his head and be by himself and as the street numbers grew higher – from the forties to the fifties, the sixties and seventies - the stronger his regrets for doing "the right thing" became. He wanted to be back in the world that he let his father keep him from – and he wanted to be back with Connie Green.

He wondered if the clock were turned back and the whole scene with Connie and Lester Duke were re-run how he would respond now. If just given the chance ... just given the chance...

There was no lesson to be learned for Clevon Nance.

As he climbed the stairs to his apartment with his take-out meal from McDonald's he raced the last few steps when he heard the phone ringing. Again, the call to battle! Reflexively, his shoulders pulled back and his feet no longer dragged as he bounded and at the same time fumbled through his pocket for the key to his apartment. As he pushed the door open with the elbow of his arm holding the food, he tripped over a bedroom slipper just inside the doorway.

Clee was on his knees sponging up the puddle of orange soda with one hand while holding the phone in the other hand when he heard what he wanted more than anything else to hear.

"Clee, you shoulda talked it out." The kid's voice was more of a plea than a command. "I told ya - and I told the Duke. I want you in my corner."

There are worse things than an orange stain on the kitchen floor, Clee told himself as he got up and threw the sponge into the sink. "Yeah, an' the man said ...?"

"He said he definitely wants you. You just have to work as a team, he says, with us, not try to change me."

Clevon Nance just had to say a soft "Yes" and everything he wanted would be out there for him but as hard as he tried to force himself, he simply couldn't do it.

"I want to, Connie. I want to be with you very badly. I just can't do it that way. I have to train you my way, not with hand-cuffs. I guess I just can't work with that man. But I do wish you the best, Connie, and I'll be rootin' for you all the way." He hung up the phone without giving Connie a chance to say anything else and he couldn't admit even to himself that his eyes were tearing. He finished cleaning up but never touched the food.

He pulled himself from his bed with such force that he almost fell to the floor. Whether it was a realization or a dream - it didn't really matter. He tripped and stumbled his way in the dark to the bathroom where he turned on the light and stared at the image in the mirror. It was his own image but he felt as though it was his father staring back at him. It didn't matter. All one and the same. He balled up his fist, shaking it threateningly for a second, then relaxed it and breathing deeply through his nostrils, knelt on the cold tile floor. "I'm sorry. I'm sorry ...Daddy." All these years he had carried the bitterness inside of himself, silently resenting that his father kept him from choosing his own path in life. It had come to him in a tortured sleep. What did his father do to him that he wasn't doing to Connie? It took him all these many years but he understood now. His father was protecting his son from wasting his time "on foolishness", at least that's what it was in his father's world. It just wasn't his way.

He grimaced and blasted his fist into his left palm. Was it any different than his turning away from Connie for not fighting the way of Clevon Nance? And he thought back to the words of Pop Chambers. "When I see him in the ring now, I have to blink. I'm not seeing Conrad Green, I'm seeing Clevon Nance in there."

He walked slowly back to his bed where he flopped down on his stomach and spent the rest of the night dreaming of his father - his father who loved him.

The next day seemed completely out of kilter; the hours dragged on as he moved his paint brush up and down like some human metronome until it was time to leave for the gym and get back to where he belonged - and with whom he belonged. The sun was still shining when he cleaned and packed his equipment, changed from his overalls to the slacks, sport shirt and sweater that he had brought along in a garment bag ... and assumed a new persona.

As the downtown IRT train lurched its way through its darkened underground world towards Times Square, he concentrated on convincing himself that the only important consideration was that he would be back with Connie, helping him in any way that he could. Right way or wrong way - that was no longer the issue. When he got off the train at 42nd Street he was thinking, "Okay, if we just work on keeping his hands up...."

Clee felt a sense of joy as he bounced up the flight of stairs. The smell of liniment mixed with sweat, the singsong whirring of leather ropes whistling through the air accompanied by the rat-a-tat beat of speed bags - he sucked it all in like a deep-sea diver breaking surface and refilling his lungs with air. Then he saw Connie who was just getting ready to climb into the ring for his sparring session, which, as Clee checked the clock on the far wall, he realized was getting off a bit early. It didn't matter, he told himself, he'll see the kid after.

It's funny how quickly joy can dissipate. He hadn't seen Lester Duke who was standing in front of the office door at the far end of the gym. Clee recognized Buck Grillo who was standing next to him. "Why isn't Conrad in the ring yet?" the Duke shouted at the kid's trainer.

"His sparring partner, Wilson, ain't here yet."

"Then get someone else in there with him. I'll want the ring for Buck in about twenty minutes."

"Okay, I got a new guy here. Looks okay. I'll move him in there with the kid."

Clee did not like what he was seeing and hearing. He kept quiet, trying very hard to fit properly into his role - not very different than the three monkeys who cover their eyes, ears and mouths. Most important, he did not want to distract Connie. As excited as he was about letting him know his decision he would wait until after the kid's sparring session.

Things do not always go according to plan. This was a lesson that Fate had drummed into Clee so emphatically that adversity should be an expectation, or, at least, anticipated. He watched as Connie climbed into the ring and pranced around waiting for the new sparring partner.

The guy he was in with was not overly impressed. He was a short, compact expressionless guy. He may have been Puerto Rican, maybe Mexican. But whatever, there was no true Latin blood coursing through his veins. The mambo was not his thing. He stood in a semi-crouch, staring as Connie went through a repertoire of moves that would have garnered him a spotlight at the Latin Quarter or the Savoy Ballroom as his sparring partner tired of trying to figure out what he was watching. Connie never saw the straight right hand that flashed out like a striking cobra and he wasn't set to take or absorb the blow. It caught him flush on the jaw as he was bouncing forward and spun him sideways.

Clee shuddered as Connie, off balance and reeling from the blow, fell into the ropes – and through the second and third strand. Reflexively, Clee ran towards the ring as Connie landed on the ring apron, then fell headfirst to the hardwood floor.

Clevon Nance kept the television on all night. He went from the talk shows to the Late Show and the Late, Late Show – without watching or paying attention to any of it. He was afraid to fall asleep and he wanted to be surrounded by noise so that he wouldn't have to think. He came back from the hospital not knowing anything other than that Connie, suffering a severe concussion, was unconscious but all vital signs were strong. They said that he wouldn't be able to see Connie and suggested that he go home and contact them in the morning.

Squinting at the clock whose glaring red numerals read 4:07 AM Clee rose from the sofa where he had spent the night, convinced himself that he wasn't hanging onto a technicality and that this was the next morning, grabbed a banana for breakfast and left for the hospital.

"They told me to come back early this morning, that I'd be able to visit Connie - that's Conrad Green - ," seeing that these were all different people than those he spoke with yesterday he realized that the night shift was still on. "How is the boy doing?"

"Oh, you must be the father," the receptionist guessed. There were times, Clee knew, when it was best to keep quiet. That's what he did.

She asked for a phone number where the family could be reached for any questions or updates on his condition. Clee gave her his number.

"Your boy still hasn't awakened but he is breathing on his own. You can go in and sit by his bedside for a few minutes and you can speak softly to him but don't expect a response. If he does show any sign of awakening please press the buzzer on the stand at the side of his bed or come out to the nurses station and let us know. But only 5 minutes, please. That's room 248, straight down the corridor, on the left side. Remember, 5 minutes."

Except for the bag of fluid hanging from what looked like a coat rack stand with a tube running to his arm, Connie looked like any innocent youngster sleeping peacefully. Clee sat at the bed for about a minute just staring at Connie, filled at the same time with a glow of contentment at just being able to be with him and an overwhelming urge to cry and pray for him. Always an obedient rule-follower, Clee spoke softly to Connie, "I'm here, son." He felt good calling him that. "You're going to be fine and we'll have some good times together." Saying that made him feel even better. He looked at his watch, not knowing whether the allotted five minutes was a hard and fast rule or not. He didn't want to leave. His eyes misted as he pictured Connie's fall from the ring and he blamed himself for not taking a firmer stand on teaching him properly. Getting up from his chair, Clee stood over the bed. He looked down and swelled with the desire to take care of this young man who he now felt such a strong bond with. He clasped the hand that was free of intravenous wires between his own. He sensed a movement, as though the hand he was holding was reaching for his in return. That's when he leaned over the bed, released the hand and bending low, cupping Connie's head, he gently kissed him on the forehead. He couldn't control the tremors going through his body as he heard a slight sound come from Connie's throat. Lowering himself and carefully raising Connie's head, he kissed him on the lips as his tears spilled over both their faces.

Conrad Green opened his eyes and pulled back in surprise, his head still cupped between Clee's hands. "Hey, what ... why, Clee?" He pulled his head back onto his pillow. "I ain't ... , I don't..."

Clee backed up as though in self defense, with his hands held up in front of him. "No, no, Connie, don't get it wrong ... I just want you to be okay. I care ..." His five minutes were up and he ran, the hurt knifing through him. He forgot to stop at the Nurses Station to tell them that Connie had awakened.

The next day Clevon Nance did something he had never done before. He did not show up for work. Three apartments were scheduled to be painted. He made phone calls and explained apologetically that he was too sick to be able to work. His second afternoon of lying in his bed and brooding, he received a call from the hospital. The doctor who had been taking care of Connie told him that he was released that morning but they were concerned about his following instructions. "His business associate, Mr. Duke, is not treating your son's situation very seriously.. I want to impress upon you, Mr. Green," Clee didn't bother to correct him, "that a concussive injury cannot be taken too lightly. There may be weeks, maybe even months of headaches and confusion. That fall that he suffered had an impact equivalent to perhaps a hundred head blows. Your son could probably lead a quite normal life, but not as a prizefighter. He should not be exposing himself to more possible head trauma. We told this to your son and Mr Duke."

Clee bounced up the stairs and stopped whistling. Perfection had unraveled. Some of the regulars looked at him as he entered the gym, then turned away uncomfortably. Connie was in the ring bouncing around like a Raggedy Ann doll, taunting, teasing and peppering a kid who looked as at home in the ring as a polar bear in the Sahara desert.

"That is the kind of razzle-dazzle the crowds love, Conrad!" The voice boomed across the gym. The trademark cloak and top hat caused Clee to draw a deep breath as he walked slowly but purposefully to the ring. Lester Duke, self-appointed ruler of the boxing world, felt that any cookie jar was there for him to dip into, but here was a cookie that wasn't even half baked yet. "Come on, son," Duke continued, making sure that he was heard by all. "Let's see some more of that magic!"

Clee walked to the side of the ring that was adjacent to where the Duke was putting on his show and waited for the bell to sound. Then he found himself squeezing his eyes shut hard again and sucked up a deep breath when Connie walked down the ring steps, and without hesitating bounded over to where the Duke was holding court, not even looking in Clee's direction. On legs that weren't as steady as they should have been, he walked to where Connie was doing his peacock prance, placed his hand on his shoulder as Lester Duke let out a "Whooee! My boy, you do have the goods!" Clee tried erasing Duke's bellowing voice, at least from his own mind. Wanting to sound calm and in command, he gently turned Connie's shoulder so that he faced him. "Didn't I ask you not to get in the ring until I got here?"

Connie made no effort to pull away. He simply moved his head so that he and Clee never made eye contact. A hole opening under his feet and swallowing him would have been a welcome comfort zone to Clee who was feeling as though he might have been invisible the way Lester Duke and Connie ignored him as they carried on a two-way conversation. "I can go out today", blared the Duke, "and get those light bulbs ready to put your name up on the marquee! You are ready for the Big Time – and Big Time is what I work with. Just give me the keys and I'll take you for the ride!"

"The boy's got learning to do," Clee cut in, trying desperately to keep his voice steady. "His first step is the Golden Gloves." From the corner of his eyes he saw a fuming Pop Chambers heading towards them from his office.

"Golden Gloves?" Duke forced a laugh. "Conrad, are you looking for some prize that looks like it's from a Cracker Jack box instead of the Pot of Gold just sitting there for you?"

Pop Chambers had seen and heard enough. "This place isn't a chicken coop where the foxes can break in ...." Clee wanted to grab Pop around and thank him. Instead, he held up his hand to stop him.

"All due respect, Mr. Duke – Connie gotta crawl before he can walk."

Lester Duke took a step back and stared at Clee as though examining some strange insect through a magnifying glass. Then he turned to Connie, "This guy, him," and he pointed at Clee with his thumb as though he were hitching a ride, "is he with you? I mean, like a manager or something ... with a contract?"

Clevon Nance moved his head ever so slightly. He didn't want to stare at Connie, but he did want to see and hear this young man who had become the most important person in his life. Clee was not breathing at all.

Connie did not look at Clee. It was strange, but all Clee was able to think about was how it was so very quiet in the gym.

"Him?" Connie hesitated. He didn't stammer but there was a hesitancy as he spoke. "My manager?" Now he did turn towards Clee. He smiled what Clee felt – or, maybe, wanted to feel - was a warm smile – almost loving. "No! He's Clevon Nance – a house-painter."

☆ ☆ ☆

Pop Chambers asked Clee to work the Golden Gloves shows with him, helping him with his team. Clee didn't like saying "no" to Pop but he suddenly felt like an intruder in a world that he was no longer part of. He spent two days at home, sharing his time between lying in bed and sprawling out on the couch, trying to blot out all thoughts. His comfort zone was not to think at all.

Connie never came back to the apartment to get any of his things. He didn't have to with a guy named Lester Duke to pay his way. Clee washed and folded the clothes neatly and put them in a pile on the shelf of the hallway closet. The hardest part was opening doors he thought he had closed forever. Making oatmeal became a chore – he didn't have much of an appetite anyhow - so he changed his breakfast to a bowl of cold cereal. The solitude – no, the loneliness of a single table at a fast food restaurant was once again his lifestyle and it was as though his overalls and work shirts were waiting for him.

Clee thought it would be easy getting back to his old routine. After all, it was just returning to habits of a lifetime. Like his return trip to the paint supply store.

It was much easier for Charlie to recognize his old friend and customer when he walked in wearing his uniform of the trade. Clee smiled and without going into detail, said to Charlie, "Goin' back to work, Charlie. Guess I'll have to buy new supplies and brushes."

Charlie's smile was bigger than Clee's. "What are you talking about? I told you I was going to keep your stuff in storage."

Slowly, Clevon Nance started rebuilding his business. He was neither overjoyed nor despondent. He simply went with the clock and calendar. He didn't watch as many ball games or go to the movies but he still went to church on Sunday. He slept a lot, striving for dreamless peace but was unable to keep out the painful images and hurt that he tried so hard to suppress. His remaining link to the world was to read the Daily News each evening. That's how he saw that Lester Duke was promoting a show in Atlantic City with his "hot new prospect, Cunning Conrad Green in an eight round semi-final."

Clee couldn't believe what he was reading. No amateur or professional experience and he was being put in an eight round professional fight?!? He knew that they had a boardwalk and benches in Atlantic City and he'd never been that far out of New York City ever, so Clevon Nance treated himself to the very first vacation of his entire life – a two hour bus ride. He left early Saturday morning. It rained so he didn't sit on a bench on the boardwalk. He sat in a hotel lobby and waited until 7 PM, then walked to the Convention Center and bought the lowest priced ticket. A five dollar tip to an usher got him pretty close to the ring. He was sorry he made the investment because from his original third tier seat he would still have seen Connie do all the aping and copycat moves that was nothing but useless fluff but he probably would have been saved the agony of seeing him throw the wide right hand that looked more like it came from an arthritic outfielder than a prizefighter as it missed its mark by about half a foot – but still his opponent keeled over and listened very carefully to hear the referee say "Ten" before getting up, running over to Connie and congratulating him – or maybe he was just thanking him. Clee caught the bus home right after the fight and closed his eyes, but he couldn't sleep. The look that he saw on Connie's face as he watched his opponent crumble from the phantom punch that whistled through the air – it was one of surprise, not joy. Clee wasn't sure but that's what he wanted to believe.

Clee was glad that he was afforded so much "think" time on his job. He told himself that he wanted to forget about Connie Green but he knew that he was lying to himself. Instead of thinking of where to place his drop cloths and blending his colors properly all he could think of was how the kid was getting along and what he was doing at that moment. He went up to the gym, telling himself that it was just to drop in to say hello to Pop Chambers but he knew the real reason. Pop knew the real reason too and told him that the Duke had moved the kid to a more upscale Times Square location. Pop Chambers grumbled about what an ingrate the kid was, dropping Clee after all he had done for him not just as a fighter but taking him in as family. "Talk about bitin' the hand that feeds you! You turned an organ grinder's monkey into a prizefighter! When I see him in the ring now, I have to blink. I'm not seeing Conrad Green, I'm seeing Clevon Nance in there."

Clee shook his head as he walked Pop back to his office. "Maybe the boy has a dream, Pop, an' he's chasing after it the best way he knows how." He turned and walked slowly towards the exit door as Pop Chambers just stopped and looked after him. As Clee walked down the stairs he thought of another young boy who, more than thirty years ago, also had a dream – but he didn't chase after it.

The next day after work, Clee walked to the subway. He was supposed to take the uptown train two stops to get home – a trip he had made so often, he should have been able to do it with a blindfold. Instead he went to the downtown side. Clee told himself it was just a mistake, he wasn't paying attention. He didn't mind deceiving himself. When he got off the train at 42nd Street he paced back and forth about three or four times on the block where the gym was before sucking up a deep breath and going inside. A boxing gym was a place where he had always felt at home. Not now, though. He felt like a stranger, an interloper. But he also felt that he had to be there, that he was drawn to the place as though a magnet had pulled him.

From the back of the gym he watched Connie work out. Everything he had worked to teach him – the basics, the fundamentals – all stored away like a discarded textbook. Connie was in the ring going through his entire routine like an auditioning vaudevillian. Actually, to a casual observer – someone who would read the front of a newspaper before the sport section – the kid probably looked great – as long as he was in there with a perfect foil, which is exactly what the situation was. It was difficult, but Clee forced himself to stay in the back and remain quiet – almost as quiet as the kid's trainer who seemed to know only four words – "Good show!" and "Nice work!"

Clee turned to leave as soon as the kid's sparring session was over but before he reached the door, "Clee, wait a sec, man." He knew that Connie had seen him but he didn't think the time was right. "Hey, it's good seeing you, Clee."

"Good seein' you too, Connie."

The kid held out his hands. He was still wearing his gloves. "You okay with … I mean … you don't feel …"

"An' if I did feel? Sure I feel bad, mostly about the way you left."

"Hey, Clee, I'm really sorry. It's just that … well, the Duke feels with my natural style he can take me right to the top. He believes in me just the way I am and he can move me now."

"Then let me wish you good luck, son. That's about all I can do – but I wish it from the bottom of my heart." Clee turned, not knowing whether the hurt he was feeling was more for himself or Connie, and headed for the door.

"Uh-huh, and what did they say?" It wasn't cold but Clevon was shivering as he pulled the blanket up around his neck.

"Your son just listened but this Mr. Duke laughed and made light of the potential dangers inherent with this type of injury. He went on and on raving about your boy being a strong young man who will be fighting for a world champion-ship soon and downplayed the seriousness of what very pos-sibly may occur if there is further head and brain trauma. I'm hoping that you can have a strong influence."

Clevon tried to answer but he wasn't sure any intelligible words came out. He wanted to thank the doctor and tell him that he would try his best to make Connie understand - even though he had no idea if he would even be able to approach and look Connie in the eye again. He hung up the phone and wondered whether the doctor heard or understood any-thing that he said.

Clee heard the knocking on the door but didn't have the desire or the energy to get out of bed to see who it was. In all these years the only knocks on his door that he cared to answer were khaki-clad youngsters selling Boy Scout or Girl Scout cookies - the butter cookies were his favorite. There was never another meaningful knock that he could remember.

"Clevon Nance! If you are alive you better open this door immediately! And if you aren't, just don't answer me for the next ten seconds and I will notify the superintendent to open your door and start clearing out what's left of you!"

Mattie Jean Williams stood in the hallway with her hands on her hip, a look of feigned anger masking her face, much like a school teacher reprimanding one of her favorite pupils.

Clee shrugged awkwardly and motioned her to come in. "I called and told you I wasn't feeling good ..."

"Clevon, when someone who has done work for me for more than thirty years without ever missing a single day sud-denly stays out for three days ...," she paused and her tone softened, "Are you alright? I mean, you look like something the milkman's horse spit out of his feed bag!"

"It ain't easy for me to talk about it. Especially with you, Mattie Jean."

Mattie Jean arched her eyebrows. "Clevon, let me tell you something. You have it for another woman? You shouldn't have a problem talking to me about it. Sure, I thought we'd make a good team. Couldn't make the deal so, yes, I felt bad at first. But I learned a long time ago to put things in its proper place and move on with life. I'm okay, so you just suck it up and stop acting like some lovesick puppy. If she don't appreciate you, then just cast your fishing pole back in the water. There's always a bigger and better fish."

It was a weak smile but the first one that Clevon was able to muster up in quite a while. "No other woman, Mattie Jean. Ain't one that could match up to you anyway."

Mattie Jean couldn't hold back a smile of her own. She turned her eyes downward as though examining her shoe tips. "Well, you don't have a dog or cat, so what in the world are you grieving over?"

A moment ago he couldn't think of talking about it. Now he couldn't hold it back. It was like a dam burst and it all spilled over. "Remember that young man Connie that worked for me about a year back?"

"You mean that jive-talkin' kid you left your business for to re-shape in your image as a prizefighter?"

It was as though an electric shock jolted Clee to alertness. "You knew?"

"Clevon, you made no secret of it. Everyone who knew you knew that that you went back to what you really loved the most - prizefighting. Doesn't mean that hardly anyone thought you were doing the right - or, better yet, the wise thing. But, Clee, everybody was wishing you well. And then when you came back and picked up your business again everyone just assumed you gave it your best shot and fell a little short. No shame in that."

"No, Mattie Jean, no shame in that." Then he turned his eyes away from her. "But I am carrying shame. Mattie Jean. I have feelings for this young man Connie that I don't understand." He stopped and looked at her, not believing that he had spoken those words - words that he had never even spoken silently to himself.

She stepped closer to him. took his hand in hers and walked him to the kitchen table and sat him down as she sat right next to him still holding his hand. Now that he had started he had to go on. He was talking and explaining to himself as well as to her. "I don't even understand it. All I know is that I want to be with him, I want to take care of him. When I'm not with him I miss him, I feel lost and keep thinkin' and wondering about him. Mattie Jean, I never knew what it was to want or care for anyone before and I don't know if it's a right kind of feeling or wrong but I just feel it can't be wrong."

He looked at her again. "I'm sorry, I shouldn't be talking this way with you. I want you to know, I always liked you a lot ... more than a lot. And I admire you, Mattie Jean. But this is different ... . How do I tell you this?" Clee lowered his head for a moment and stared at the floor. "Like the other day, he was in the hospital ... hurt, sick ... and my heart went out to him. He was sleeping, unconscious, and I kissed him. It wasn't a kiss like to a brother or son or friend. Mattie Jean, I kissed him a real kiss - I mean on the mouth. I don't ever remember kissing anyone with that kind of feeling ever before, not ever. And he woke up ... and God, Mattie Jean, I am so ashamed ..."

"There is nothing to be ashamed of." Her grip on his hand tightened. "Just remember, Clevon, Love is not a prize fight. There are no set rules. There are no three-minute rounds; no referee to say 'fair' or 'foul.' Tell me, why is this young man Connie in the hospital? Did you say he was unconscious?"

"He's out of the hospital now, but he ain't outta the woods." Clee explained to her about Connie and Lester Duke; how Connie asked him to come back as his trainer and how he had refused, saying he couldn't work with Duke. "But I think that was just an excuse I was using because I wasn't really training Connie. I was rebuilding him into ... into ...me! Even you - and you ain't a fight person - saw it. You said I was I was trying to re-shape him in my image. And you know what? That's the real reason I turned away from him - because he wanted to be Connie Green, not Clevon Nance."

Mattie Jean stood up and placed her hand on Clee's shoulder. "I am not a doctor and I am not a priest but I do think I am able to give you a bit of advice on this one. Go to Connie and start from Square One - train the boy. He wants you and you want him. Do not be a stubborn mule and stand on ceremony!"

"Connie shouldn't be fighting." He told Mattie Jean about Connie's head injury and how the doctor, thinking he was Connie's father, explained the danger of his taking head blows. "But the worst part is  that this slime, Duke, is pushing the kid on. He's fattening him up like the goose ready for the kill. He's lined up a bunch of payroll stumblebums who play dead better than any Hollywood actor so he can throw the kid in with the champ, Buck Grillo for an easy title defense. And it looks like he has the kid believing his fairy tale plot over the doctors' warnings."

With hands on hips, Mattie Jean Williams glared at Clee. "So what is it, Mr. Nance? Looks like this Mr. Duke is not the only one believing in fairy tales. You expect someone to come around waving a magic wand? Or you just want to lie in your bed and cry for Clevon Nance?"

Clee stared up at her, jolted out of his lethargy by her sudden turning on him.

"Clevon," she picked up, "if you are anywhere near the person I thought you were you will get your butt out of that sack and do something other than crying for Clevon Nance? It's about time you learned that the ring isn't the only place where a person fights. If I recall properly, it used to be that it was your Daddy who kept you from what you was meant to be and turned you into a housepainter. Ain't it about time, Clevon, that you stood up and started fighting for what you want?"

Clee got off the bed where he was sitting, stared hard at Mattie Jean, then grabbed her shoulders, pulled her close and kissed her - on the mouth!

Mattie Jean rubbed the back of her hand across her lips and watched as Clevon Nance bolted out the door.

All the sounds in the gym didn't really stop when Clee entered. He knew it was just his imagination - even though he was able to hear his left shoe squeaking as he walked to the ring. He saw Connie shadow-boxing at the mirror on the the far side of the gym and walked towards him but stopped as he saw Lester Duke step out from the office door next to the workout area. "Ready to spar a few rounds today, Conrad?"

"I don't know. Got another one of those headaches," the kid shrugged.

Duke laughed. "What do you think God made aspirin for? That's okay. You're always in shape. Save it for the big night."

At that moment, Clee had an option - he could either puke or talk. He chose not to mess up the gym. "The boy shouldn't be fighting!"

Connie and the Duke both turned and stared at him. Connie was momentarily speechless. The Duke had no such problem. "You are unwelcome in this gym and you are not to poison the mind of this young man!"

"Connie, listen to me. You're good but you should not be fighting any more. Did he tell you what the doctors said?"

Connie stood there, expressionless and motionless. He didn't move as the three burly security guards closed in on Clee and ushered him to the street.

Mattie Jean was waiting outside his building when he got home. She asked him how it went and he told her. He shook his head and spoke in slow but emphatic words describing the abbreviated session. "But it don't end here. I gotta get him to understand."

"Do me a favor. Take a breather tomorrow. I got a two-room apartment in my building at 127th Street that has to be done tomorrow."

"I can't concentrate on work, Mattie Jean."

"Sometimes it pays to think and develop a well-conceived plan. Give yourself some breathing room and give the boy a chance to think, also."

Mattie Jean gave Clee the keys to the apartment. He got there early the next morning, still heavy of heart and just missed Mattie Jean who was walking to 125th Street to catch the subway downtown. Even though she had known Clevon Nance all thse years she had never been to a boxing gym before.

Clee was doing the best he could but simply couldn't concentrate on the job at hand. He began moving the drop cloths to the other side of the first room when there was a knock at the door. "It's not locked. Come on in but be careful - fresh paint." He knew that was unnecessary - Mattie or the super.

He was prying the lid off the can of beige paint. Fortunately it was sitting on a double layer of drop cloth because he wound up knocking the can over when the door opened.

"Hey, Man, got an extra brush? Whooie, look at that mess you just made!" Conrad Green dropped his small canvas bag with his overalls to the floor. Clevon Nance wished that there was a sliced onion around to explain away the tear trickling down his cheek as he stepped over the puddle of paint and embraced the young man who he knew would be working with him for a very long time.

He smiled thinking of the Glory Days that were still ahead.

# MRS. ELIZABETH GREEN

*By Ron Ross*

The first time I saw Elizabeth Green was a humid, overcast summer night. The last I ever saw of Elizabeth Green was a humid, overcast summer night. It was the same night, a fact over which I shed no tears. Elizabeth Green was not the stuff that dreams are made of. Nor was she a girl whom I could ever have brought home to mother, Although, who know? They might have made great Mah Jong partners. Anyhow, on this night Elizabeth Green was the object of my desire.

Looking back, I blame it on uniform fixation. It's funny what affect a uniform can have on a person. It doesn't even matter what kind of uniform - in this case it being a Mobil Service Station uniform. You can sort of relate it to what happens to Clark Kent when he goes into a telephone booth wearing a dark, conservative business suit and comes out in this uniform of blue tights and a red cape. He is a totally different person; his shoulders are thrown back proudly, his chest is puffed out with confidence. Don't get me wrong.

I'm not comparing Superman to a gas station jockey – after all, who ever saw a Mobil attendant fly. Then again, there is Pegasus, the Flying Red Horse. But, as they say, that is a horse of a different color.

As soon as I see myself in my bedroom mirror in the blue coverall uniform with the sleeves rolled up to my elbows, I am transformed. Graduation from Tilden High School is a week behind me and my Freshman year at Brooklyn College is a summer ahead of me. Lost somewhere in the shuffle, or rather due to the donning of this uniform, is a nice punchball-playing Jewish boy from East Flatbush who runs errands to the grocery store and butcher shop, follows the rules by calling on Monday night to ask out his Saturday night date and to whom tempting the fates is going to a Friday night clubroom party in a finished basement of a one or two-family house somewhere in the East 50's where almost everyone starts out by dancing in the dark to Eddie Fisher, Tony Bennett and Vic Damone, then necking very competitively until a little past midnight at which time hunger pangs overwhelm desire, leading to an abrupt exodus to Garfield's Cafeteria on Flatbush Avenue where all the young stallions give with the sly winks over a corned beef on club and in confidential whispers relate conquests that never occurred.

The mirror-image mutation confronting me is a cool, actions-speak-louder-than-words dude. Gone is the schoolboy with the hesitant, unsure gait and sinewy but skinny, almost pipestem arms. These same arms, framed by heavy blue linen, are now a gently rippling network of well-articulated muscles that form a natural complement to this quietly confident very savvy young man that I have seemingly become. He is a guy who very obviously sees what he wants and quietly goes after it. No fanfare, no bragadoccio. Wherever he goes, room is made for him and he is looked upon with respect.

These feelings do not just spring upon me spontaneously. They evolve. A guy working on a gas station, wearing a uniform of the trade, is not spoken to as a wet-behind-the-ears, namby-pamby momma's boy. Immediately, it is taken for granted that such a guy with grease stains on his hands and smudges on his face, an oil rag dangling from his back pocket and forever poking the nozzle of a gasoline hose into a car's rump is one very mechanically-minded individual who spends all his spare time tinkering with screwdrivers, wrenches, spark-plugs and carburetors. The reponse to this person is totally different than that accorded to a spoldeen-chasing schoolboy whose greatest apprehensions are walking into a chemistry test unprepared or discovering a new zit on his cheek on Saturday afternoon.

It is of no great consequence that the only tinkering I have ever done on a car was to fill the tires with air which is not the simplest of tasks because unless you insert the air hose properly you can lose more air than you put in and truthfully, it took me almost a day to learn the sequence in filling up a car's gas tank - rewinding the meter on the pump (it was not automatic in 1950), flipping up the nozzle lever to start the pump motor, flipping down the nozzle lever when finished and most important - remembering to get paid. All of these things one can overcome if his father happens to own the gas station.

Anyhow, on this cloudy, sticky July night I decide not to go straight home from the station but instead, drive to the hub of East Flatbush - Utica and Church Avenues. This was not an unusual path for me or anyone else to take especially if you wanted to pick up the early evening edition of the News or Mirror which was dropped off at Goody's Candy Store before any other place in the area. Since most of the Yankee and Dodger games were now being played at night I had no use for the evening edition so that really was not my reason.

I don't think I knew of any real reason. It was more of a sense that going home was old routine. I'd walk through the front door and there I was again. By 'there I was' I really mean ' who I was ' as in 'who I was' past tense, not present tense. It is no single obvious or intentional act. It is not even anything specific, just a set of dynamics that is absolute, not subject to change. If some genius in a laboratory solves the mystery of the biological clock tomorrow and because of that I, someday in the future, at the age of two hundred and twelve, come home after a hard day's work, I'd still have to explain to my then two hundred and thirty seven year old mother why I didn't put my sox and underwear in the hamper that morning.

Utica Avenue was not Times Square but this is not to say you could cross the street without looking both ways. All the shops stayed open late, even on weekdays and you never had to worry about starving, as long as there was some loose change jingling around in your pocket, not with three restaurants (one an all-nighter) in a half-block strip. Even though this was familiar territory it was not home turf. I was a visitor here, not a belonger. I grew up going to Saturday matinees at the Rugby Theater, spent many teenage hours bowling and shooting pool at Guy Burkland's Lanes and slurped more black and white ice cream sodas at Silver Rod's Drug Store than I could ever dream of keeping count of, but this was still a place with an aura of difference, a flavor of enticement.

Goody's, for instance, was a candy store that did not sell too much candy. The clientele that is always hanging out there all hours of the day and night are not, let us say, run-of-the-mill shoppers. It is a crowd very big on toothpicks and Sen-Sen. Toothpicks, I know, are free and I do not know how much Sen-Sen costs but if you look on the sidewalk and wastebasket in front of Goody's what you will find are plenty of wrappers from these two items. For Hershey Bar wrappers you would be much better off looking in a hay stack, which is something you will not find on Utica Avenue or its environs no mattter how hard you look. Besides Sen-Sen, which is a staple additive very necessary due to the dietary habits of this crowd and which causes the local atmosphere to smell like a licorice onion,  Goody obviously does okay from newspapers and cigarettes. This inventory gives a pretty good insight into Goody's clientele. The rest of their purchases are generally made at the pari-mutuel windows of establishments like Belmont and Aqueduct. I do not talk to these people because if you do not talk horse talk then you are just not talking. They speak a language that is altogether from another place. It is my honest belief that if Goody ever replaces his stock of candy with apples, sugar and oats, inside of two months he can close up shop and spend his days on a Carribean Island which he will, of course, have bought with cash.

I am now beginning to feel like maybe I should have gone home and settled in front of the TV with a Mrs. Wagner's Blueberry Pie and a cold bottle of milk as all I am presently accomplishing is becoming an expert in the various ways that mouths, teeth and lips can dangle toothpicks. Toothpick-dangling could be considered interesting and, who knows, even exciting to some people - at another time in my life, maybe even to me - but at this moment my life was at a crossroads  So, realizing that my departure would probably not bring about great frenzies of wailing or mass hysteria, with hands in pockets, I turned and walked silently towards Church Avenue leaving a small arsenal of dueling toothpicks behind.

Hurley's Tavern was the fourth store from the corner on the other side of Church Avenue. If it was on the Moon it would not have made any difference as far as my being able to pass through its front door - or its back door, if it had one - or even its chimney.  The inherent dangers of such a place were implanted deep in the recesses of my mind, without

173

explanation or reason but the warning message was clear nevertheless. My parents could possibly have settled in the Louisiana bayou country instead of New York City in which case I would have been warned of the dangers of quicksand bogs. Places like Hurley's were the urban equivalent. I remember, as a little boy, walking past the Beverly Bar & Grill which was between Chris's Deli and Spiegel's Pharmacy on Ralph Avenue while shopping with my mother. The door was open so I stopped and looked inside, then inquired, "What do people buy in this store?"

"Nothing - and you should never even think of buying it."

At the advanced age of seven this was not an easy answer to digest. "What kind of people pay money to buy nothing?"

"Not our kind of people." It suddenly dawned upon me why I still did not know why the sky was blue. "You would never see your father in a place like this."

This was the clincher that converted all Bars and Grills into quicksand bogs. My perception was that there was no place in this whole world where my father couldn't go except to the Ladies' Room, which, to me, became a symbol of inviolateness. Therefore, to learn that there was yet another place of such ominous importance made it forever out of bounds to me - until now.

Not that I was never in an establishment that served alcohol but there was a difference between a cocktail lounge with music and entertainment and a place where there was ... well, like my mother said ... nothing. Nothing but drinking and ... whatever goes with drinking when there is nothing ... like talk ... plain down to earth talk in a real man's world. I sensed that this was my kind of place and these guys were my crowd.

Walking through the front door was an act of courage in itself and I considered my options carefully before making my move. There was the Edward G. Robinson entrance

- collar pulled up, hands thrust in pockets with shoulders hunched together, beady eyes glaring straight ahead and walking with a brisk, determined stride. Or the Errol Flynn, with a warm captivating smile, twinkling eyes greeting everyone, a sprightly bounce to his step and yet an air about him that let you know he was top dog. And I could not discount John Wayne, who would push open the front door, then just stand there, arms folded in front of him, slowly eyeballing everyone in the room, eliciting a challenge to one and all without so much as uttering a single word. However, I settled upon Claude Raines – you know, "The Invisible Man". This should not be misconstrued as fear or timidity but should be recognized more as humility.

After all, I was the new kid on the block, so to speak. My presence would be more than just felt by the natural course of events. The cream always rise to the top, doesn't it ? Meanwhile, I had to hand it to them - these guys were some cool piece of work. No matter how badly they wanted to turn around and grab a look at the "stranger" - me - they acted as though they didn't even know I was there. That was okay by me.

The place smelled like one big beer bottle and my eyes kept tearing from the cigarette smoke that looked like it hung from the ceiling and did a slow little swirling dance around the room. The last thing I needed right now was for these guys to think I'm crying so I try most inconspicuously to wipe my eyes.

"Hey, you gonna sing 'Mammy', Mr. Jolson?" It was this tall geek with no front teeth playing at the shuffleboard table. I had no idea what he was talking about until I looked at the mirror behind the bar and saw both my cheeks smudged with grease. I forgot when I wiped the tears away that I still had some grease on my fingers. That's because I hate to wash with Gre-Solvent at the end of the day like the other guys. It makes me feel like I'm scraping away my skin with sandpaper. I console myself by rationalizing that at least I was now noticed. Again I try to be very inconspicuous as I take out my handkerchief and scrub away at my face until I am sure I must be down to bone. When I turn my attention back to the bar I feel like the Number One Stripper at Minsky's as nobody is watching the Brooklyn Dodgers on the Dumont TV behind the bar but all heads are turned my way watching me do my scrub-a-dub-dub. I think wouldn't it be great if I waved my hands like an orchestra conductor and led the whole place in singing, "This is the way we wash our face, wash our face ...". But it turns out I am a gutless wonder. I know I would be able to do this without thinking twice in the lunchroom at Tilden High, but in Hurley's Tavern I do nothing but think and shrink while my face gets redder and redder. Silently, I thank God when Gil Hodges poles one to Bedford Avenue and everyone turns back to the game and away from me.

Perhaps, I think to myself, that I am not quite projecting the right image. Maybe another night should be a consideration. But I recognize that what I am really doing is thinking of quitting on myself so I take a deep breath and convince myself that I am magnifying in my mind a couple of incidents that probably no one else noticed or even gave a second thought. Looking in the mirror again I am relieved to see that the grease smudges are gone and I quickly replace them with a slight curl at the left corner of my lip, a flare to my nostrils and a narrowing of my eyes. This automatically converts my walk to a swagger as I move to the bar, now quite comfortable with who I am.

There is an empty stool next to this mountain that looks very much like a person and I decide this is where I will sit. If he would appear on "What's My Line?" I am certain that everyone on the panel would venture to guess that he was a wrestler – but not Gorgeous George, that is for sure. Actually, and this I discover by looking at the back of his shirt, he works for Smolowitz Brothers Movers and Haulers. It is very possible that he is their one-man piano-moving department.

I take note that the place is about half-filled and everybody is watching the game but nobody seems to be concentrating on it. There is some talk about the new war in Korea and a lot of talk about money, jobs and women but I am sitting in a pool of silence. For the sake of congeniality I am thinking about saying something to Mount Everest but cannot think of anything to say. It is then that I look at his arms for the first time. This guy is a walking, or sitting, moving picture theater. He has so many tatoos, you would have to use the Dewey Decimal System to catalogue them. There are snakes, lions, sinking ships, broken hearts ... and it is very touching ... he really loves his mother and is not ashamed to let the whole world know as she is engraved in three colors on each of his arms. He is of such size that to catch the whole show would probably take as long as seeing "Gone With The Wind."

I hardly get a chance to see the coming attractions when the bartender breaks in with a, "What'll it be, buddy?" Truthfully, I was not from the drinkers. In fact, I was just getting used to acquiring a taste for beer but in a place like Hurley's I didn't want to be looked at as unsophisticated. It was just a couple of weeks ago that I had my first night club date. We went in a group of four couples to Ben Maksik's Town and Country club on Flatbush Avenue and I was very impressed by my date who ordered a drink called a Singapore Sling. I went right along and said, "I'll have the same" and I was proud because I had no problem holding my liquor. So I look this bartender right in the eye, act as though I am running a whole drink menu through my mind, then purse my lips and say, "Make it a Singapore Sling." I am not too sure whether the look he is giving me is of great respect or whether he is contemplating what planet other than Earth I might come from. As it develops, I recognize that he is just not a master of his trade because he finally says, "I do not get a request for that drink too often, maybe once on Ladies' Night. I think it's made with sloe gin and I am out of sloe gin."

Not being a very picky drinker I give him a not-to-worry smile and answer, "It doesn't matter to me. I can handle my liqour. If you don't have slow gin, fast gin will be fine." This turned out to be a real mountain-mover as my neighbor made his stool creak and groan as he turned in my direction. I was now desperately wishing that I had ordered a beer and the bartender must have been part genie because he looked at me in a very funny way and suggested, "Why don't you let me get you a beer?" There was another creak and groan as the mountain resettled.

Midway through my second beer, which, under other circumstances would have been exciting by itself as I was approaching my personal beer-drinking record, I became acutely aware of the fact that not only wasn't I jubilant but I was depressed. The red "Exit" sign over the rear door seemed to be blinking and beckoning to me and I was smiling back at it but I thought that if I moved towards it every eye in the place would be following me. All that cool confidence and eye-catching street savvy was quickly and surely evaporating into the air and I couldn't understand what was holding me back in this place. These jokers are watching a ballgame and half of them probably don't even know any more about the game than four balls are a walk and three strikes - you're out. Meanwhile, I can name the entire rosters of all sixteen major league teams and can run off the complete stats for every Yankee and Dodger player. I can show these guys stuff that would stand them on their ears. Just picture me getting their attention and saying, "Hey, guys, how about a spelling bee?" What a walk-over that would be! Then again, I figure this may not be one of their favorite pasttimes.

Instead I spent some time twiddling my thumbs clockwise and when that got tiring I changed pace and did a little counter-clockwise thumb-twiddling. After that I spent some time enjoying the picture show on the human art gallery next to me which I followed by  taking another large swallow of my beer.  The timing of this was not too good as I had just popped a few peanuts in my mouth which had not yet gone down  and which also stopped the beer from going down, thereby causing a great deal of hacking and coughing which is very helpful in clearing the throat but not too helpful in clearing the air.  For some reason, maybe it is a reflex, I turn my head to the right and a couple of peanuts with a spray of foamy beer are very forcefully expelled from my throat. You would never believe that something or someone so large could move so quickly as the man-mountain did in dodging the peanuts.  Unfortunately, as he ducks backwards he goes a little too far - past what you would call the point of no return. All of Hurley's shakes and rumbles.  The hanging light fixtures, the bottles behind the bar,  for a minute even the lights on the jukebox are flickering as my neighbor crashes to the floor.  He is truly the strong, silent type because not a sound comes from him as he goes down.  I am immediately very upset. Maybe more than he is because I am uncertain about how good-natured he will be over such an occurrence.

This turns out to be a problem I never have to contend with as when he arises he does not even know of which country he is a citizen, let alone for what reason he awakens on a barroom floor.  He gets up, section by section, brushes off a few pounds of sawdust and wobbles, as only a mountain can wobble,  to, and barely through, the front door.  Meanwhile there is a good deal of whispering and soft chatter around the room, with all eyes now darting glances in my direction. As no one was paying any attention to me before the great clap of thunder, no one really saw or knew what happened regarding the ducking of the peanuts and beer. This gives rise to the very erroneous assumption that there was some sort of major difference of opinion between the mountainous picture show and myself which resulted in a lowering of the boom.

It's not that I don't want to set the record straight; I am not given the opportunity as no one asks me about it. So now I am one of the guys. At least I am asked such probing things as to please pass the peanuts, do I know what the score is and even "What time ya got, buddy?" Although I should be very happy to finally be passing peanuts in Hurley's I am very reluctant falling into this role in such a manner. But as I continue drinking beer, and breaking my record, of course, playing an occasional game of shuffleboard with the toothless geek who no longer calls me Mr. Jolson, and being the devil's advocate by expounding on why the Whiz Kids from Philly were going to beat the Dodgers for the National League pennant it seems there is an overabundance of oxygen or maybe helium in the place which makes my head very light and easy to handle. It spins a little bit, then stops as I look at the "Exit" "Exit" sign. I also notice that the bartender is now working with his twin brother right at his side and think to myself that a family that tends bar together … . Little by little all the reluctance starts filtering off into space. For a moment it feels like maybe my head is going to float off after it so I decide to very gently lie it down upon the bar.

Indisputably, heads are among the most discriminating parts of the anatomy. True, there are differences in the degree of authority a particular head may carry. I personally know people whose heads may issue forth the warning, "No way! Forget about it!" or "Ugh!" but another body part will rebel and say, "I want her" or "Let's go for it anyhow" and the head will be overruled. That is why I have always been particularly proud of my head as it always assumes a role of leadership and is never seriously challenged. However, hazy eyes and a fuzzy cranium can do a lot in mitigating the judgemental prowess in the best of heads. This may somewhat explain what occurs when a sound somewhere between a bugler blowing Reveille and a tugboat pulling into New York Harbor is converted into a melodious clarion-like heralding, "Any gentleman care to buy a lady a drink?" My head slowly arises from the bar top, eyes straining to focus and what they finally settle upon can be described as a vision of loveliness – CAN BE described as a vision of loveliness – under the haziest and fuzziest of conditions and even then could be open to much conjecture.

The backlighting from the Wurlitzer Jukebox framed her in a rainbowed halo and for a moment I thought I was looking at an angel. It was a valid deduction based on a flawed hypothesis. She was not an angel. I stared at her, thinking how thirsty she must have been to make herself dispense with pride and plead for a drink. As our eyes locked, she floated – the lighting not being too effective perhaps she floundered over towards me. "You're a real gentleman. Probably the only one in the place."

It was amazing. I hadn't uttered a word, yet our minds were seemingly on an open wavelength. Only I realized that it was not chivalry or kindness, but lascivious self-indulgence on my part. "I'll ... I'll get you a drink, Miss." I had to force the words out and I was slightly unsettled by the higher-than-normal pitch to my voice. In order to compensate I followed that by reaching way down in my stomach and offered in a deep, resonant bass, pointing at the mountain's now empty stool, "Why don't you make yourself comfortable and sit down?"

She clasped her hands, marvelling at what I said, "What are you – half of the Four Inkspots?" I wondered to myself whether two Inkspots were as desirable as one Al Jolson. As she seated herself upon the stool I began to truly grasp the meaning of 'distance lends enchantment'. However, the harshness of reality and acuity of vision was muted enough by the unaccustomed flow of alcohol through my veins to negate what I was actually looking at and transform it into what I wanted to be looking at. Wrinkles and sallow, mottled flesh were seemingly airbrushed by the mind's eye. I was not sitting next to a Calendar Girl by Vargas but at least she didn't have a beard or mustach.

"What'll you drink, Madam?"

"Madam?" She arched her eyebrows. "Who do you think I am? Polly Adler? I do not run any establishments. I am Mrs. Elizabeth Green – formerly of the Bronx, New York."

I felt the red creeping into my face and was hoping it wouldn't be noticed with the dim lighting. "Don't get me wrong, Mrs. Green. I meant 'Madam' as a term of respect. It's really a generic ..."

"Forget it. My drink. My drink."

"Oh, sure. How about a ginger ale or maybe you'd prefer a real cold glass of juice." I knew juice was very big with girls. She looked at me the same way the bartender did when I ordered the Singapore Sling. "I really have no preference. You order for me. I see you are a real man of the world." Oh, my God, I thought to myself, I am in like Flynn!

"Bartender, one ginger ale, please."

Then, from over my right shoulder, "And send along a chaser with that – four fingers of Johnny Walker."

I wasn't sure what she asked for – a Bela Lugosi movie or a drink. It didn't even help when the bartender set it down because she swallowed it so quickly I hardly had a chance to see it. The Johnny Walker that is. The ginger ale may still be sitting there.

Looking around the bar I noticed that a lot of the guys were sneaking glances in our direction which I interpret as being envy. It does not even dawn upon me that they could be thinking - "There but for the grace of God go I." It does not even dawn upon me because at that moment I am deluding myself. "What you see is what you get" should not always be taken at face value. Sometimes it is "What you think you see is what you get." I am sure that I was the only one in the place that was seeing Mrs. Elizabeth Green as a rosy-cheeked, barely-wrinkled cheerleader doing a stirring sis-boom-bah, as a high-kicking Rockette smiling down at me from the stage at Radio City Music Hall ( her thighs jiggling in time to the music went unnoticed by me) but as I said, no one else was seeing what I was seeing. At any rate my pulse quickened at the sight of her - and the thought of what was going to transpire between us.

What all this brings about is more than just a little guilt on my part as I realize that my intentions are not completely honorable. Not that I wouldn't get a thirsty person a drink with no strings attached. I am not that kind of guy even though it turns out she is much more thirsty than I could have believed. I don't think a camel lost in the desert for a week could have drank more than Mrs. Elizabeth Green. I wanted to tell her to consider some salt tablets also but I decided not to because I realized I would probably be the one who would have to go out and find them.

When Mrs. Elizabeth Green relates to me her misfortunes and grief and how she is taken advantage of, my guilt grows to a point where I find myself staring and focusing on a spot on the the sawdust-covered floor as I cannot look her in the eye. It is such a touching story that it is necessary for her to have some physical bond which is why I discover her hand upon my thigh. Though understanding the innocence and need for compassion that brings about such contact I am ashamed at some of the thoughts that are now racing through me.

It seems she was out walking the streets in search of Mr. Green, who had disappeared.

"Why didn't you call the police?" I asked.

"I did. Lots of times. Probably a hundred times over the last ten years," she explained.

"Did you say ten years?"

"That is what I said. There is no quit in me." This she said very emphatically. "I have become quite well-known by the entire police force. In fact, I am on the tip of the tongue of almost every cop in the Bronx."

I felt that maybe some elaborating was in order but I just kept staring harder and harder at the floor.

"They call me Lizzie when I call. They know me so well some of the boys from the precinct stop by for coffee late at night and sometimes stay over."

"I guess this makes you pretty certain, at least, that your husband is not lost somewhere in your house?"

"Oh, there is no chance of that. They always check around very carefully. In fact, even though we are on what you would call more than friendly terms, every once in a while they have to do a strip search of me just to keep the record straight. I am so cooperative that they realize my dedication in finding Mr. Green."

My eyes were now raised from their focal point on the floor. "Do you really expect to find him after ten years?"

"I don't give up like my next door neighbor."

"Your next door neighbor?" Why, I asked myself, was I playing straight man when I couldn't care less about Mr. Green. It was Mrs. Green that I was zeroing in on.

"It was such a coincidence," she went on, now that I had opened the door for her. "Mr. Buckley's wife - they lived in 3B, right next door to us - disappeared on the very same night as Mr. Green and they never found her either. But the police recognize how much more sincere I am than Mr. Buckley because they never ever go to his apartment."

Even though ten years had passed I didn't want to be the one to cause any friction in this marriage so I tried to be as diplomatic and tactful as possible."Did you and Mr. Buckley ever discuss this, what you call, coincidence?"

"I told you, he's not sincere like me. In fact, he has found himself a new Mrs. Buckley a long time ago." Then she adds with a smile, "He was always more concerned about Mr. Green than his own wife. I remember he said to me he wouldn't take her back no matter what, but he couldn't wait to find Mr. Green. Wasn't that a sweet thought?"

I feel it is better to smile than to answer because a smile is wide open to interpretation. Then I repeat the question, "Then you still expect to find him after ten years?"

"I don't but it gives me something to do, especially since my television set broke. Also, it is good exercise. So tonight I am walking in search of Mr. Green when a car pulls up with what I assume to be three very goodhearted samaritans and they invite me into their automobile to assist me in the search."

I shake my head and sigh, "Mrs. Green. You never get into a car with strangers."

"Now you tell me!" She leans forward and her hand is taking a quick ride up my leg which makes concentrating not too easy. "Where were you with this advice when I needed it? Anyhow, they weren't strangers. I asked them their names and they were all part of that cough drop family ... ooh, you know ..."

I took a wild guess. "The Smith Brothers."

"Oh, you are so smart." There was a look of true admiration in her eyes. Somehow, I knew it wasn't going to be the Ludens family.

When Mrs. Elizabeth Green told me the whole story of what she went through I should have felt very sorry for her but instead I was visualizing myself as one of the Smith Brothers. I know that makes four Smith Brothers but if I could be two Inkspots why couldn't I be one of four Smith Brothers?

"At first I couldn't get over how concerned they were," she went on. "They drove all the way from Fordham Road in the Bronx to the marshlands off the Belt Parkway - a place called Canarsie."

"Why did they go to Canarsie when your husband got lost in the Bronx?"

She leaned over again and whispered in my ear, "What if I told you that their intentions were not honorable?" This puts me in the terrible dillemma of condemning what, deep down, I really condone. "That is unbelievable. Guys like that really deserve to be punished."

"Oh, they were. They certainly were. The Lord works in mysterious ways," she winked at me confidentially. "There was a laying on of the hands but it was not at all in a reverend way. The Lord, knowing I would some day be faced with such an ordeal provided me with very sensitive nerve endings to which every touch is a tickle and in this case there was so much touching, it caused me to laugh as if I am being tickled to death and these nerve endings, which control my hair-trigger sphincter muscle caused their repentance."

"Don't tell me."

"I am so going to tell you. I pissed all over the back seat of their car - with the lambs' wool upholstery. Which is how I wind up stranded on the side of the Belt Parkway in Canarsie." Immediately I am thinking that it might be best for me to alter whatever course of action was bouncing around in my head as I did not take into consideration weak sphincters.

It was as though she read my thoughts. "Don't you worry, though. My sphincter works very selectively." I think that she is telling me that she pees on who she wants. She then tells me how she hitches her way from Canarsie to Utica Avenue turning down proposals ranging from instant stardom to marriage because she senses there is something far greater in store for her on this night. I feel as though an army of caterpillars are crawling over my body at this moment. Who would ever believe this? A woman of the world like Mrs. Elizabeth Green openly, unashamedly announcing her desires for me. Was it the uniform - the Mobil uniform - or what was in the uniform?

I wondered to myself if after this night I would ever again be able to look at or be attracted to another bobby-soxer or girls of the clubroom society? Would I feel out of place at frat parties and college dances and from this day forward move in on the mah-jong and canasta set? Mrs. Elizabeth Green had extracted a nickel from my pocket, popped it in the juke-box which was now playing "Body and Soul" and then pulled me off my stool to dance with her. I did not want to dance, mainly because I did not know how to dance but as it turned out I did not have to know how to dance because I do not think what we were doing was called dancing. We did not move our feet. We just stood in front of the bar and she held onto me while we swayed back and forth.

The beer was still rolling around inside of me, probably all settling in my brain because my head was on a merry-go-round of its own. The strains of "Body and Soul" made me think of John Garfield and Lilli Palmer standing alone on a tenement roof with her purring, "Tiger, tiger, you are my tiger" while she runs her hand across his fist and he looks at her and answers, "But I don't have claws for you." I was waiting for Mrs. Elizabeth Green to give me the chance to say that now but I couldn't wait forever, especially knowing that with her being so busy the past ten years she may not have even seen the picture, so I figured I may as well change it around a little and say her part for her. "Tiger, tiger, I am your tiger", at which point I stop for a moment, give her that look where I let my eyelids slide halfway down, then follow with the clincher, "But I don't have claws for you." She shakes her head, not quite understanding the beauty of it. "What do you wanna do, scratch me now?"

This upsets me, embarrasses me and hurts me all at the same time because I was saving that line, that scene to be used at a highlight moment of my life and this was not it. I blew it and I just wanted to bury my face somewhere - and I did without even realizing it - in the only available place for me to bury my face, Mrs. Elizabeth Green's very soft and cushiony bosom. Actually I did realize it - as soon as I felt her hands grabbing on tightly to my cheeks, and I do not mean on my face. As I have never been held in such a manner before I do not quite know how to react. Swaying slowly to the music I see that a few new people have entered the bar and again I am outdrawing the Brooklyn Dodgers or maybe it is my dancing partner who is the real attention-getter. Probably, some of these guys would know exactly how to respond to being held in such a way and would very much like to be in that position. But they obviously have been clued in to the tale of my demolition of the man-mountain and at the moment seem content to live a little vicariously. Mrs. Green also notices how they are looking at me and I tell her of how I disposed of my oversized neighbor with a mouthful of beer and peanuts while everyone thinks I did it with my right hand or possibly, my left. I then felt it necessary to add, "But do not think that if the situation called for it I could not have done it the way they thought I did."

Somehow, I dig up the nerve to place my hands on Mrs Elizabeth Green's cheeks the same way hers are on mine. I am in total shock. Hers move. They are soft like a bagful of jello would be and they move in every direction. She, in turn, must think that my body is very achy after a day's work as she is now massaging me and I, once again am feeling very strange. It turns out that she is also a very private person as she is whispering in my ear. "Poor me. I am like a lost soul. It's too late to go back to the Bronx and I have no money and no place to stay. If I only had a big, strong man to take care of me."

The only things that penetrated was 'place to stay' and 'big, strong man'. First, I tried flexing my biceps in as subtle and inconspicuous way as possible, then I can't believe that I dug up the nerve to say what I did. "I ... I have this place, you know." I was talking about our clubroom on East Fifty-first Street, which we only used on Friday nights and, thank God, this was not Friday night. I was now thinking of "The Spider and The Fly".

"You have your own place?" She looked at me, smiling, realizing I was much more sophisticated than she thought.

I lied. "Sure I do. You didn't think I still lived with my parents, did you? I mean, I visit them a lot because they miss me ... and I support them ... but live with them?"

She stopped swaying and said, "I love having a strong he-man to take care of me. We are going to have a real good time tonight!" Then she hugged me so hard that it caused all the beer in me to be pushed into one spot - my bladder. This, combined with the excitement of thinking what tonight held in store for me reminded me of Mrs. Elizabeth Green's adventure on the lamb's wool upholstery of the back seat of the car that she was in earlier this evening. So I excused myself and weaved my way to the Men's Room at the rear of the bar, wishing that everyone wasn't staring at me right now.

After relieving my bladder and splashing cold water over my face, hoping to help me see one of everything again instead of two, I tried to think rationally but my heart was pounding from excitement. The Spider and the Fly, The Hunter and the Prey, To the Victor goes the Spoils. This was not a goodnight kiss at the front door, nor petting at a drive-in. This was going to be the real thing. I pictured myself at Garfield's Cafeteria with everyone gathered around me. I was ignoring them, just drinking a cup of coffee - black, of course. Somehow, they had gotten wind of my night at Hurley's - from one of the guys sitting around the bar, obviously, and pleaded with me to tell them about it. I merely smiled, got up and left, feeling it very important to protect the good name of Mrs. Elizabeth Green.

I braced myself, tried squaring my shoulders and putting just the right look on my face before walking out to, by now, a most anxious Mrs. Elizabeth Green. Taking a deep breath, I opened the door. A few heads turned my way, smiling strangely - obviously about some secret they were sharing - but not with me. My woman was dancing with a guy in a red flannel shirt. I walked back to my stool, signalled her with a little wave of my hand to let her know I was ready. She saw me but ignored the signal and turned away, laughing at something he said. I knew he wouldn't dream of messing with me after seeing what I did to the mountain.

At that very moment I noticed his hands clutching her ass and knew something was wrong. I couldn't think of what to do so I ordered another beer. When the bartender put down the foamy stein he asked with a grin, "You want a refill on the peanut bowl, too?" All I could do was return his grin, but in very weak fashion. Maybe I should have told Mrs. Green it was a secret. I didn't touch the beer because I was sure that if I did everything that I drank that night would wind up on the barroom floor and this bartender did not seem like the kind of guy who would be overly accommodating about cleaning up messes. I heard Mrs. Elizabeth Green screaming and laughing at the same time. From the corner of my eye I saw her flannel-shirted dancing partner running his hands up and down her body. I was considering telling him about her very sensitive sphincter, but decided to let him find out by himself.

What a hand fate had dealt me! Sort of like a man without a country - lost somewhere in time and space. Being with a real woman like Mrs. Elizabeth Green made me feel that I could never again be comfortable with or settle for the brace-wearing, pony-tailed Junior Miss set. I shook my head at the thought of them waving their pom-poms at football games and giggling at any move you made towards them. Still, I no longer wanted to be in Hurley's but I didn't know how not to be there. At least not in a graceful, face-saving way. Finally, I settled on very dramatically looking at my watch and simultaneously slapping my forehead, which I did much too zealously - it really hurt - and yelping, "Oh, Christ!" I capped this off with a flourish - a loud snap of my fingers. Now everyone knew that I had forgotten a very, very important appointment - much more important than spending the night with Mrs. Elizabeth Green. Bouncing up from my stool without skipping a beat, I headed for the door. As I passed the dancing, grappling couple, in a final try at redemption I barked, "Sorry, Lizzie, forgot about something very important." Then to flannel-shirt, "Take over for me, Buddy." I was out the front door before anyone could answer.

I walked towards Church Avenue as quickly as I could without running. All the lights looked a little blurry but I wasn't sure whether it was the beer or if my eyes were still teary from the cigarette smoke. There was a bitter taste in my mouth and I wanted to get rid of it so I was glad to see that Silver Rod's was still open, especially since it was still humid and the thought of a nice air-conditioned place seemed very appealing. Just being inside these familiar, brightly lighted surroundings made me feel a little better, almost like I was in my own living room. The thought of a tall, whipped-cream-topped ice cream soda made me smile without realizing I was doing so. As I walked, actually it was more like skipped, to the soda fountain I noticed that the place was almost empty, except for a young, cute girl in a light cashmere Tilden High School Booster sweater seated on a stool, studying the fountain menu.

At an earlier time in my life, such a sight would have set in motion ... "Don't even bother looking at the menu," I could not believe what I was doing - this was a child - seventeen at best. "You can't do better than a double-dip black and white soda." She looked at me, hesitated for a second, then smiled. "What if I don't like chocolate or vanilla?"

"Then you will go through life a most bitter person, missing out on its greatest pleasures and you are also probably a communist." I cannot believe all the charm and savoir-faire that spewed forth from me over the next few minutes. All wasted on youth, I told myself, but for some reason I could not stop myself - it was like a voiding process or an exorcism. She really had never had a black and white ice cream soda before (and I thought I was lost in time and space) so I convinced her to let me treat her to her first ever. I thought how it would be buying Mrs. Elizabeth Green a black and white soda and her polluting it with a Johnny Walker. Ugh!

I didn't want the night to end yet so I suggested going from Silver Rod's to the Rugby Theater down the street and catching the double feature. She laughed, no, it was more a giggle, not a mature laugh, "Are you crazy? Do you know what time it is?"

"It's summertime. No school. You can stay out late." This is what you are faced with when you play with children.

"But the first picture is almost over by now. We'll only be able to see one picture."

"Don't worry. My treat. So we'll see one picture."

She was really shocked. "I don't believe it! You're willing to see only one picture and pay for the price of two?" Someday she would be a very good homekeeper with budgets, money in the cookie jar and everything. Meanwhile, I made such a big impression splurging four bits to see only half a show that she could not refuse me. As she got up from her stool I couldn't take my eyes off her perky little behind which I was sure was nothing like a mushy bag of jello and definitely would not move around. As we walked towards the Rugby I saw that the same crowd was still standing in front of Goody's. They were probably dangling fresh toothpicks, though. Nothing was blurry any longer as I looked at the marquee of the Rugby Theater. The second feature was a rerun and I saw it already but It didn't matter. It was "Body and Soul".

I looked at my new date who was holding my hand and I was glad that she had clear, firm skin and nothing jiggled on her. She told me that she had never dated a mechanic before and I told her it was just a summer job on my father's station - that I was starting Brooklyn College in the fall. Maybe, once we're sitting in the dark and we get to know each other a little better, I'll even get to do my "Tiger, tiger" line before John Garfield does it - or maybe we'll do it together. Who knows, maybe I'll even get up the nerve, even if it is the first date, to slide my hand down around her shoulders and try to touch ... well, maybe that's moving too fast. It felt good just being with her. I decided to just wait and see what happens, you know, let Nature take its course. Anyhow, it didn't matter. I was really happy. I was on home turf.

# THE KIND MAN AND THE BLIND MAN

*- by Ron Ross*

Irving Pelofsky didn't try to make excuses or defend himself when Milty, shaking his head, handed him the container of coffee over the candy store counter and asked – even though it wasn't meant to be a question – "What are you, out of your head, even in this weather, delivering coffee to a beggar?"

Still shivering from the bitter cold, Irving grasped the container, luxuriating as its heat, starting from his palms and fingertips, filtered through his body. "You wouldn't understand, Milty. It's something I gotta do."

"*I* don't understand? I think you got it a little mixed up, my friend. Doing a mitzvah is something you should want to do, something that comes from the heart. Not something you *gotta* do."

Irving didn't answer. Some things you can't share. They're just too personal. As long as he understood and so did his Sophie – God rest her soul – what else mattered? It was shortly after his wife Sophie passed away that Irving Pelofsky moved to a smaller apartment on Hopkinson Avenue and was walking towards the elevated train on Livonia when he saw him sitting in an alleyway midway down the block, wearing a stocking cap, two or three layers of sweaters and large dark glasses masking an emotionless leathery, dark brown complexion. The tin cup in front of him was half-filled with coins. Irving passed without contributing. Then he stopped, turned back and stared at the black glasses as though challenging its wearer to respond.

"You want some coffee?"

"Sounds good. I like it sweet 'n black."

When Irving came back with the coffee from the corner grocery he enjoyed watching as the Blind man gave a sigh of satisfaction – "Aaah!" - as he tasted the fresh brew. Irving repeated this act the next day and the day after.

Not being of a generous nature – after all, who comes through a Depression losing all he has saved and worked for without being suspicious and skeptical of everyone and everything – Irving, with Sophie's life slipping away, made a silent covenant with God - A kind act, a good deed every day of his life, hoping it would be his guarantee to spending eternity with Sophie.

Now he decided to simplify carrying out his "good-deed-a-day-act of-kindness" by ritualizing the act in concert with the blind beggar on Hopkinson Avenue. This would be his act of kindness and generosity every day of his life –and, naturally, the life of the blind man.

It was a strange bond – more than a bond, it was a friendship. A unique friendship, but one that suited the needs of both. Seven years passed and neither missed a day. Weather, health, holidays – Irving Pelofsky always came and the Blind man was always there waiting.

Walking from Milty's candy store, headlong into the howling wind, clutching the container of coffee tightly, he was just about fifty feet from the Blinder when someone jumped out of a nearby alleyway, knocked Irving to the ground and quickly went to his pockets. Irving realized that he must have seen him leave the check-cashing store on Sutter Avenue where he cashed his monthly Social Security check, all that he had to live on.

"Stop! Thief! Bandit!"

The thief ran down an almost deserted street, turned once to look and laugh at his distraught victim. Irving, who was stumbling after him, now stopped and stared in disbelief.

The Blinder stepped from the alleyway and snapped out his arm, nailing the fleeing crook right on the throat, abruptly ending his flight. When Irving staggered up to him, the Blind man, with Irving's money in his fist, booted the bedraggled thief on the backside, sending him on his way and turned to Irving, handing him his money.

There was no "Thank You." Irving couldn't believe what had just taken place. Shock had replaced gratitude.

Finally, he regained the ability to speak, breaking what seemed an endless silence. "You caught him!"

"Uh-huh." The Blinder smiled.

"All this time you lied to me. You can see."

"No," the blind man assured him, "I cannot see. But I hear better than you can; in fact, all my other senses are better tuned than yours. They help me see, just in a different way."

Irving shook his head, embarrassed at his still suspicious nature. He smiled at his friend. "Look, I spilled your coffee. Instead, today let me give you a reward. Here, five dollars. Tomorrow I'll see you with coffee." He turned and walked away.

"Hey, wait, friend," the Blind man called after him. "Five Dollars! Ain't that Abe Lincoln?" Then, holding up the bill, "This is George Washington!"

Irving's face was frozen. "You're kidding!"

Once more, the Blind man smiled. "Uh-huh!"

*The prize ring, a roughly twenty-square feet roped-off enclosure, has always seemed to me to be a microcosm of life. It is a world unto itself where the very struggle to survive, the dramas, the pathos and the joys of success – as well as handling failure or defeat are reduced to its most basic elements.*

*And those gallant performers on this stage of life often appear to me as poetry in motion and there are times that I feel compelled to tell their stories in a more lyrical style. Apologies to Muhammad Ali, the true poet laureate of the boxing universe.*

# THE CLUB FIGHTER

*by Ron Ross*

He stood under the marquee, satchel in hand
His name in lights for another one night stand.
As the city's cold winds bit through his coat
He gathered his threadbare collar closer to his throat.
He'd been here before, long years ago,
A much younger buck swimming in life's flow.
The winds didn't chill him in those years, he thought.
His blood was too hot and there were fights to be fought.
He took one last look at his name in lights
"Catman Miller" it shone, "Veteran of One Hundred Fights".

Through a side entrance, down a dank hall he went
His eyes groped in the darkness, his nose curled at the scent.
The smells of stale urine, of wintergreen, of sweat ;
These were the greetings with which he always was met.
The sounds of men's voices and a flickering light
Led him to the locker room, his home for this night.
He pushed the door open to a scene that he knew

And entered a world familiar to so few.
A world filled with men primed for the wars
With the sweat of anxiety oozing from their pores.

The Catman was here, he announced with a wave,
And stood in the doorway, soulfully grave.
All eyes turned his way and acknowledged his might.
Old to be sure, but still the big name tonight.
"Hi there, Catman," a young fighter said.
"You gonna show us the way? Knock the bum dead?"
The Catman smiled sagely and had this to say,
"I just does my best to earn a night's pay."
He walked to a corner to be by himself
And emptied his belongings on a bare wooden shelf.

Slowly, he undressed, amid the small talk around
And studied his body, thickly muscled, still sound.
Like a great tree, he stood massive and tall,
His punch-bloated face bringing a shudder to all.
Though not a stranger to smoke or cheap wine
He worked himself hard and kept toein' the line.
The shell was a good one, belying his years,
This, certainly, was not the cause of his fears.
If fears you would call it, probably not,
The Catman was as brave as any of his lot.

A premonition of something had crept into his mind
Whether doubt or fear or youth left behind.
It lived with the Catman from day unto night,
And muddled his thoughts right up to each fight.
But he'd stifle these thoughts and shut out the gloom
And he knew to relax, not pace 'round the room.
He lay upon the rubbing table cradling his head
And soon slept so soundly you'd think he was dead.

And as other's pulsebeats raced wildly, quickened by a third,
Catman Miller's soft breathing could barely be heard.


☆　☆　☆


"Go! Catman! Go!" the crowds used to scream.
But now these were sounds heard only in a dream.
He fought like a fury, lust in each punch.
Bound to be the champ, was everyone's hunch.
He thrilled as the crowds roared out his name ;
Here was the Catman and this was his game!
But the road to the top takes many a twist,
And somewhere along this path the Catman missed.
He fought the best, the crowd's cheering him on,
But somehow the fury and the passion were gone.

Buses and trains raced him to faraway towns.
The Catman fought on, having his ups and his downs.
Wherever he went, he packed the crowds in,
"This guy's a fighter - he c'n take it on the chin!"
No more talk of his winning the crown ;
Just, "Let's see some blood - someone go down!"
He soon grew accustomed to losing a fight ;
It no longer kept him up half of the night.
But as long as he fought hard and showed his stuff
He kept the crowds coming and that was enough.

Then came the blow, the hardest of all
It was no ordinary punch that made Catman fall.
A jolt to the heart - nay, not a punch
It landed, nonetheless, with a sickening crunch.
The dispatcher of such a powerful blow
Was, of course, a woman. By now you know!

She was the fairest of fair, a beauty to behold
For whom the Catman's greatest glories began to unfold.
So, once again, born out of desire
A tiger called the Catman caught on fire.

He saw Seneca first from a Chicago ring,
And knew at once it was the real thing.
When the final bell rang she smiled his way
And for the Catman was born a new day.
She waited for him after that glorious fight
And they walked Chicago's streets late into the night.
Seneca was his, as was the world
And win after win he soon unfurled.
Just to be bathed in the warmth of her glow
Was more important than vanquishing any single foe.

The Catman and Seneca were soon to be wed
But first he wanted the Champ, he said.
No ordinary bride would Seneca be
But the Champ's wife for the world to see.
So, with Seneca's warm kiss fresh upon his lip
He headed back East upon a momentous trip.
For in New York City, his old home town,
Catman Miller signed to fight for the crown.
With the contract signed, his lease on life,
The happy warrior returned to his soon-to-be-wife.

But life is filled with strange and wondrous tricks
As well as hucksters, hustlers and loads of slicks.
So no one's surprised with jazzmen around
That more'n one romance is apt to be drowned.
Some guy who talked fast and played a good sax
Applied to the Catman the sharp end of tha axe.
He returned to Chicago on a rainy summer night

Only to learn that he was one girl light.
She skipped with the jazzman, took his money and clothes
And broke his heart, the cruelest of blows.

The Catman was broken and shattered and dead.
He couldn't believe that his Seneca had fled.
He'd have given her the world, let alone his life.
Might as well have sliced him with a jagged, rusty knife.
He cursed her name and spat at his fate
Where he felt warmth and love, he now knew to hate.
The hate filled his soul 'til he was ready to burst
And then he felt nothing - this was the worst.
He floated in a trance, the fires grew cold ;
And in this zombie-like state, the Catman grew old.

As you probably know, he never fought the champ.
He was the original guy cut from a hard-luck stamp.
Two months before the fight, needing to eat,
He fought in some hick town and was knocked off his feet.
So for a penny-ante fight, he threw it all away
And for the Catman there wasn't to be another day.
He bummed 'round the country fighting for his keep,
Knowing full well the road back was too steep.
A journeyman fighter, he won and he lost;
He desired no more than to cover his cost.

The hurt over Seneca left him in time,
But he never regained the form of his prime.
He only regretted that he threw it all away
On a dame that should have been just an enjoyable lay.
His face grew puffed and scarred with the years
And soon the crowd's roars turned into jeers.
They came to see the Catman fight – but not win;
"Come on, Local Boy, poke him on the chin!"

But win, lose or draw, he was always a tough test
Because every time out he gave it his best.

✬  ✬  ✬

A deafening roar roused the Catman from his sleep.
He looked 'round the room. No one uttered a peep.
All eyes were now trained on the locker-room door,
Awaiting a sight seen many times before.
The fighter staggered in with the help of his second.
He took more of a beating than anyone reckoned.
Besmeared with blood, a crimson-masked face,
He was covered with welts, as though raked by a mace.
Somewhere in the next room a guy bounced aroun',
Telling how he busted up that stumblebum clown.

The Catman got up - he'd be out there soon ;
And started to move, getting his muscles in tune.
"You lookin' good, man," his second cooed low.
He held out his hand to test Catman's blow
Who snapped out a left into the poised, open palm
And as it smacked on the flesh, the Catman felt calm.
Then somewhere inside he felt it again ;
That feeling of doubt, a voice asking "when?"
He'd slowed with age and it was harder each fight.
And he'd felt something coming - maybe tonight.

But his face showed no sign of this feeling inside.
There wasn't an emotion that his face couldn't hide.
He held out his hands for his second to tape,
The size of those fists caused near everyone to gape.
"About five minutes, Miller," cried a voice from outside.

204

"That's me," he smiled, "and there's no place to hide."
Next door some young buck was getting ready to go
This was the local boy headlining the show.
The Catman was fighting Young Jackson tonight
And it promised to be one helluva fight.

Young Jackson was the boy the crowd came to cheer.
They all were his neighbors and their thinking was clear.
These farmboys were tough in their own backyard
So the Catman knew he'd have to fight hard.
He'd heard of this Jackson - the kid wasn't bad.
Nobody'd beat him. He was ripe to be had.
He heard the crowd whistling, stamping and such.
This meant the semi-final wasn't showing them much.
The door was flung open, "Okay, Miller, let's go!"
"C'mon baby," said his second, "let's show 'em what you know."

The crowd was ugly and they greeted him with jeers!
And he knew they'd get worse as they swilled down their beers.
He walked down the aisle, a towel 'round his head.
"G'wan, ya big bum! They'll carry you out dead!"
He climbed the ring steps and ducked through the ropes.
It was now his job to shatter the kid's hopes.
He looked across the ring as Young Jackson climbed in.
One look and he knew the kid wanted to win.
His eyes were set hard, his mouth a grim line,
And his back muscles rippled so supple and fine.

The Catman studied the kid and liked what he saw,
You knew he was tough by the set of his jaw.
Then the spotlight was on him, the announcer called out,
"Ladies and gentlemen ... and now, the main bout."
He called out their names in a voice loud and clear.

No sound for the Catman, for the kid a loud cheer.
Then to the center of the ring they walked
And shifted nervously as the referee talked.
"No backhands ... no laces ... break when I yell ..."
Then back to their corners awaiting the bell.

The lights grew dim and there was a silence so loud
That all you could hear was the breathing of the crowd.
In this longest of moments the whole world stopped.
The Catman gulped air as his stomach flip-flopped.
Was this to be it - his last lonely night?
This was the question that plagued him each fight.
And then in a shattering cacophony of sound
Rang out the bell to start the first round!
All other thoughts were voided from his mind -
Catman Miller had ten rounds to grind.

He moved to the center ; Young Jackson was there.
Staring deep in his eyes, he saw no sign of fear.
He started a left but the kid danced away,
"Hey, there, Catman, don't ya wanna play?"
He narrowed his eyes and leaned to the task.
"I'll play, boy. All ya gotta do is ask."
The left flashed again, followed by a right
But Jackson moved with the speed of light.
Suddenly the Catman got tagged by a hook
And this was followed by every punch in the book!

He was seated in his corner, a cold sponge on his neck,
Still in one piece but pretty much a wreck.
He looked up at his second and smiled a sad grin,
"Bet this is the shortest fight there ever has been."
"There's nine more big ones still left to go.

You just try slug him standin' toe-to-toe."
"You kiddin', man! I'm really still aroun'?"
"He hit you with everythin' but couldn't put ya down."
The Catman arose before the sound of the bell.
"Okay, kid. Now I'm gonna fight ya like hell !"

He moved quickly out, his right hand held high
And glared at the kid waiting to let it fly. '
But he waited too long and the kid landed first,
And he tried for the kill with an unquenchable thirst.
The Catman was no plain babe in the woods ;
He'd fought 'em all, he had the goods.
So with the crowd's roars ringing in his head
He countered with his right, almost knocking the kid dead !
The kid staggered back, eyes troubled and glazed.
Not a sound from the crowd, now completely amazed.

Down low in a crouch, the Catman moved in
But the kid was still up and he wanted to win.
The Catman scored well with a left to the face
Then the kid moved in close and raked him with his lace !
Seeing the blood, the crowd came to life
Catman felt like he was sliced by a knife.
He moved at Young Jackson with a snarl in his throat,
Not giving the kid a second to gloat.
Incensed by his blood he tore at his man
But rather than fight, Young Jackson ran.

In his corner, the Catman was at ease
He felt he was ready to take Jackson in a breeze.
"You fightin' hi good," the second smiled.
"He shoulda known better than to get you riled."
He doctored the cut and bathed the hot face

And wondered how each lump was put in its place.
He knew there was a story for each bump and scar.
Maybe they're better untold,  better by far.
He was workin' him tonight,  probably never another,
But for this single shot he felt closer'n a brother.

Now the kid wasn't running ;  they told him to fight,
And the crowd let out a yowl that pierced through the night.
"He's an old man,  Jackson.  Go get him now !"
"Come on there,  baby,  he's slow as a cow."
So they locked heads together like two angry rams,
And let loose the furies of two separate dams.
Now the kid was on fire ;  his eyes were ablaze,
As the crowd cheered him on and sang out his praise.
Not an inch would one give,  this was a war ;
They'd punch and they'd stagger and then punch some more.

The Catman no longer kept track of the round.
He was doin' his best to just hold his ground.
The hot lights beat down atop his bare head
And his hands were so heavy they felt made of lead.
But he kept right on punching,  how he knew not
And the kid threw them back from that very same spot.
He thought of a breeze and a bed and of sleep
But these were things that would just have to keep.
There was a taste in his mouth that was salty and wet ;
He knew it was a mixture of his blood and his sweat.

He was now in a crouch,  holding his hands low
And he pounded Young Jackson's gut with a mighty
    right hand blow.
He heard the kid grunt from way deep inside
And he followed with a left,  or at least he tried.
The years are unkind,  they treat one with disdain ;

This the Catman learned in a lesson filled with pain.
A fist that before, always followed his command
Now moved from his side like a paralyzed hand.
As the slow-motion punch moved towards its mark,
All the bright lights exploded and then there was dark.

This wasn't sleep and it couldn't be heaven
Then he heard the count of, "Five .. Six .. Seven.."
He knew it wasn't heaven, that he could tell,
But why, in the Lord's name, did it have to be Hell ?"
He pulled himself up like a puppet on a string.
"Okay," he sneered, "let's finish this here thing."
The mob was going mad, screaming for the kill,
But in just another second everyone was still.
The Catman feinted with his left, and feinted one
    time more,
Then he threw a whistling right and the kid was on
    the floor !

They dragged the kid to his corner, saved by the bell.
So the Catman still had something, though just a
    hollow shell.
He hobbled to his corner and flopped upon the stool.
"Do somethin', man," he croaked, Jes' make me cool."
They bathed his weary body and snapped capsules
    'neath his nose,
And in sixty precious seconds, both battered fighters rose.
The Catman was mighty weary, but one thing he knew ;
If he was feeling tired, the other guy was, too !
Thus, they continued their mortal combat in the
    center of the ring
Two bruised and butchered warriors whose clubs
    had lost their sting.

Through some miracle of nature, both men regained
   their strength
And now they waited for the finish, the final
   round - the tenth.
"Only God c'n whup ya now," Catman's second said.
And suddenly the Catman felt that awful, awful dread.
He froze there on his stool, cold sweat upon his brow,
The feeling was back with him, only even stronger now.
The bell beckoned both fighters to the center of the ring.
"Okay," called his second, "show this cat who's King !"
The Catman shook the feeling as quickly as it came,
Not through undue bravery, but fighting was his game !

Now they leaned into each other with everything they had
And everyone was roaring, nearly going mad.
The Catman's fists were lightning as they bit into his foe,
But the kid was real gritty and traded blow for blow.
Catman's fist was buried deep in belly-skin
And as Young Jackson groaned his agony, he took one
   on the chin.
But Catman couldn't follow up, blinded by his blood
As the final bell sounded and the cheers fell like a flood.
Blood-splattered warriors clasped in a warm embrace,
And of all the hate between them ... no longer a trace.

Everyone was quiet, awaiting the call,
Was this to be the night, then, for Young Jackson to fall?
In this hushed arena, the Catman stood alone
And listened, as in the rear was a growing, buzzing drone.
"Jackson !" they all chanted. "Jackson got the fight !"
The mob was getting surly as the chorus grew in might.
The Catman merely smiled. This wasn't new to him.
Unless he scored a k.o. his chances were mighty slim.

Catman's eyes turned slowly and looked upon the crowd ;
Never batted an eyelash,  for this he was too proud.

"You fought too good to lose - you won it goin' away,"
His second kept on saying, but his mood was far from gay.
The announcer had the cards and climbed into the ring
The decision,  knew the Catman, would be the usual thing.
The announcer cried out loudly,  "The winner of this fight
Is our own Young Jackson !" to everyone's delight.
The Catman's second embraced him,  eyes brimming
   with tears,
The Catman only shrugged,  "Who the hell cares !"
"You wuz it tonight,  baby. You wuz the real thing."
But Catman didn't hear him.  He already left the ring.

The Catman let the shower play upon his skin.
What the heck's the difference - ya lose 'em or you win !
He toweled off and dressed in the smelly, sweaty room
And sat by himself - no one to share his gloom.
Slowly,  out of habit,  he packed his bag himself,
Carefully removing his belongings from the bare
   wooden shelf.
He played his hand tenderly across his pulpy face
And took one final look at this God-forsaken place.
Then out stepped Catman Miller into the cold of the night,
And slowly started his journey to another town –
   another fight.

# BEAU JACK

*By Ron Ross*

You hadda be there to hear them shout for Beau
An' if you wuz, you'da seen one helluva show.
'Cause the kid fought with all get-out, that was his way
You'd never hear no one grumble 'bout not gettin'
for what he'd pay.
Wuzn't no Fancy Dan moves when Beau was in the ring
Just every punch in the book, y'see, fightin' wuz his thing.

They'd all be stompin' and yelling" – "Beau! Beau! Beau!"
Didn't matter who he wuz in with – he'd be goin' toe-to-toe.
Like when Zivic gave him the thumb, near
turned his eye inside out,
Beau only shrugs, "That's what fightin's all about."
He learns his lessons good when Zivic takes him to school
And smiles, "I'm born on April First but I'm no April Fool!"

Oh, how that Garden rocked as they cheered on their Beau
Who then taught the teacher some things he didn't know.

213

He showed him his left and his right over and over again
And when the final bell rang, all Zivic said was "Amen!"
He fought 'em all the same, from pillar to post,
This little Georgia Peach who became New York City's toast.

There's a new Garden now and new fighters on the go
But there ain't never gonna be another like Beau.
Whoever he wuz fightin', an' he fought the very best,
It wuz always a war, not a second to rest,
"Cause he only knew one way – never step back!
And that's why they loved the one and only "BEAU JACK"!

# A Visit To St. Nick's

# ('Twas The Night Before Saturday)

*by Ron Ross*

It was the night before Saturday and the Garden was shut
    down
The fights were moved uptown as the circus was in town.
Still the crowds came pouring in – by bus, by cab and rail
These were the real fans – Blood and Guts were on sale!
No mink coats or diamonds were found among this crowd
Just stale sweat and cigar smoke and God! They sure were
    loud.
They were here for real punchouts, not fancy tricks
And they never, never were let down – not at a visit to St.
    Nick's.

The opener was usually two young kids going four
Who had an awful lot to learn but they put on a real war!
They only knew to punch away, not to clinch or to grab
(Somewhere down the road they may even learn to jab.)
There were punches in bunches, roundhouse swings galore
And an occasional uppercut brought up from the floor.
It never mattered which kid won – both got in their licks,
That's how it always started – any night at old St. Nick's.

Now the crowd was warmed up – "Let's get on with the show!"
And swilling down their beers helped them put on a glow.
Soon the fists were flying and not only in the ring
As the guys in the balcony were doing their favorite thing.
Wherever you looked – whether up, down, left or right
You were always bound to see one rousing helluva fight.
A broken nose here, a split lip there, scrapes from punches
    and kicks
You certainly got more than you paid for any night at old St.
    Nick's.

Remember all the young warriors who climbed through those
    ropes
With only one thought in mind – to shatter the other guy's
    hopes.
Oh! The courage that they showed and the battles that they
    fought –
Tino Raino, Patsy Giovanelli, Sammy Farber, and Julie Bort.
There was Paddy DeMarco, Terry Young, also Artie Levine,
Johnny Saxton, Ernie Durando and Brownsville's Harold
    Green.
Fading memories now on which one's mind has to fix
In order to never forget those nights at old St. Nick's.

Seeing a whistling left hook, even today, sinking into the belly
Brings back the spectre and memory of East Sider Joey Miceli.
And as for crowd-pleasing fighters with punches unerring
Who could top Chico Vejar or Ridgewood's Jimmy Herring?
We learned Coney Island's biggest scare wasn't the Cyclone
    alone
Once we saw Herbie Kronowitz and Bulldog Tony Pellone.
There was Billy Graham and Johnny Colan, with moves so
    very slick
That they gave graduate courses to one and all at old St.
    Nick's.

There were those legendary cornermen readying their boys
    for the bell
Whitey Bimstein, Charley Goldman and the dean – Ray Arcel.
For those who weren't able to see the live toe-to-toe show
Sam Taub and Don Dunphy were at ringside, calling it
    blow-by-blow.
And to all those silent warriors for whom the ten-count bell
    did toll
Let us hoist a cup o' kindness now to Boxing's Honor Roll.
Let's remember those who graced her ring, from the cities to
    the sticks
As we travel down memory's lane on a visit to St. Nick's.

CPSIA information can be obtained at www.ICGtesting.com
Printed in the USA
LVOW13s1457221213

366444LV00003B/509/P

9 781470 002190